Praise for the Midnight Breed series by LARA ADRIAN

BOUND TO DARKNESS

"While most series would have ended or run out of steam, the Midnight Breed series seems to have picked up steam. Lara Adrian has managed to keep the series fresh by adding new characters . . . without having to say goodbye to the original ones that made the series so popular to begin with. Bound to Darkness has all the passion, danger and unique appeal of the original ten books but also stands on its own as a turning point in the entire series with new pieces to a larger puzzle, new friends and old enemies."

—Adria's Romance Reviews

"Lara Adrian always manages to write great love stories, not only emotional but action packed. I love every aspect of (Bound to Darkness). I also enjoyed how we get a glimpse into the life of the other characters we have come to love. There is always something sexy and erotic in all of Adrian's books, making her one of my top 5 paranormal authors."

—Reading Diva

CRAVE THE NIGHT

"Nothing beats good writing and that is what ultimately makes Lara Adrian stand out amongst her peers.... Crave the Night is stunning in its flawless execution. Lara Adrian has the rare ability to lure readers right into her books, taking them on a ride they will never forget."

—Under the Covers

"...Steamy and intense. This installment is sure to delight established fans and will also be accessible to new readers."

blishers Weekly

Praise for the 100 Series
contemporary erotic romance
from
LARA ADRIAN

Look for these titles in the *New York Times*
and #1 international bestselling

Midnight Breed series

. . . and more to come!

Other books by Lara Adrian

Paranormal Romance

Hunter Legacy Series
Born of Darkness
Hour of Darkness
Edge of Darkness *(forthcoming)*

Contemporary Romance

100 Series
For 100 Days
For 100 Nights
For 100 Reasons

100 Series Standalones
Run to You
Play My Game *(forthcoming)*

Historical Romance

Dragon Chalice Series
Heart of the Hunter
Heart of the Flame
Heart of the Dove

Warrior Trilogy
White Lion's Lady
Black Lion's Bride
Lady of Valor

Lord of Vengeance

BREAK THE DAY

A Midnight Breed Novel

NEW YORK TIMES BESTSELLING AUTHOR

LARA ADRIAN

ISBN: 978-1-939193-30-8

BREAK THE DAY

www.LaraAdrian.com

Available in ebook and trade paperback. Unabridged audiobook edition forthcoming.

BREAK THE DAY

CHAPTER 1

Rafe stroked his fingers over tender female flesh, his thumb lingering at the carotid, where the human's pulse pounded as hard and fast as her panting breaths.

As blood Hosts went, this one was more than willing to give him her vein. She either didn't notice or didn't care that they were seated at the bar in full public view of the other patrons at Asylum tonight.

Which suited Rafe just fine.

Lowering his head to the side of the woman's bared throat, he took a long moment to savor the scent and sound of coppery red cells rushing just beneath the surface of so much fragile skin. His fangs elongated in reflex, pushing out of his gums in anticipation of the first bite.

"Feeding curfew ended at midnight, warrior."

On a growl, Rafe paused and swiveled a dark look at the bartender who'd issued the warning. The man was

Breed, like him. A big male with a shaved, tattooed head and shoulders as wide as a tank.

Asylum mainly catered to a human clientele, given that the Breed had only one drink of choice: blood taken from a freshly opened vein. Still, in the twenty years since Rafe's kind had been outed to man, the tavern in Boston's old north end had become a popular gathering place for members of both races.

At this late hour, the place had thinned out to a few dozen diehards and the usual smattering of inebriated newcomers who'd evidently grown tired of the flashy dance clubs and sim-lounges in the tourist areas and had wandered deeper into the city for a taste of the local color.

From time to time, Rafe and his teammates from the Order had hung out here as well, sharing some laughs together after their patrols.

Damn, how long had it been? A few months by now. Not since the summer, when he'd been pulled off all Order missions.

Not since his epic fuck-up in Montreal.

Worse than a fuck-up, the near catastrophe had almost killed him. And it might also have cost the lives of everyone closest to him if Opus Nostrum's beautiful, but treacherous, mole hadn't been stopped by Rafe's best friend and comrade, Aric Chase.

Rafe had been played for the worst kind of fool, blinded by a pretty face and a seductive mouth that had spewed nothing but lies.

Never again.

He shook off the bitter reminder with a curse uttered low under his breath. Self-directed anger put an even sharper edge to his voice as he glared at the big bartender. "Why don't you do us both a favor and get off my dick? I don't hear the lady complaining about feeding curfews."

The male scowled. "Listen, man, I don't make the laws."

Rafe grunted. "Neither do I."

"Yeah, but isn't the Order supposed to enforce them?"

"He ain't Order. Not anymore. Rumor has it they bounced his ass."

The comment came from a group of Breed civilians from area Darkhavens occupying one of the tables behind him. Affluent and useless in their polo shirts and khakis, they were the vampire version of rich frat boys. Rafe had earned the scorn of the five young males the minute he arrived and the human blood Host they'd been plying with alcohol for most of the night decided she'd rather spend her time in Rafe's lap.

He swung his head around to glance their way now, sensing the contempt simmering at his back. A couple of the ego-rankled boneheads actually looked stupid enough to want to take him on.

Rafe had to curb his smile. He was ready for a fight tonight.

Hell, it was the reason he was there in the first place.

"My father works in law enforcement," the mouthpiece of the Darkhaven males added helpfully. "He says it's been all over JUSTIS for weeks that Golden Boy here got his ass handed to him by Lucan Thorne and they cut him loose. Evidently 'gross insubordination and conduct unbecoming' isn't a good look, even for the members of the Order."

"That true? You're not one of the Order's warriors

anymore?"

Rafe pivoted back to the scowling bartender. "Do I look like I am?"

He knew damn well he didn't. His dark blond hair was grown out in loose waves that broke at his shoulders, windblown from the ride on his motorcycle, which he'd parked outside the bar. Thick whiskers shadowed his face and jaw. He hadn't put on the Order's black fatigues and weapons belt in months.

Tonight he was dressed in jeans and a dark T-shirt under his black leather jacket. He more resembled one of the cluster of menacing-looking gangbangers playing pool and slamming back shots near the other side of the room than a member of the elite warrior team from the Order.

The humans in studded black leather had been watching him since he walked in, mistrusting and cautious. Rafe felt their eyes on him now, in particular the muscled, goateed man lording over the bunch, and the sole female of the pack, a tall, leggy brunette with an angel's face and mouth-watering curves beneath her biker's leathers and black turtleneck sweater.

As for Rafe, his rough appearance was as deliberate as his presence in the bar tonight.

All part of the plan. Just like his removal from his team's patrols after he returned from Montreal, and the more recent, carefully constructed rumor that had been allowed to spread like wildfire through both human and Breed law enforcement communities that he had been dishonorably ousted from service.

Only a few in the Order who knew the truth. Namely, the architects of Rafe's current deep undercover mission: Lucan Thorne at the D.C.

headquarters; Gideon, the Order's technology genius; and Sterling Chase, the commander of the Boston operations center.

Lucan had agreed on one concession at Rafe's insistence—his parents, Dante and Tess. Although Dante commanded the Seattle operations center for the Order, there would be no keeping him away from Boston if he truly believed his son had strayed so far off the path.

Allowing his parents to think the worst of him would have been hard, but it damn near killed Rafe to be required to keep the truth from his teammates and friends Nathan, Elijah, and Jax. He could only imagine what they thought of him now.

Letting Aric Chase believe he was a washout and a failure was even worse. Especially when he owed his life to his best friend. Fortunately, the male was still in Montreal with his new mate, Kaya. The pair were busy recruiting a new team for the Order, one comprised of daywalkers, those few and rarest of the Breed like Aric and his twin sister, Carys, and their mother, Tavia.

Rafe only hoped that once the dust settled after the solo operation he was launching tonight, he'd be able to redeem himself in everyone's eyes.

Not just for his covertly orchestrated fall from grace with the Order, but for the very real one that had preceded it.

Ironically, it was the shame he brought down on himself in Montreal that made him the only suitable candidate for this mission now.

And he would not fail.

Not this time.

Even if it meant staking his last breath on that vow.

Behind him, Big Mouth from the Darkhaven only seemed emboldened by the fact he wasn't getting more of a rise out of Rafe. "I don't know, boys, he doesn't seem like such a hardass to me. Guess he ain't so tough without the other Order thugs around to back him up."

Rafe exhaled a heavy sigh, if only to mask his satisfaction at the predictability of his target tonight.

Calmly, he moved the clinging woman off his lap and onto the stool beside him. Then he tossed a sneer at the table of civilian vampires. "You know the best thing about getting axed from the Order? Not having to treat entitled Darkhaven fucks like you as if you matter."

A couple of them scoffed at the insult. Rafe heard the abrupt scrape of a chair in the instant he turned his attention away from them. He knew the attack was coming even before he felt the shift in the air as one of the Breed males launched himself at him from behind.

No surprise, it was Big Mouth. And shit—the asshole had a knife. It would have been buried in Rafe's back if he hadn't dodged the strike in the same moment his attacker lunged. Rafe grabbed the male's wrist in the vise of his fist and twisted hard.

The male screamed and let go of his weapon.

Rafe caught the blade in his free hand, using the other to wrench his assailant's arm around to his back. He could have snapped the limb with a flex of his wrist or turned the knife on its owner, but he wasn't looking to do real harm to the Darkhaven punk or his friends, no matter how satisfying it might be.

He had escalated the situation for an audience of one.

And he had the guy's full attention too.

While half of the bar cleared out in a hurry, a few

panicked tourists shrieking as they fled to the street outside, the gangbangers remained. From Rafe's peripheral, he saw their goateed leader watching as he calmly continued his game at the pool table.

Rafe increased the pressure on Big Mouth's elbow joint, making him squawk for good measure. And yeah, because the bastard deserved a little pain.

He was just about to toss the male back at his companions when the bar's front door opened. Another pair of Breed males strode inside, no doubt alerted to the trouble by the crowd pouring out of the place moments ago.

Rafe groaned inwardly.

Ah, fuck. Just what he didn't need.

Jax and Elijah.

His two teammates—*former* teammates, as far as they knew—were suited up in patrol gear and armed to the teeth. Whatever they thought of him now, they were clearly shocked to find Rafe standing in the middle of Asylum holding a whimpering Breed civilian in one hand and a dagger in the other.

"What the fuck's going on in here?" Eli's low, Texas-tinged drawl was practically a snarl.

Jax's ebony brows were drawn together over his dark, almond-shaped eyes. "This is the last place we expected to see you, Rafe."

"No shit." Last place he expected to see them too.

He didn't miss the fact that one of Jax's razor-sharp hira-shuriken glinted in the warrior's hand, ready to let fly. The move to palm a throwing star was pure reflex for the lethal male, but this was the first time Rafe had ever stood in the crosshairs of his comrade's cold skills.

Fortunately, the pair had arrived without Nathan, the

team's captain. As much as Rafe dreaded the thought of a confrontation with Eli or Jax, his odds of walking away in one piece would diminish drastically if the former Hunter were standing here with them.

"Good thing you showed up," the bartender muttered from behind the counter. "This one's been itching for a fight with someone since he got here."

Rafe couldn't deny it. The plan had been to cause a ruckus in front of the gang, make it known in a very public, even violent, way that he was no longer on the right side of the law.

He kept his hold on Big Mouth, only because his mind was busy formulating the best way to defuse the situation without unraveling his sole purpose for being there tonight.

Meanwhile, he was caught in an unwanted standoff with the two warriors he still considered his brothers.

"Let him go, asshole!"

The shouted command didn't come from Eli or Jax, but rather one of Big Mouth's buddies.

And the dumbfuck had the poor judgment to draw a gun from somewhere on his person. The shiny stainless-steel semiautomatic pistol wobbled in his grasp as the civilian vaulted up from his chair and squeezed the trigger at Rafe.

Or, tried to.

In that same moment, Jax's hira-shuriken zipped through the air. It ripped into Dumbfuck's forearm, knocking his aim off. The weapon fired a short spray of rounds toward the ceiling, the ricochets ringing over the beat of the music thumping on the sound system.

The two Order warriors moved quickly on the table of Darkhaven males. In seconds, they had them rounded up and searched for other weapons.

Eli strode up to Rafe and pulled Big Mouth out of his grasp, shoving the male over to his friends. Then he grabbed the dagger from Rafe.

"You're already walking a razor-thin line, man. Don't do something you can't take back."

His deep voice was level, but there was no mistaking the warning it carried. He turned back to the Darkhaven males. "As for the rest of you ladies, get your asses home before some jackass like the one over here wastes you just for being stupid."

Rafe watched as Big Mouth and his friends shuffled out of Asylum. Jax followed behind them, but Eli lingered for another moment. He pinned Rafe with a grave stare.

"You know if the command ever comes down from Lucan to deal with you, we're gonna have to carry it out."

Rafe held his comrade's sober gaze. He knew how he had to act right now, what he had to say. But knowing it and pushing the words off his tongue were two different things.

"You think I actually give a fuck anymore?" His mouth twisted from the bitter taste of the lie.

"No, man. I guess I don't." Eli frowned, then slowly shook his head on a curse. "So you'd better fucking watch yourself."

He turned away then, and stalked out of the bar without a backward glance.

A few seconds after the Order was gone, a pained groan drew Rafe's attention to the area near the pool table. One of the gangbangers pawed at his midsection in a frenzy, his face going ashen with shock.

"Oh, fuck! Cruz, I think I'm hit. Son of a bitch, I'm

bleeding!"

The olfactory punch of fresh hemoglobin hit Rafe's nostrils at the same time the scrawny man tore off his leather jacket to reveal a blooming red stain across his stomach.

Just fucking great.

Rafe's fangs erupted in response. It was next to impossible for a Breed vampire not to react to the sensory blast of spilled blood. His eyes burned amber, his vision sharpening with the vertical narrowing of his pupils as everything Breed in him came to dangerous life.

The gangbanger's wailing intensified. A couple of his companions gathered around him, including the one in charge. A few others moved farther away, including the pretty brunette who averted her gaze from her wounded comrade and wheeled away from the others as if she were on the verge of throwing up.

Behind him, the Breed bartender growled through his fangs. "Fucking hell. That son of a bitch is gonna bleed out in another minute."

Rafe couldn't pretend he actually cared. He glanced back at the human with the likely mortal gut wound and the grave faces of his comrades. A few more seconds was probably all the life their friend had left.

Rafe had been studying the hard-partying, petty-thieving crew for weeks, looking for a way to win their attention—and their trust. The plan he'd put together with Lucan and Sterling Chase required patience he didn't really have. Maybe this unscripted opportunity might be his best chance to grease the wheels of his mission.

Rafe glanced down at his hands. He'd been born with his mother's gift for healing. As much as he hated to use his personal ability on vermin like these, it would all be worth it if it got him closer to his ultimate goal: the destruction of Opus Nostrum and everyone loyal to their cause.

The bartender uttered a harsh curse. "If that human dies in my bar, I'm holding both you and the Order personally responsible, asshole."

Rafe shook his head. "He's not going to die."

Fisting his hands at his sides, he headed across the bar.

CHAPTER 2

Her stomach seized up as if she'd been punched.

Bloody hell. Devony Winters wheeled away from the rest of the group on a groan. She was barely able to resist the urge to run from the sight of the gushing bullet wound in Fish's skinny gut.

Not because she was squeamish around blood.

Far from it.

The reaction she strove to conceal was something much different, and a lot more damning than fear or sickness. Her fangs surged behind her tightly closed lips. Her vision sharpened, everything tinged with an amber glow.

She was Breed—a daywalker, rarest of her kind. It was a truth she'd been hiding from Cruz and his gang since she first joined up with them five weeks ago.

Far as she could tell, the group of law-breakers were more interested in thievery and partying like kings off the proceeds than wholesale hatred of the Breed. That didn't mean she wanted to test the theory, or lose the trust she'd been cultivating since they took her on as one of them. Now, all her meticulous caution was on the verge of being undone by an errant bullet and a pointless bar brawl.

All of it caused by the arrogant, tawny-haired behemoth across the room.

Fucking brilliant.

Too bad the pair of warriors from the Order hadn't bounced him from Asylum at the same time they'd ejected the trigger-happy Darkhaven idiots who'd been so eager to goad him into a fight.

Devony struggled to tamp down her body's automatic response to the sound of Fish's drumming heartbeat and the scent of the lifeblood pooling beneath him on the floor. Daring a quick glance over her shoulder she saw that the source of all her problems tonight was now heading across the tavern. Not leaving at all, but striding toward Cruz and Fish and the others in a long-legged swagger, his large hands fisted at his sides.

Shit.

The Breed male—Rafe, his comrades from the Order had called him—was no less affected by Fish's rapidly spilling blood than she was. But he made no effort to hide it.

His transformed irises threw off fiery heat, his pupils narrowed from their normal state to catlike slits. The tips of his fangs glinted diamond-bright behind the generous cut of his parted lips. And his *dermaglyphs*, the Breed skin markings that wrapped his forearms and tracked up onto his throat from below the collar of his black T-shirt, were now pulsing and alive with dark colors.

Devony's own *glyphs* itched beneath her long-sleeved turtleneck. In public, she always took care to keep them covered, particularly in front of Cruz and the others. Right now, it was her fangs and glowing eyes that were going to out her to the gang if she didn't pull herself together.

Of course, there was a chance they might not pay any attention to her. Especially if the Breed male stalking over with such purpose meant to end Fish's misery by opening his carotid right in front of them now.

Devony moved farther away from Cruz and the others as they huddled around Fish, who howled and writhed on the scuffed plank-wood floor. She sat down at an empty table, holding her head in her hands if only to shield her face from view. Better if they judged her weak-stomached than learn the truth. She willed herself into a state of forced calm, but it wasn't easy. The blood was still pumping fresh and warm behind her, a siren's call to her Breed senses.

"Move away from him." Rafe's command was a deep, otherworldly growl.

Devony lifted her gaze in time to see him stepping between a couple of the guys. Ocho and Axel weren't the kind of men to be pushed around by anyone, but neither of them seemed willing to stand up to this scowling Breed male and his bared fangs. Not even Cruz made a move to defy him, though his hand rested on the pistol concealed beneath his leather jacket.

Fish erupted in a sputtering panic. "Oh, shit! Get me outta here, guys. This bloodsucker's gonna kill me!"

"He doesn't have long." In a toneless, dispassionate voice, the Breed male addressed Cruz alone as if he understood everyone in the gang answered to him. "I can help him."

Cruz said nothing, but he took a measured step back, making room for the male in front of Fish.

"S-stay away from me!" Fish wailed. He tried to sit up, but only slipped in the puddle of slick red cells beneath him. "Don't drain me, man. I'm begging you!"

Rafe sank to his haunches on the floor and placed his hands on Fish's abdomen. "Calm down. Your panic is only making you bleed out faster."

Devony held her breath and watched, confused and curious. She tried to crane for a better view, but all she could make out was the big Breed male leaning over Fish, his hands holding steady over the wound.

After a moment, she heard the soft rattle of a spent round clatter onto the floor. Then the pungent scent of fresh, flowing blood began to fade. Fish's panting slowed, his pain and fear dissipating into a muted moan.

"Holy shit." It was Cruz who spoke first, amazement in his eyes as he stared down at the two men. "You healed him."

Now that the flow of red cells had dried up, Devony's thirst abated. Her fangs no longer filled her mouth. Her vision, still inhumanly sharp, no longer burned like embers. She got up from the table and drifted over to the rest of the group.

"I'm okay," Fish gasped. He ran his hands over his sticky, stained midsection, searching for the wound. It was gone. Not a trace of it on his pale white skin. He let out a whoop. "Son of a bitch, I'm really okay!"

The Breed male rose from his crouch beside him while Ocho and Axel helped Fish up from the floor, all of them marveling at what they'd just witnessed.

Cruz nodded, clearly awed by what he'd seen. "That was . . . impressive."

"I can't believe it," Fish murmured, still shell-shocked. He stared at the Breed male as if he were looking into the face of a saint. "I was dying, I know I was. Another minute or so, and I—" He shook his head on a quiet curse. "What you did is a miracle. You fucking saved my life. Why?"

"Because I could, I guess."

Fish blew out a sigh. "Well, I don't care why you did it, man. I owe you. And I make good on my debts. I'm gonna repay this somehow, you have my word."

"Don't worry about it." Rafe shrugged off the promise like pulling someone out of the clutches of death was something he did every day.

With Fish recovered, Ocho and Axel called for a fresh round of drinks for their resurrected comrade. While the men carried on with one another, the Breed male's gaze swung away from them to settle on Devony.

Shrewd aquamarine eyes studied her beneath the tousled waves of his dark honey-blond hair. She had never been inspired to call a man beautiful before. Especially not a dangerous looking Breed male who stood six-and-a-half feet tall and whose immense body was wrapped in heavy muscle and a low-simmering menace.

But this male was beautiful. His handsome face carved in lean angles, his squared jaw bristled with the thick shadow of a beard. His lips were decadently lush, almost too tender-looking on a man. But that was where the softness of his face ended.

Those questioning blue eyes held a trace of disdain. It was the same edge of couched contempt she felt radiating off him from the moment he first walked into Asylum tonight and spotted Cruz and the rest of them at the back of the tavern.

Maybe she wasn't the only one with something to hide.

"Feeling better?" His deep voice rolled over her senses like a caress. "You still look a little green, if you ask me."

The uninvited observation drew the attention of Cruz and the others. They all stared at her now. Expectant, waiting to see how she would respond.

Alarm shot into her veins. For one jolting heartbeat, she worried that the Breed male could see through her. That he might be able to tell she wasn't quite what she seemed.

But a surreptitious flick of her tongue along the edge of her teeth assured her that her fangs had receded completely. And her vision held no trace of amber anymore.

To him and the other men looking at her, there was nothing to give her away.

"I didn't ask you," she muttered tightly. "And how I feel is no concern of yours."

She gave him her back for a moment and finished the shot of whisky she'd been nursing most of the night. Being a daywalker, her uncommon genetics allowed her to consume human food and drink. Right now, with the heat of his eyes still boring into her from behind, she was eager to look as commonly human as possible.

What she really wanted was to get the hell out of Asylum and as far away from this male as she could.

From her peripheral, she watched with a growing sense of concern as the exchange between the men continued, becoming chummier and more relaxed by the minute. It wasn't good. Passing herself off as human with Cruz and his gang took some effort, but it would be nearly impossible to hide what she was for long from another member of the Breed.

The fact that he'd been trained as an Order warrior only made her dread—and her suspicion—intensify.

The last thing she needed was him hanging around the group any more than he already had tonight. She wanted him gone, and the sooner the better.

Setting the glass down on the table, she folded her arms over her breasts and eyed the Breed male with a mistrust she hoped would be picked up by her comrades. "Healing seems like an ironic skill for one of your kind."

Her comment halted the conversation as effectively as another round of gunfire.

"One of my kind?" he asked, those sharp eyes narrowing almost imperceptibly. "You mean Breed?"

She arched a brow. "I meant an Order warrior, but now that you mention it . . ."

He stared at her. "Well, newsflash in case you missed it, sweetheart. I'm not a warrior anymore. As for my genetics, I take it you don't approve."

She lifted her shoulder. "Your words, not mine."

"Sure." A smile tugged at the edge of his beautiful mouth. "Don't knock what you haven't tried."

The men chuckled. Devony's face burned, and for an instant she wanted nothing more than to give them all a flash of her fangs—right before she leapt on the Breed male to take his arrogant ass down a peg or ten.

Fish guffawed and clapped his new best friend on the shoulder. "Hey, man, word to the wise. Don't piss off Brinks here, or next thing you know she'll be serving your balls to you on the end of her dagger."

Brinks was the nickname they'd given her, the one she'd had to work damn hard to earn in order to be part of them. And now here was this smirking vampire—this former Order warrior—making jokes at her expense and ingratiating himself with the gang in a matter of minutes.

She didn't like it.

And she damn well did not like him.

Ignoring their amusement, she caught Cruz's gaze. "I thought we had somewhere to be tonight. We going, or what?"

He nodded. "She's right. Let's pack it up and get out of here."

Devony zipped her leather jacket, giving the interloper a satisfied, sidelong glance as she stepped past him and the pool of blood that was coagulating nearby. "I'll be waiting outside."

The cool autumn air and wide open night sky of the parking lot was a welcome reprieve from the humid, blood-tainted confines of the tavern. She walked over to her motorcycle and swung her leg over the black Triumph's seat. For a moment, she simply sat there, taking in deep, cleansing breaths with her head tipped up to the moon and stars.

As she reached for her helmet that hung from the handlebar, she heard Cruz and the others exit the back door of Asylum.

And dammit, they weren't alone.

Rafe strode out with them. Fish clapped the former warrior's bicep before following Ocho to his red Ferrari and climbing into the passenger seat.

"Meet you there," Cruz called to Devony as he and Axel walked to the gang leader's brand-new gunmetal gray Lamborghini and revved it up. The two vehicles rolled out of the parking lot and headed up the street.

Devony always preferred to ride alone, but she deeply regretted that choice as the Breed male walked over to a sleek monster of a BMW bike parked in the space next to hers.

"Where the hell do you think you're going?"

"Same place you are." He climbed onto the motorcycle and heeled the kickstand up with his boot. "Cruz invited me to come hang for a while. Guess that means I'll follow you."

Not if she had anything to say about that.

Without answering him, she slammed her helmet down onto her head and started the engine.

Then she opened the throttle and tore out of the parking lot, leaving him in the dust behind her.

CHAPTER 3

Rafe had spent many nights chasing from one Boston rooftop or another while on patrol with the Order, whether in pursuit of Breed vampires gone Rogue or other bad guys who'd run afoul of the law and thought they could elude capture on the city's maze of zig-zagging streets and twisting alleyways.

But he'd never seen the city from the perspective of the multimillion-dollar, sixtieth-floor penthouse where he stood now.

He wasn't told the name of the rich fuck who owned the place. He didn't know any of the hundred-plus people partying and dancing inside or spilling out to the open air rooftop terrace with him. Near as Rafe could tell, he was the only member of the Breed there. The crush of humanity—inebriated, sweaty, and loud—had driven him outside not long after he arrived.

As for his newfound companions, Cruz was in a meeting behind closed doors with a few other men from the party, while Fish and his two buddies were busy continuing the celebration they'd started at Asylum. All three were well on their way to shit-faced and surrounded by a group of similarly impaired, attractive women.

Ocho lifted his right hand, the one that had likely earned him his nickname on account of the fact it was missing the last two digits. He gestured for Rafe to come in and join them, but the invitation held little interest or value. Despite the need to fortify the men's trust and friendship, Rafe's attention would be better spent elsewhere right now.

He flicked his glance away as if he'd missed Ocho's signal, then walked farther out onto the terrace.

There was still another member of Cruz's gang he needed to win over.

Back at Asylum, the brunette called Brinks had eyed him with suspicion from across the tavern even before he'd healed Fish. Afterward, her animosity toward him only seemed to increase. He was used to raising a few hackles in people on the wrong side of the law as a member of the Order, but this woman seemed to hate him on sight.

Apparently, ditching him in the parking lot was only the start of her avoidance of him. Since he'd arrived at the penthouse party, Rafe hadn't been able to catch more than a fleeting glimpse of her.

He could have sworn he saw her slip outside not more than two minutes ago.

Weaving through the clusters of men and women chattering over their drinks near the illuminated pool and surrounding seating areas, Rafe spotted the briefest hint of black leather and glossy sable hair retreating into the darkness. He wouldn't mistake that tall, knockout body for anyone else. She disappeared into the shadows at the far end of the long terrace.

He homed in on her with single-minded purpose.

He found her seated on a stone bench tucked into a gloomy corner. With her arms wrapped around her bent knees and her combat boots planted before her on the bench, she glanced up as Rafe approached. "You just don't take a bloody hint, do you, *vampire*?"

She leaned a bit heavily on the word, as if to remind him of their difference. Not to mention her disdain.

Rafe smiled and lifted his shoulder. "Just trying to be friendly. In case no one told you, the whole point of a party is to socialize."

"So, go socialize. In case no one told *you*, the whole point of doing that is to find someone who's actually interested in talking to you."

"Ah. And you're not."

One slender brow arched, she touched her finger to the tip of her nose. "Look at you, learning to take a hint after all."

He chuckled. "Why aren't you inside with everyone else?"

"I came out here to be alone," she said, slanting him a flat look when he made no move to leave. "Besides, I'm just waiting for Cruz to wrap up so we can get out of here."

Rafe grunted. "Where'd he go, anyway? Looked like he had serious business to take care of with someone."

"Did it?"

When she didn't respond any more than that, he

decided to take a different tack. Exhaling a sigh, he turned his head to look out at the city lights competing with the stars and moon overhead. "This view must cost some bank, eh? What'd Fish say the guy's name was who owns the place?"

No one had mentioned the penthouse owner's name to him, and unfortunately the cagey brunette staring holes in his skull wasn't even tempted to take the bait. He glanced at her and was met with a narrowed stare.

"You ask a lot of questions."

"What can I say? I'm naturally curious."

And if he had to use his Breed powers to trance the woman in order to get those answers, he wasn't above stooping to do that right here and now.

Earlier tonight at the tavern, he'd considered her attractive. Now, with only a few feet to separate them in the secluded corner of the moonlit terrace, he realized just how inadequate the term was in describing her.

Her face was lovely, creamy skin accentuating a delicate bone structure and lips the color of a dark, dusky rose. Her warm bourbon-hued eyes were too large for her face and infinitely expressive—even when Rafe was certain she was doing her best to shut him out.

All of that beauty was framed by a mane of thick, rich brown waves that tumbled over her shoulders and down her rigid spine. The glossy strands gleamed like silk under the starlight, a mesmerizing contrast against the studded black leather of her biker's jacket.

The woman herself was a study in contrasts, right down to her voice, which was measured and sophisticated, a sexy purr that stroked over his senses more than he cared to admit.

When she let the silence lengthen between them, he

stepped closer and took a seat on the bench. "I'm Rafe, by the way."

"I know who you are." She tilted her head and studied him. "I heard one of the Order warriors call you that back at Asylum."

He gave her a grim nod. "What about you? Is Brinks your last name or something?"

"Just a name."

It wasn't exactly an answer, and she obviously wasn't in the mood for sharing.

He didn't know what he'd done to trigger her animosity—aside from having been born Breed. Her comments back at Asylum left no question that she wasn't going to make it easy for him to establish any kind of footing in Cruz's gang.

If he thought he was going to win her over with a few smiles and some small talk, he'd apparently overestimated his charm. Or underestimated her instant dislike for him.

He was in uncharted territory now. Blessed with a combination of his mother's golden looks and his father's bulk and swagger, Rafe was accustomed to having the undivided attention of any female he wanted.

Not this one.

And damn if that didn't make him all the more determined to find out why.

"So, you and Cruz. You together?"

"As in a couple? No." She denied it so fast it might as well have been a scoff. "Why? Do you assume because I'm female I must be sleeping with him? Or maybe you think they're all sharing me?"

An instant, uninvited image of her being passed between those four rough men filled his mind before he could stop it. He had no right to feel the spike of aggression, of protectiveness, that swept through him on the heels of that unwelcome possibility.

He shook his head, if only to dislodge the vision. "Just trying to understand the situation."

And yeah, he wanted to know why a beautiful, clearly intelligent woman like her was wasting time hanging around a criminal element like Cruz and his pals. If not out of personal involvement, then what brought her to them?

What made her protective of Cruz and his criminal endeavors when Rafe wasn't sure she even liked the man?

Or was it her own secrets she was trying to protect?

The whole reason he was there was to find out if the gang had a connection to Opus Nostrum, and, if so, who was at the other end of the string. That meant no one could be above suspicion. For all he knew, he might be looking at that connection right now.

As if sensing his increased scrutiny of her, she glanced away from him and didn't look back. "I'm not with Cruz or anyone else. I don't mix business with pleasure."

Rafe grunted. "Smart policy. So, what kind of business are we talking about?"

"We aren't. You're the only one who keeps talking."

"Must be lucrative," he pressed. "Maybe there's room for me in there somewhere."

"There's not."

Something resembling fear flashed across her face in the instant she swung her head around to look at him. But she tamped it down just as quickly, shuttering her expression.

Rafe believed she wasn't involved with Cruz or any of the other men in his gang, but he wasn't buying for a second that her defensiveness had anything to do with loyalty to them. Her reaction right now was personal.

And so was her desperation to get away from him and his questions.

Because she was hiding something.

Lying about something.

Hell, right now he wasn't sure he could believe anything that was coming out of her pretty mouth.

That didn't mean he was ready to accept that fact and walk away. Far from it.

Sensing her secrecy only made him want to peel her apart layer by layer until he was satisfied he had the answers he needed. Whether he did that by charm, force, or some other means to his advantage, he damn well didn't care. All that mattered was his mission.

Until he had a name or a face that would lead him to Opus Nostrum's inner circle, everything else was just a matter of clearing obstacles.

Even if they were beautiful ones like her.

Hell, especially then.

She swung her legs off the bench and abruptly stood up. "This conversation is over. You want to know anything about Cruz or his business, ask him yourself."

She started to walk away. Using preternatural speed, Rafe moved off the bench and planted himself in front of her before she had taken her next breath.

She sucked in the gulp of air on a gasp, her big eyes going even wider as he blocked her path. He needed honest answers and he didn't have the patience to risk waiting for them.

Which meant he was going to have to trance her and

take the truth from her.

He reached for her arm and she flinched out of his hold on a curse. "Get out of my way."

Her voice was a low, dangerous growl. And she was strong. His fingers had clasped nothing but pure, lean muscle in that brief moment of contact. There was more power in her than he would ever have imagined possible in a human.

Unless . . .

Rafe reeled back from her, scowling. "What the fuck?"

"Heeey, man!" Fish's drunken greeting announced him as he approached their tension-wrought corner of the terrace. "There you two are. I've been looking all over for you, Rafe."

He had a pair of giggling women under his arms, and a bottle of beer sloshing precariously in his hand. His shirt was still torn and stained from the gunshot he'd survived, but his companions didn't seem to mind.

"Here, I brought something for ya." Fish shoved one of the women at him.

As soon as Rafe's attention was diverted, Brinks ducked away, as slippery as a ghost.

Biting off a tight curse under his breath, he watched her vanish into the crowd.

He wasn't going to find her again tonight. She would make certain of that now.

But she couldn't avoid him forever.

He wasn't going anywhere. Not until he'd unraveled all of Cruz's secrets . . . and hers.

"Come on, man." Fish clapped him on the back. "These chicks have never partied with one of the Breed before."

"Is that right?" Rafe grinned, totally disinterested. "Then let's go back inside so I can show them what they've been missing."

CHAPTER 4

Sunrise came early, especially considering he only made it home to his shitty rental in Southie a couple of minutes before the first rays began to break through the dark.

Rafe pushed open the door of the dumpy studio apartment and stepped inside. "Home, crap home."

The unit on ground level of the old triple-decker boasted few windows, all of them covered in state-of-the-art ultraviolet-blocking shades. It was one of the first improvements he made his first night in the place.

The other upgrade he'd added was just as essential.

Bypassing the fold-down Murphy bed in the living room, Rafe walked into the kitchen where a cabinet with a false facade concealed a computer workstation. He stared blearily into the retina scanner, then waited for a moment as the device launched an encrypted, highly secured connection to the Order's headquarters in

Washington, D.C.

Gideon's face filled the screen. Sharp blue eyes shaded by similarly tinted, round glasses stared back at Rafe from under the spiky crown of the Breed male's short blond hair. "Christ, about time you reported in. You look like roadkill, by the way."

Rafe grunted at the warrior who was also his godfather. "Good morning to you, too."

As Gideon's fingers clattered over a keyboard on the other end, Rafe's screen split to accommodate the other two Order elders who were looped in on the call.

Lucan Thorne's expression was grim, his black hair accentuating the harsh angles of the Gen One's face. In the other video window, Sterling Chase looked equally sober. Both the Order's leader and the Boston commander peered at Rafe like disapproving fathers.

"Where the fuck have you been?" Chase demanded.

Lucan seemed equally pissed off. "This debriefing was supposed to happen more than four hours ago, son."

Rafe reeled back at the undue reprimands. "If I hadn't still been in the field and undercover until now, it would have. Sirs."

What the hell? It wasn't like any of the Order's chiefs to lay into a warrior for simply doing his job. Rafe knew he had some ground to make up after the way he'd screwed up in Montreal, but this kind of micromanagement was ridiculous.

"All due respect, but if any of you feel you can't trust me to undertake this mission, you should've said so up front."

Chase bit off a curse. "That's not it, Rafe."

"You sure? Then what the fuck is it . . . sir?"

Lucan lowered his chin, a wry glimmer seeping into his stormy gray gaze. "You've got your father's blood running through your veins, no doubt about that."

But his deep voice was oddly sober.

And Rafe still didn't know what this was about.

"We're dealing with a . . . situation on our end," Lucan said. "It has nothing to do with you or your mission, and, frankly, until we get our arms around it I want to keep it contained."

Rafe wasn't going to press. Judging from the look of gravity in the Order leader's eyes, whatever it was had not only him concerned but the other two males as well.

Chase cleared his throat. "Now that you're here, Rafe, tell us how things went last night. I understand Eli and Jax walked in cold on the operation at Asylum. Shitty timing. Sorry about that."

Rafe shrugged. "Under the circumstances, I can't say I was happy to see them. But it actually couldn't have worked out better."

He explained what had happened, and how he'd gained crucial credibility with the leader, Cruz, and the others by healing the wounded gang member.

"They invited me with them to this place." He typed in the address of the building where the party was held, and an area map came up on their displays with the high-rise highlighted.

A moment later, Gideon had scoured the internet and assembled a full dossier on the owner, which displayed onscreen. "Judah LaSalle. Age thirty-two. Single. Sole heir to a French billionaire industrialist. No less than a dozen residences around the world, not counting a megayacht he purchased last year from a Saudi prince for a cool two-hundred million."

Lucan's brow furrowed. "This guy Cruz has interesting taste in friends."

"Or is it the other way around?" Chase asked.

Those were questions Rafe had been asking himself all night. "Cruz and the others like expensive toys too. They've got a few hundred grand tied up in their vehicles and that's only the start, based on what I was able to get out of a couple of them last night after the drinks had been flowing for a few hours. Hopefully, I'll have the chance to squeeze them for something more substantial soon. I told Fish, the guy I healed, that money's been tight since the Order gave me the ax and I'm looking for something to do. We'll see if they take the bait."

"What about LaSalle?" Lucan asked. "Any reason to think he might be part of Cruz's band of merry men?"

"They've got business together, no doubt about that," Rafe said. "Cruz disappeared into a closed-door meeting with him almost as soon as we arrived. He stayed in there for a couple of hours before LaSalle left the party with his bodyguards."

"Any idea what was discussed?"

"Not yet."

"Well, find out. And if we need to put dedicated eyes on Judah LaSalle, we'll make that happen." Lucan paused, staring at Rafe for a moment. "Healing that gangbanger in the bar was quick thinking. And now we've got this new lead to run down too. If this mission turns up even one additional lead in our hunt for Opus Nostrum's inner circle, it will be more than we've had in months. Good work. We couldn't do any of this without you."

Rafe hadn't been expecting praise. Nor was he prepared for how deeply it impacted him to hear Lucan

Thorne express his gratitude, his trust.

He wasn't worthy of it.

But he would be one day.

He would make sure he redeemed himself in everyone's eyes, even if it cost him his last breath.

"I'm not going to rest until we're able to unmask every one of those Opus bastards," he vowed to the three Order elders.

And he wasn't going to let anything—or anyone—stand in his way.

His thoughts went back to the leggy brunette with the face of an angel. The woman who had as much coiled power in her as she had attitude. And that was saying a lot.

In truth, she hadn't been far from his mind all night.

"They've got a female running with them," Rafe said. "They call her Brinks."

Gideon frowned. "We're not aware of a woman being part of the gang."

"Well, she is. And she sure as hell doesn't want me around. I tried to get information out of her, but she stonewalled me at every turn. She made it clear she doesn't want me hanging around."

Chase's eyes narrowed. "You think she's on to you?"

Rafe shrugged. "I don't think so. I think her problem is something personal."

He wasn't ready to voice all of his thoughts about her yet, least of all the one that had been haunting him since he clashed with her on the rooftop.

All of his warrior instincts were telling him she wasn't what she seemed.

All of his Breed instincts were telling him something even more troubling.

She was an immortal. Probably not Atlantean, since members of that race didn't react to spilled blood the way she had at Asylum. Which only left one other possibility.

And that possibility not only raised a hell of a lot of questions, but put him at a risky disadvantage if he meant to embed himself as one of Cruz's gang.

In Rafe's grim silence, Lucan studied him. "Figure the woman out, get her story. Report back with your findings next time we talk."

"Yes, sir."

It was a command Rafe intended to pursue with ruthless determination.

And if she continued pushing back on him or impeded his mission, he would take whatever steps necessary to remove her from his path.

~ ~ ~

The tea kettle whistled, the sharp complaint piercing Devony's daydream as she stood in the kitchen of her brownstone in Boston's affluent Back Bay.

Although to call her dark thoughts a daydream was far from apt.

She hadn't slept more than a couple of hours after coming home last night. Every time she closed her eyes, her mind flooded with images of the Breed warrior, Rafe. She couldn't shake the memory of all his probing questions, or the jab of dread she'd felt when he grabbed for her on the terrace and she saw the flash of confusion in his aquamarine eyes.

That instant flicker of suspicion . . . and dawning realization.

He knew.

He knew she wasn't human. Whether or not he'd guessed she was Breed or something close to it, she couldn't be sure.

Devony didn't stick around to find out. She hadn't been able to get away from him fast enough. She'd fled the penthouse party for home, and for the rest of the night she worried about what he might say to Fish or the others.

She still worried now, because if he had given Cruz or anyone else a reason to doubt her, it would undo everything.

All her hard work and planning. All the sacrifices she'd made to get even this far.

All the promises she'd made through bitter tears and a seemingly bottomless pain.

Devony steeled herself to the anguish that still had a firm hold on her. Taking the kettle off the heat, she fixed herself a cup of strong tea and carried it through the spacious first floor of the Darkhaven.

The brownstone was hers now, but had been in her family for decades. She had lived in it on her own while attending university in Boston the past two years. Her plans for a career in music were over now, although that was the least thing she missed. She hadn't stepped foot in her classes in months, but she stayed in the old house because she couldn't bear to return home to London.

Not after what had happened.

Not until she had upheld her vow to make it right, to make someone pay.

Maybe she wouldn't even return then.

In the grand, bookshelf-lined study her father's carved oak desk stood like an immense, unbreakable sentry. Fitting, considering she'd always thought of him in much the same way. Her protector, her champion, her shining knight.

She smiled wistfully, picturing him in the room that was filled with so many of his cherished treasures. His books and collectibles, his chessboard where he used to patiently teach her and her brother about logic and strategy and the patience required to win a war. Across from the big desk hung a painted portrait of her beautiful, dark-haired mother, a piece he'd had commissioned especially for that very spot on his study wall so he could see his beloved mate even when their work kept them apart.

Devony's gaze sought out another picture, the framed family photograph on the edge of her father's old desk. It greeted her in this room each morning, a reminder of those better times.

Devony pressed her fingertip to her lips, then touched each of the three smiling Breed faces that surrounded her in the photo. Her handsome, ginger-haired father, Roland Winters. Her daywalker mother, Camilla. And her older brother, Harrison, who'd also been born a daywalker, just like Devony.

They were all the family she'd had. She let her fingers rest on the cold glass that covered them.

"I love you," she whispered in the emptiness of the room.

Then she slid her hand beneath the edge of the desk and pushed the button that was concealed on the underside.

One of the enormous built-in bookcases opened silently on its hinges. Behind it was a room her father had designed as a security feature of the large home. The hidden space had been constructed during the time not long after the Breed's existence had been revealed to mankind. Back when wars between the races had been a terrifying new normal.

Daytime raids on Breed households by humans afraid of their night-dwelling neighbors were epidemic. Retaliations were brutal and blood-soaked.

Those wars that followed First Dawn had been mostly extinguished in the twenty years that passed since then, thanks in no small part to the work of the Order. The law enforcement officers of the Joint Urban Security Taskforce Initiative Squad around the world had helped too.

But hatred was a difficult disease to wipe out completely. It festered in silence, invading wherever it found the slightest purchase.

It waited for the opportunity to spread.

Waited for a new carrier to come along and give it fresh life.

And now it had found one in the terrorist group calling themselves Opus Nostrum.

Devony walked inside the former panic room and let her gaze travel over the maps and photos and dossiers that covered each of the four walls. Red strings attached to pins connected some of those individuals to others on the wall. Drug dealers, gangbangers, petty criminals. Corporation heads, politicians, community leaders. A few weeks ago, she'd added photos of Ricardo Cruz, Wayne Fishbaugh, Vincent Axelrod, and Eugene "Ocho" Snyder.

Many of the faces she'd added to the walls now had a large "X" drawn on them.

Before this was over, she expected to eliminate

numerous more.

Because this room served a new purpose now.

No longer a place for panic, but one for cold and steady justice.

It was aiding in a new war—a very personal one.

Devony took a sip of her tea as her gaze moved along the images and connecting lines she'd established between groups and individuals. Eventually, she would find the link that led her to Opus. One day, she would pay them back for what they had taken from her.

Until then, she had to have patience.

And she was not about to let the former warrior from the Order knock her off that course.

CHAPTER 5

Devony rode her Triumph into the parking lot behind Snyder's Exotic Auto in Roxbury.

At 10 PM on a weekend, Ocho's garage had been closed for several hours but a dim light glowed from the small windows above the two bays out front. Cruz's dark gray Lambo was sitting in the nearly empty lot next to the rest of the group's vehicles.

They were all here ahead of her. That didn't exactly ease the niggle of anxiety that had been troubling her from the moment she'd received Cruz's text, instructing her to come for a meeting at the gang's unofficial headquarters.

All day, she'd been plagued with paranoia about her standing in the group.

It was bad enough that she nearly revealed herself to them at Asylum. Then, at Judah LaSalle's party, she had practically bolted from the place after her unnerving run-in with Rafe on the terrace.

Had anyone noticed her extreme discomfiture around the Breed male?

Had she given them any reason to suspect why he made her so nervous?

Or, worse, had he voiced his suspicions about her to Fish or the others after she was gone?

"Get a grip," she muttered to herself under her breath. If she had been compromised, she would just have to deal with that swiftly and on her own terms.

She hadn't yet found solid evidence that Cruz and his friends were in league with Opus Nostrum, but they were far from choir boys. If things went south with them here tonight, she had no problem counting them as collateral damage in her quest for answers . . . and for retribution.

Devony killed the Triumph's growling engine and swung off the seat. With her helmet secured on the back of the bike, she headed for the rear entrance of the garage and went inside.

The door was unlocked, the low rumble of conversation and intermittent chuckles leading her to the manager's office where Cruz, Ocho, Axel, and Fish were seated.

She met their inquisitive stares with cool, measured confidence. "Looks like I'm late."

Fish carefully shook his shaggy head. He was wearing sunglasses and looked to be nursing a protracted hangover. "I just rolled in five minutes ago. What happened to you last night, Brinks? One second you were chatting it up with Rafe, the next you were gone."

"Gone?" Devony shrugged as if she hardly recalled. "No, I hung around for a while. Not that any of you would've noticed the way you three were sucking down the drinks and drooling over the women."

Axel chortled. "You jealous, Brinks?"

"Excuse me?"

From behind his metal desk, Ocho smirked. "If you prefer chicks, that's cool. It'd be even cooler if you let us watch sometime."

"What the hell are you talking about?"

He held up his hands in mock surrender and it took all she had not to reach out and snap off the three fingers he had left on his right hand.

Fish snickered. "Rafe told us what happened between you two last night."

Oh, shit. The statement made some of the blood drain from her face. She had no fear of these human men, but confusion and dread had her pulse hammering in her temples. "He told you what, exactly?"

"Said he made a move on you," Axel said. "He told us you shut him down hard."

Fish grinned. "Actually, what he said was that he thought you were gonna try to kick his ass, and that's about the time I walked up. I saw you were pissed at him, but damn, girl. Are you suicidal too? You couldn't touch him if you tried. He's a fucking Breed."

So, they didn't know anything. Thank God.

They didn't know, because Rafe kept their conversation to himself.

She wasn't sure if she felt relieved or even more deeply concerned. Why would he lie for her? And what did he think he could demand in return? All she knew was, she didn't want to find out.

Devony kept her silence as the three men continued making jokes and laughing.

Cruz didn't seem to share their amusement. His text to her had seemed all business, and his sober attitude now only confirmed it. "You three boneheads about done? I didn't bring you all here for shits and giggles."

"What's going on?" Devony asked him.

"We've got a gig on the docket for tonight. A big one." He pulled a brochure out of the pocket of his leather jacket and held it out to her.

She stared at the advertisement for an upcoming Impressionist art exhibit on loan to one of the city's museums. Nearly a dozen masterpieces soon to be on public display, each one easily worth millions. But not in the hands of a bunch of thieves like Cruz and his gang.

She glanced up at him. "You can't be serious. Even if you get your hands on them, they'll be worthless to you. You'll never be able to fence them."

His mouth quirked in the center of his goatee. "Don't worry about that. I've got it covered."

"What about security? We'll never even make it inside, let alone get close to the art." She shook her head, not wanting to be a party to this at all. "There'll be guards posted around the clock. Alarms on the doors and windows, even on the exhibits."

"Yeah, I know," he said. "Got all that covered too."

"Covered how?"

"Rafe," Fish said, looking at her over the tops of his dark sunglasses. "Turns out, he's looking for work. Lucky for us."

"Lucky?" She gaped at Fish, then swung her disbelief in Cruz's direction. "Tell me you're joking."

But he wasn't. His face was pure resolve. "You said it yourself, we'll never get inside unless we can take care of the guards and the security systems. We need the vampire to get it done."

No, no, no. This couldn't be happening.

Her stomach sank, cold and leaden. All her hopes of keeping Rafe at a safe distance—not only for her personal goals, but for her state of mind—were evaporating by the second.

"He's a Breed warrior, Cruz. Are you forgetting that until recently he was part of the Order?"

"I haven't forgotten that for a minute."

She pushed the brochure back at him. "I don't like any of this. Have any of you even stopped to ask yourself why he's hanging around? He just shows up in the right place at the right time, and now you open the door and invite him in?"

"Ain't that what we did with you, Brinks?" Ocho asked, a note of challenge in his voice.

She sank her teeth into her tongue to keep from letting him goad her. That's all she needed right now, to lose a grip on her emotions and show them her fangs or the heat of her Breed irises.

Cruz got up from his chair to face her. "You don't make the rules around here. I do. And before you go thinking I'm stupid, think again. I'm not about to trust a goddamn vampire without testing him first."

There was a threat in his airless voice, in the way he practically spat the word 'vampire.' Devony knew Cruz was dangerous. Right now, the menace rolling off him was lethal.

"What do you mean, you're going to test him?"

He merely smiled. "Go get your toolbox, Brinks. You're gonna need it. I'm putting you to work tonight too."

It was a dismissal without so many words. A

reminder that she was not yet part of them, only an asset they intended to use just as long as it suited them. When she was no longer needed, she would be out. She knew that before, but tonight the message was loud and clear. Which meant she needed to ramp up her efforts to find out what, if any, their connection was to Opus.

She wouldn't be able to do that once Rafe was in the picture.

A selfish part of her hoped that he would fail whatever test Cruz had in mind for him. It was the only way she could continue her work on the inside without discovery.

Devony left Cruz and the others behind in Ocho's office and went out to the parking lot to get her safecracking tools from the lockbox on her bike.

Being Breed, she didn't need drills or magnets or other implements in order to break into a safe. All she needed was the power of her mind. But they could never know that, so she'd faked her way through her first job with the gang several weeks ago and never looked back.

Overhead in the moonlit parking lot, storm clouds bunched sooty against the black night sky. In the distance, she heard the low rumble of thunder. Except it wasn't the weather vibrating all the way into her boots now.

It was him.

Rafe, roaring up on his BMW like a shadow in the darkness.

He was the last thing she needed to deal with right now.

She tried to hurry collecting her kit from her bike but there was no avoiding him. As he entered the gravel lot, she felt his intense eyes on her like warm hands moving over her body. A shiver that had nothing to do with the autumn nip in the air shuddered through her as she glanced his way and their gazes collided.

Heat arrowed through her, uninvited.

Ocho and the guys thought she had no use for men. She only wished that were true as she watched Rafe roll toward her now.

It didn't help that he was as handsome as Adonis. His dark blond hair was a wild tangle from the ride, the lack of helmet only making his thick mane look even more untamed and luxurious as it danced around his impossibly broad shoulders. Irrationally, her fingers itched with the urge to find out if the tousled waves were as soft as they looked.

His hair wasn't even his best feature. Every inch of him was powerful and immense, pure male perfection that was barely contained beneath his black shirt and leather jacket. Dark denim clung to his muscular legs, which were spread wide to accommodate the bulky body of his motorcycle. Desire coiled inside her and a sudden vision of him, naked and magnificent, invaded her senses before she could stop it.

Bloody hell. What had gotten into her?

Devony pivoted away from him as he slowed to a stop next to her. Her fingers were usually nimble and unerring. With awareness of him sending a dangerous arousal through her senses, she was all thumbs, fumbling to retrieve the compact pack that held her tools.

Behind her, the BMW's motor quieted, then stopped. The leather seat creaked softly as Rafe got off it and his heavy boots hit the gravel as light as a cat.

"Looks like a storm's on the way."

She nearly groaned in agreement. Doing her best to

tamp down her body's reaction to this male, she determinedly left him at her back as she continued struggling to unfasten the snaps and bungee on her toolkit.

"Need some help with that?"

He reached around her and the heat of the near-contact felt like an open flame to her heightened senses. "Leave it," she bit off without looking at him. "I didn't ask for your help."

Amber sparks tinged her vision. Not good. The spike of her irritation was too sharp. She had to contain herself around him.

She'd already given him enough cause to suspect she was hiding her true nature. She couldn't afford to confirm it to him now. Not when Cruz was practically rolling out the red carpet for him to be part of the gang.

"I see you're still upset with me from last night," he murmured. "I want you to know, I didn't tell them your secret."

Even though she already knew that, hearing him say the words was jolting. She continued working furiously on her gear. "I have no idea what you're talking about."

"Really?" He scoffed under his breath. "That's how you want to play this?"

He was standing too close, crowding her against her bike. Finally, her impatience hit its limit. With a pulse of mental power, she freed the last cord holding her pack of tools and yanked the kit free. She held it against her like a shield as she pivoted around to face Rafe.

"We done here?"

"No," he said grimly. "I think you and I are just getting started."

"Like hell we are." She stepped past him but didn't

get far. His hand wrapped firmly around her arm, the same way he'd taken hold of her at the party last night. "Let go of me. Now."

He shook his head. "Not until we talk. We can either do it here right now, or inside, in front of everyone else."

She glared. "Are you trying to threaten me?"

"Just trying to get to the truth. You're not what you're pretending to be."

"I don't think you are, either."

His handsome face remained impassive, but he didn't deny her accusation. And his grasp on her arm went a bit tighter. She tested his hold, confident she could break free if she really wanted to, but not without proving his point.

His eyes searched her face before moving lower. "What are you hiding under your long-sleeved turtlenecks and barbed-wire attitude?"

Devony's pulse raced. She braced herself for fury or violence, but instead his deep voice was gentling, almost soothing. So was the dark-lashed gaze that lifted back up to her face.

"I know you're not human, no matter how much you want to pretend you are. I'll bet anything that underneath all these concealing clothes, your soft skin is covered in Breed *dermaglyphs*. Am I right?"

A strangled sound escaped her throat. "You're crazy."

If he had snarled at her or treated her with even a trace of brutality, she would have fought him with everything she had. Instead, his low, quiet tone and penetrating eyes called to something deep inside her.

A preternatural connection.

A longing to have someone she could trust.

A yearning to feel that she wasn't all alone in the world.

Things she often dreamed could be hers one day . . . before everything she had was ripped away from her.

She shook her head, reminded of where she'd come from and how far she still had to go.

"Take your hands off me."

He held her gaze. "Tell me I'm wrong."

"Okay. You're wrong."

A scoff curled his lip and those incredible aquamarine eyes flashed with a crackle of amber heat. He moved closer, leaving less than an inch to separate them. The pointed tips of his fangs gleamed in the moonlight. "Now, try to tell me I'm wrong without lying about it."

"Damn you, vampire. I said you're wro—"

His mouth came down on hers without any warning. Firm, forceful, a total shock to her system. But his lips were infinitely soft, his kiss moving from power to possession.

Devony melted under the tender assault. She wanted to pull away. She wanted to fight him.

God knew, she wanted to deny everything she was feeling.

Desire.

Hunger.

A marrow-deep need that rocked her to her core.

That need ignited her blood like flame to tinder. She couldn't hold it back. Every cell in her body lit up, sending fire into her veins. Her fangs erupted from her gums. Underneath her clothes, her *glyphs* came to life, pulsing like living tattoos on her skin.

And as Rafe drew back from their kiss on a hissed

curse, her glowing eyes bathed him in the hot glow of her transformed irises.

"Holy shit," he uttered tersely, his own fangs gleaming in the darkness. "I knew it. You are Breed, a daywalker."

His hold on her went slack now. Devony yanked out of it on a low growl.

All he'd done was kiss her, yet every fiber of her being felt electrified and raw. If she had thought having him around was dangerous before, now she understood it was something far worse.

Because now he knew unequivocally what she was.

And she wanted him in spite of what that knowledge could cost her.

He lifted his hand to her face, his expression one of disbelief . . . and potent desire.

Before his fingers had a chance to brush her cheek, the garage's back door opened and the gang filed out dressed in head-to-toe black and armed with heavy firearms.

Cruz hailed Rafe from across the lot. "Good. You're right on time. We're rolling out now."

Devony could feel Rafe's big body tense in front of her. He was positioned to shield her face from their view, giving her the moments she needed to bring her transformation to heel.

"What's going on?" he asked the men. "We got plans or something?"

Cruz chuckled as Ocho clicked a remote starter and a parked delivery van with a linen company logo on its side fired up. "Hop in, both of you. We can cover the logistics on the way."

With the other men climbing into the vehicle, Rafe

cast a surreptitious glance at Devony. "What's going on?"

She didn't answer, mostly because she couldn't find her voice to speak. All of her energy and focus went into the effort of schooling her features back to a state of calm before she had to make the trek over to the waiting van.

That kiss had shocked her. Not only because of Rafe's audacity in doing it. Her own response was just as jarring.

His brows furrowed as he waited for her reply. "What's Cruz got planned tonight?"

"I guess we're going to find out," she told him tightly.

Part of her wanted to clue him in. After all, he had shielded her from discovery for the second time when he could have just as easily hung her out to dry. But how could she help him make inroads with the gang when her goals depended on keeping him out?

After that kiss, it wasn't only her goals she wanted to protect.

She clutched her safe-cracking kit tight against her hammering heart, even though she was certain his acute hearing couldn't be fooled.

As she stepped past him, she paused to level a glare on the Breed male's maddeningly handsome face.

"If you ever try something like that with me again, vampire, I will fucking ash you."

CHAPTER 6

Rafe tried to assure himself that the kiss he'd laid on Brinks didn't mean anything. He sure as hell hadn't intended it to mean anything. Just a tactic to throw her off guard, force her to let go of the fierce hold she seemed to maintain on her Breed nature.

He'd needed a weapon to combat her stubborn denial and he had reached for the first one that came to mind.

Now, it was all he could do to sit beside her in the back of the delivery van and pretend that kiss hadn't short-circuited his brain along with the rest of his anatomy.

He wanted her.

Fuck, he'd wanted her the moment he walked into Asylum the other night and saw her running the pool table over Cruz and the others. Those luscious curves and long, lean legs. That cascade of silken, dark hair framing those big bourbon-colored eyes that made him hard no matter if she looked at him in fury or in tormented desire.

Shit. Thinking about what she did to him only made the problem worse.

And he'd be damned before he'd let himself walk right into a seductress's trap.

Though to be fair, Brinks—or whatever her true name was—behaved less like a seductress than a combatant. He didn't doubt for a second that she meant it when she threatened to ash him.

He would trust that more than sweetness and honey any day.

Especially after he'd barely survived the trap the Opus bitch had set for him in Montreal.

Yet as the van left Roxbury heading north onto Columbus Avenue, Rafe couldn't help but wonder if he was being led into a different sort of trap tonight.

He leaned forward to get a better look at Cruz in the passenger seat. "You mentioned logistics back at the garage. What's going on?"

A few moments of odd silence fell over everyone on the heels of his question. Rafe flicked a glance at Brinks, but she turned her head to stare at nothing.

"You like art, vampire?" Cruz asked, nonchalant.

Rafe grunted. "Sure. Depends what kind."

"Fine art," Fish said from across from him. "Monet, Renoir. Classic shit like that."

Behind the wheel up front, Ocho snickered and shook his head. "You wouldn't know a fucking Monet or a Renoir from an Elvis on black velvet."

"Who cares, asshole?" Fish scowled. "I'm not planning to hang one on my wall."

Rafe's hackles were already up on instinct, so the idiotic back-and-forth only increased his impatience. "You told me we were going to discuss business tonight, Cruz. Lucrative business, you said. So, what is it?"

Instead of answering, he reached back to hand him a flyer for an art museum exhibit that would be opening in a couple of days in Boston.

Son of a bitch. Rafe's veins tightened as he realized what he was seeing. "This is from the Museum of Fine Art."

Cruz stared at him. "So, you're familiar with the place? That's good."

He knew damn well Rafe was familiar. No doubt, that was the whole point of the conversation. The whole point of this entire exercise.

Ah, Christ. That explained the route Ocho was on. The MFA couldn't be more than another five minutes across town.

"Yeah, I imagine you might've been there a time or two," Cruz remarked, hardly masking his smugness. "Didn't I read somewhere that the bitch of one of your old buddies from the Order is the curator for that place? Could swear I also heard that the daughter of the Boston commander works there on occasion too. That hot piece of daywalking ass, am I right?"

Rafe nodded tightly, his teeth set on edge at the disrespect this bastard was showing not only toward Nathan's blood-bonded mate, Jordana, but Aric Chase's twin sister, Carys, as well.

Beside him, he noticed Brinks had gone stock-still at the mention of daywalkers and members of the Order. Yet she didn't seem shocked at all by the subject of the museum and its on-loan exhibit of priceless art.

If Rafe was being tested—and he was damn sure he was—then it appeared he was the only one in the vehicle who hadn't been aware of that fact until now.

He grunted, unsure why Brinks's participation should bother him as much as it did.

"Why don't you just get to the fucking point, Cruz."

The human's grin split the center of his dark goatee. "Someone I know wants to add those paintings to his private collection. And he's willing to pay big for them. So, we're going to get them for him. Right now."

Rafe didn't have to guess where their bankroll would be coming from. Evidently, this was the business Cruz and Judah LaSalle had been discussing at the party last night.

"You want to run with us?" Cruz challenged. "You get us inside, past the guards and the security systems. We've got word that the art is being kept in a vault room in the basement of the building. You clear the way for Brinks here to crack it open, then make sure we all get out with the art and don't get our asses shot or arrested."

Rafe scoffed. "Sounds like I'm the one doing all the heavy lifting."

"You want in? This is the price."

He held the criminal's scrutinizing gaze. As much as it offended him to play this role, if he didn't, his mission was over here and now. Cruz and the others were asking him to prove his loyalty, so that's what he was going to do.

As for the art, he was certain the pieces were insured. Regardless, he would put the Order on their recovery as soon as possible.

"They keep five armed guards on the clock twenty-four-seven during business hours," he said. "After closing, that count goes down to three. But with an exhibit of this magnitude in-house, I'd expect the full detail to be on duty at all times."

Cruz nodded in acknowledgment. "Can you take out that many at a time?"

"Please." Rafe smirked. He wasn't about to kill anyone, but he could render a human unconscious and tranced in less than a second. He'd make sure the guards all stayed down as long as needed. "I'll handle the guards and shut down the security system. Everything's wired. There are motion and heat sensors throughout, all of them triggering silent alarms. That includes the vault room."

As he spoke, the museum came into view up ahead, its campus illuminated by security lights in the parking lot and outside the building. Ocho drove around to the receiving docks in back and reversed the van into one of the bays.

"Grab the props," Cruz told Axel and Fish, gesturing to the bins of folded, laundered linens on wheeled hand trucks that shared the back of the van with them. He pivoted out of the passenger seat and came into the back with them. "They'll get the guard's attention at the back door. Then it's your show."

He handed Rafe a semiauto pistol, a weapon he had no intention of using. Tucking the gun into the back of his dark jeans, he sent a cold glance at Brinks, then gave Cruz a nod.

"All right. Let's do it."

The gang moved in concert, as if they had done this kind of job a hundred times before. Maybe they had. Fish and Axel opened the rear of the van and climbed out, each wheeling a large supply of linens. Rafe followed close behind, and when the night watchman opened the door to tell them they must be at the wrong address, Rafe took the man down and put him in a lifeless drowse on the floor.

He acted quickly then, using the power of his Breed mind to disable the dock's alarm system and kill the cameras for the receiving area. "Stay here until I give you the all-clear."

Moving with preternatural speed, it took him all of two minutes to shut down the rest of the museum's alarms, monitors, and sensors.

He had been right about the guards. Another four security men were posted inside. He disabled them all, trancing them into a heavy sleep that would last well after he and the gang were gone tonight.

Flashing back to the receiving dock, he motioned Cruz and his crew forward. "Come on. The vault room is this way."

They fell in after him. He led them to the freight elevator and down to the basement. The huge vault was at the back, a locked, temperature-controlled storeroom for all manner of priceless pieces not currently on display in the museum.

Rafe could have gotten the gang into the heavily secured vault as easily as he got them inside the building. Being Breed, all it would take was a silent mental command and the locks would spring open.

That's all it would take for Brinks to breach the reinforced, polished-steel door as well, but only if she wanted to out herself to her comrades. Instead, she moved in front of Rafe and hunkered down to unfasten the pack of tools she had retrieved from the back of her motorcycle a few moments before that kiss he'd stolen from her. A kiss that was still wreaking havoc on Rafe's senses as he watched her work.

He had to give her credit for making a convincing effort to seem legit in front of the gang. She carefully laid out a set of delicate implements, compact magnetics, electronics, and listening devices. The kit looked like something off a movie set, which probably wasn't that far off the mark.

"Impressive collection. Guess I don't need to wonder anymore why they call you Brinks, eh?"

She slanted him a withering look and he could hardly hold back his chuckle.

Fish clapped a hand on Rafe's shoulder. "You're looking at the best safe-cracker you'll ever meet, man."

He smirked. "I don't doubt that."

"Shut up and let her work, both of you." Cruz scowled, his hand fidgety where it rested on his holstered gun. "This is taking too long already. Snap to it, Brinks."

She pretended to struggle with the lock for a few tense minutes before announcing she was in. As soon as the door was open, Cruz and the other men hurried into the vault and began raiding the crated masterpieces stored inside. With the linens dumped off the hand trucks, Fish and Axel started loading up some of the art.

They worked in silence, but even if they had been shouting to one another, Rafe's keen hearing would not have missed the sudden shift in the air.

The elevator was moving.

Not the freight elevator they rode down in. The main lift, the one used exclusively by museum staff.

Brinks picked up the vibration too. Her head swiveled in his direction, a stark look on her face.

He nodded. "Fuck. We've got company. Everyone

out. Now."

"What are you talking about?" Cruz drew his pistol. "Who's coming? I thought you said you took out all of the security detail?"

"I did. This is someone else."

As soon as the words left his tongue, a female voice sounded from another part of the basement. "Hello? Who's down here? Is it you, Arnie? I just wanted to let you know I'm finally wrapping up for the night and heading home."

Ah, shit.

Jordana.

It wasn't unusual for Nathan's mate to put in long hours at the museum. Art was her passion, along with her devotion to the former assassin who captained the Order's patrol team in Boston.

"I can't find Louis or Max anywhere," Jordana said as she approached the area of the vault. "Where is every—oh, my God."

She stopped short on a gasp. Her beautiful face went slack with shock as her ocean-blue eyes took in the scene with one swift glance. "Rafe. What are you doing?"

"Get out of here." He wasn't sure if he was talking to her, or to Cruz and the rest of the thieves surrounding him. All he knew was this was the worst scenario he could've imagined tonight.

He was friends with Jordana. To him, she was family, the blood-bonded mate of one of his best friends. And now she was staring at him in disbelief, in utter contempt.

He glanced away from her to glare at the gang. "I said, get the fuck out of here right now!"

Fish and Axel scrambled into motion. Shoving past

a stunned Jordana with the wheeled hand trucks, they sped toward the freight elevator.

She watched them, then swung her outrage back at Rafe. "This is how low you've sunk? I can't believe this. What's happened to you, Rafe?"

"Jordana, just go. Please."

Instead of obeying, she took a step inside the vault. Her breath grew rapid as anger began to replace her confusion and fear.

"She's prettier than I expected, vampire." Cruz leered, swaggering toward her with his gun in hand. "Maybe we ought to take her with us too."

Jordana lifted her hand and the weapon flew out of his grasp. It clattered onto the floor several feet away.

Ocho made the next stupid move. The big man lunged for Jordana, but another flick of her hand sent all two-hundred-plus pounds of him sailing out of the vault as if he had wings. As soon as he had gotten up from the floor, he took off running after his comrades.

Cruz was only an instant behind him.

"You too," Rafe muttered to Brinks when it was only the two of them left. "For fuck's sake. Go."

She didn't budge. And he didn't have time to argue with her.

The way Jordana's fury was mounting, he was going to have a much bigger problem very soon. Not only from this female who was pure Atlantean, but from the assassin who was bonded to her by blood.

Because by now Nathan would have felt every spike in his mate's emotional state. And there would be no stopping him from coming to her rescue, no matter where he might be.

"Jordana, calm down."

It was a lame thing to say, but it was all he had. He wanted to explain everything, but he was still in play and unable to breach his commanders' faith in him. And while he and the Breed female at his side had reached some kind of mutual dependence inside Cruz's gang tonight, that didn't mean he was ready to give her any added leverage over him.

Not that it mattered.

Jordana was looking at him like a stranger now, an enemy.

"Nathan told me you'd hooked up with some lowlife criminals. I didn't want to believe it."

Rafe swore under his breath, his reply tasting like bitter acid on his tongue. "Yeah, well, I'm sorry to disappoint." He glanced at Brinks. "We need to go now."

He took a step forward and was stopped by a pulse of powerful energy. It shoved him back on his heels.

Jordana's hands were down at her sides, her fingers curled into loose fists. Light emanated from within her palms, growing stronger. Not merely light, Atlantean power.

Rafe grabbed Brinks by the wrist and tried to haul her past Jordana.

A bigger blast hit him, jolting his nervous system and knocking him flat on his ass.

"Rafe!" The sound of Brinks's concerned shout penetrated the haze of his rattled skull.

He lifted his head and saw that Jordana's hands were aglow now, her palms and fingers engulfed in bright halos of unearthly light.

Rafe tried to get up, but invisible chains held him down. He cursed, fighting to break loose from her power. It was no use. She was far stronger than he imagined. No doubt, her blood bond with Nathan had only enhanced her abilities.

He would be damn impressed if he wasn't glued to the floor of the vault.

"Let him go." Brinks's cool demand shocked him. Her face was anything but calm. As she stared at Jordana, her bourbon eyes threw off amber sparks like a bonfire. The tips of her fangs gleamed like diamonds as her lip curled back on a snarl.

Jordana glanced at the other female, but the force of her energy didn't relent. Not even a little.

Brinks didn't give her a second chance.

She launched herself at Jordana with a speed that surpassed anything Rafe was capable of. One instant she was standing off to his side in the vault, the next she was planted in front of Jordana, seizing her by the shoulders.

Jordana made a strangled noise as Brinks's hands locked on to her and didn't let go.

"Don't hurt her," Rafe shouted, but he wasn't sure Brinks was listening. And as hard as he tried, he couldn't shake loose from the telekinetic force that held him down.

Fuck, this wasn't good. He didn't think it could get much worse.

Then, upstairs in the museum came the crash of breaking glass.

A deep, unearthly roar shook the building. Unmistakably Breed.

Nathan.

The massive, black-haired Gen One seemed to materialize from out of nowhere.

And Rafe had never seen him so enraged.

Nor more starkly terrified as his mate began to sag against the unfamiliar Breed female. "Get away from her."

The light in Jordana's palms extinguished. As it faded, the power that had been holding Rafe down subsided. He leapt to his feet. "Nathan, this isn't what it looks like."

Smoldering, murderous eyes skewered him. "Then what the hell is this bitch doing with her hands on my mate?"

On a bellow, Nathan charged at Brinks in homicidal rage.

She lifted her hand away from Jordana and the massive male flew backward, tumbling ass over tea kettle before crashing into the far wall. He moaned, but didn't—or couldn't—get up.

"What the fuck?" Rafe gaped at her.

Brinks's palms now glowed with the same light that had filled Jordana's.

Rafe grabbed her hand and turned it over, trying to make sense of what he was seeing.

He could feel the power circulating through her, hot and bright and almighty. Atlantean power.

Except it didn't belong to this Breed female. She had drawn it away from Jordana.

"They will both be all right," she said, gently lowering Jordana's slumped, unconscious body to the floor. "But we should go now."

CHAPTER 7

The storm that had threatened earlier was in full swing as Devony and Rafe burst out of the museum on foot. The delivery van was gone from the receiving dock, Cruz and the rest of the gang having left Rafe and her to make their escape on their own.

Fat raindrops soaked them as they ran, sheets of water rolling across the football-sized parking lot and turning puddles into almost ankle-deep pools on the asphalt.

Devony couldn't stop shivering.

Her legs felt increasingly rubbery beneath her, her black boots seeming to gain an extra pound of weight for every step she took as she hurried to keep up with Rafe's long strides.

Her hands were no longer glowing. The power she had siphoned off the woman Rafe had called Jordana had begun to leave her even before they'd made it out to the parking lot. Now, she was paying the price for using her ability.

In another few minutes, she would be completely drained.

Rafe glanced at her and frowned. "You okay?"

"I'm fine," she shouted through the rain. At least, she thought she shouted. Her voice sounded weak, hardly more than a croak. "Keep going. I'm right . . . behind . . . you."

"Like hell you're fine."

She took a sluggish step and stumbled. Rafe's hands were underneath her before she had a chance to hit the pavement. Scooping her into his arms, he stared down at her, his handsome face pinched with concern.

"You need help. First, I need to get you out of this rain."

She wanted to argue against needing anything from him, but her mouth had gone dry as all of her energy faded away. Her head was too heavy to hold up now, even though it felt as if it were stuffed with cotton. Resting against Rafe's muscled chest, she had no choice but to give in to the comfort of his strength.

His heat warmed the chill that gripped her. His body was firm and solid as he carried her, his arms holding her aloft as if she weighed nothing at all. And Lord, he smelled good too. Even in her weakened state, her senses responded to everything male in him.

"There's a park across the street," he said, his deep voice vibrating against her ear. "I'll find us some shelter to wait for the storm to clear. Then you're going to tell me what the hell I just witnessed back there in the museum."

In moments, they were beneath the timber roof of a

covered picnic shelter in a secluded corner of the empty park. Rain pattered in the surrounding trees and on the shingles overhead, while the dark sky rumbled with thunder.

Rafe set her down on the wooden bench seat beside him. Her head was still woozy, her skull throbbing from a pain that was building swiftly now that she was sitting upright. Or trying to, that is. The post-ability crash was coming on fast now, sapping what little strength she had left.

"Shit," Rafe hissed as she listed toward him. "Come here."

She couldn't fight him as he drew her close, settling her across his lap on the bench. It had been years since she used her psychic ability, mainly because of the price she paid afterward. But she had never experienced pain and depletion like this.

She had never experienced the kind of awesome power she'd pulled from Jordana, either.

Devony moaned, shuddering and cold as the last of that power leached out of her, leaving her as helpless as an infant. She hated this weakness. Hated it even more because Rafe was seeing her this way.

"Christ, you're ice cold." Shrugging out of his leather jacket, he laid it over her. The added warmth felt nice, but not as good as the intense, permeating heat of his body beneath her, or the soothing comfort of his hands moving tenderly over her face and brow. "Does that feel better?"

It did, she realized. The savage pound kicking up inside her skull was ebbing under his touch. She nodded, not yet able to form coherent words. Her eyelids lifted and she stared up into the face of a golden angel. A scowling angel, whose grim concern was focused entirely on her.

And he was still touching her. His fingers stroked her forehead and temples, while his gaze clung to hers.

It felt more than good. It made her crave the feeling in a lot of other places on her body.

A weak moan escaped her as she struggled to lift up from his lap.

"Relax, Brinks. You're not in any shape to even think about moving yet." He shook his head and exhaled a curse. "Tell me your name. Your real name this time."

It leaked out of her in a whisper. "Devony."

He gave her a nod, the edge of his mouth quirking in response. "Devony. That's a hell of an improvement over Brinks. Now, stay put, Devony. Let me help you."

Accepting his help was the last thing she wanted, but she didn't have the strength to refuse. He slipped his hands under the jacket he'd covered her with, moving his palms over the length of her arms then along her center.

"What did you do to Jordana back there?"

"I didn't hurt her, I promise. I just borrowed her ability . . . temporarily."

"Borrowed it." His brow furrowed. "You mean you absorbed it into yourself? Explain."

She hesitated, uncertain how he would react. "I can siphon someone else's ability. I can use it as if it's my own. Not for long, though. I can only hold it for a few minutes."

"That's what you turned on Nathan when he came at you? Jordana's power." He shook his head, his expression grave. "No wonder. That's about the only thing that could stop a former Hunter like him. Don't make the mistake of thinking he'll give you a chance to do it again."

Devony wasn't surprised to hear that Jordana's mate had been one of those formidable assassins. When he'd come at her, explosive in his fury, she had almost resigned herself to the fact that her next breath might be her last.

But Jordana's power had protected her.

Not even a massive, clearly lethal Breed male like Nathan was any match for the light that had manifested in Devony's hands.

"What is she, Rafe? Jordana . . . she isn't Breed like you or Nathan. She isn't a daywalker like me, either."

"No."

"But she is an immortal?"

His lengthy silence neither confirmed nor denied it. But he obviously wasn't going to give her any more than that. The message in his stony expression was clear enough.

He didn't trust her. Not with information about people he once cared about. He probably didn't trust her with anything.

Not that she should blame him, considering the way Cruz had set him up tonight. Choosing the MFA had been Rafe's test. She doubted Cruz could have anticipated they might run into someone he knew. The gang leader was cruel at times, but she wasn't ready to give the man that much credit.

And while Devony didn't have an obligation to clue Rafe in about Cruz's intentions, she couldn't deny that her guilt had been gnawing at her the entire time.

"I'm sorry I didn't tell you where we were going tonight."

Rafe grunted. "Don't worry about it."

His reply was clipped, toneless. She couldn't decide if that was because he expected everyone to betray him, or only her.

"Well, I'm saying it anyway, Rafe. I am sorry. Cruz told me he was going to test you somehow, but I didn't know the details. And I didn't know there was a chance we could run into friends of yours."

His gaze clashed with hers. "I said forget it. And they're not my friends. Not anymore."

"But they were once?"

He blew out a harsh sigh. "Yeah, they were. Nathan is the captain of my old patrol team. He was one of my best friends."

"Then why aren't you still with them? How could the Order just cut you loose?"

"I fucked up, all right?" His eyes flashed, hot and fiery. "That's all you need to know."

His curt, defensive reply jarred her. Whatever he'd done bothered him deeply. He may not trust her with information about his former friends or anything else, but there was no denying the honesty in his voice now. Nor in his handsome, tormented face.

Yet for all his irritation with her probing, his hands remained warm and soothing on her.

She sighed and let her eyes drift closed for a moment, hating how easy it was to melt into the pleasant heat of Rafe's touch. Energy flowed back into her by the moment, drawing away her pain. With the power of his bare hands, he was reversing the physical toll she paid for using her ability.

Healing her, much like he had done for Fish the other night.

"You saved my life back there," he murmured. "Hell, you saved both of us tonight. I should be thanking you for that, not snarling at you."

"It's all right." She lifted her lids and found him watching her. The intensity of his gaze unsettled her, even as it stirred something deep inside her. Something more than just the remarkable energy of his healing hands.

His eyes searched hers as he continued to restore her depleted body. "I've never seen an ability like yours before. Jesus, Devony. Do you realize what you could do with a gift like that? No enemy could stand against you. You could be unstoppable."

She never had enemies, not until a few months ago. As for using her gift? From the time she was a child, she had been cautioned to take care with her unique Breed ability. Her brother too. Both daywalkers, both the children of their genetically enhanced mother, Camilla, she and Harrison shared this incredible, inherited gift. They had been raised to respect the power they could wield at their will.

"I don't feel very unstoppable now," she said, mortified to still be lying helplessly across his lap. "As you can see, once the effect wears off I'm useless for a while. Total crash and burn situation."

"So, this always happens to you afterward?"

"Yeah. More or less." In tonight's case, it was definitely more. Her limbs had felt stretched, wrung out. The rest of her body had felt sapped and deflated, a husk that was only now beginning to come back to life. Her vitality was returning swiftly now, energy moving through her veins and bones.

All thanks to Rafe.

And while there was nothing sexual about his touch, it was impossible for her to ignore the pool of heat that began to bloom in her core as his palms skated over her clothed body. She shifted on his lap, unsettled by the quickening of her blood and the arousal that was licking through her senses.

A quiet moan escaped her before she could curb it. Rafe answered with a low, strangled groan. His hand went still on her belly, and she felt the outline of his broad palm and each strong finger as if his touch were branding her.

"Rafe . . ." She didn't know what she was going to say.

His eyes met hers, something unreadable flickering through them now. Her throat jammed with a hundred unsettling thoughts, words she hardly dared to speak out loud.

Especially to him.

His glance drifted to her parted lips and hesitated there. Was he thinking about the way her mouth had felt on his in the parking lot outside Ocho's garage?

God knew, she had been unable to put that kiss out of her mind for even a second since it happened.

And in spite of her outrage at the time—in spite of her threat to ash him for it—right now, she couldn't think of anything she wanted more than to feel his lips pressed against hers again.

Now that her limbs were her own to command once more, she slid her hand tentatively over his.

Rafe's expression darkened into a scowl. But in his eyes, embers smoldered. A tendon pulsed in his rigid jaw, as if her tenderness confused him.

Or worse, piqued his mistrust.

On a gravelly, uttered curse, he drew his hand out from under hers.

Clearly, he hadn't intended their kiss to be anything more than a means to an end. Just his way of forcing her to reveal herself as Breed so he could use the knowledge against her.

If she had read anything more into it, the mistake was all hers.

"How do you feel?" he asked as his touch left her completely.

"Better." She felt foolish, honestly. Naïve to have imagined his care with her tonight was inspired by anything other than gratitude. Lifting off his lap, she pushed his jacket toward him. "Thanks for the help. We'd better get back to Ocho's. Cruz will be wondering what happened to us by now."

He gave her a dark look and cleared his throat. "Before we do that, we need to talk."

"About what?"

"You can start by telling me what you're doing with men like them in the first place. You have no loyalty to Cruz. If you were truly one of his gang, you wouldn't be deceiving them about the fact that you're Breed."

"I have my reasons."

"What are they?"

"Personal."

He shook his head. "Maybe before, but not now. Not when I have to decide whether to keep your secret from Cruz and protect your interests, or tell him and look out for my own."

So, there it was. He'd just played his best card. The one she had personally handed to him earlier tonight.

"I knew it wouldn't take long before you threatened

to expose me to them," she said, feeling stung and cornered. "To think, just a few minutes ago you were thanking me for saving your ass. I guess it's good to know what your gratitude is worth."

She rose from the bench, but Rafe stood with her. Face to face, with only inches between them, there was no way to avoid his probing stare.

"You're in over your head, Devony. What happened here tonight has only increased the odds that you're going to get hurt. Or worse. You need to know you're dealing with some very dangerous individuals."

"Does that include you?"

He didn't have to confirm it. The sheer starkness of his expression took her aback. There was a bleak truth in his eyes, one that chilled her.

"You say you have your reasons for being here. So do I," he said, speaking with the calm smoothness of a diplomat rather than the lethal male he'd just reminded her he was. "I'm not here to make friends . . . or anything else. But I don't want us to be enemies, either."

She scoffed. "What a relief. Either way, it appears we're at an impasse."

"Maybe it doesn't have to be that way."

She eyed him warily. "Then what would you suggest?"

"A truce, for now. A mutually beneficial one. I keep your secret, so long as you have my back inside the gang. That means you keep me informed of all activity, and you alert me if Cruz has plans to cross me or test me the way he did tonight. In return, I'll provide cover when you can't show your true nature in front of the men."

She wanted to balk at the proposal, but what other choice did he leave her? And while she wasn't looking to make friends either, the thought of having someone to confide in, to lean on, was sorely tempting.

Especially when the alternative was forfeiting months of effort in trying to find a link to her true enemy, Opus Nostrum.

Rafe held out his hand. "Do we have a deal?"

Devony slipped her fingers into his grasp, hoping she wasn't making the mistake of her life in allying with him, even under the confines of their wary truce.

"All right, Rafe. We have a deal."

CHAPTER 8

The parked delivery van was still warm in the lot behind Ocho's garage when Rafe and Devony made it back there on foot some forty-five minutes later.

Soaked from the rain, Rafe's mood following the near-disaster in the museum and his conversation with Devony afterward hadn't been improved by the three-mile trek in the cold drizzle. He vibrated with anger as they entered the garage and found Cruz and the rest of the crew in the midst of pouring shots and celebrating as if the whole caper hadn't almost gone as far south as it could have.

Rafe wasn't usually the kind to lose his shit, but thinking about how Nathan and Jordana must feel about him now ignited a volatile rage inside him.

That fury only amplified when he considered that in testing his loyalty, Cruz had also risked the lives of five innocent museum guards and Jordana.

Not to mention Devony.

And her life was still at risk, because after what happened with Jordana at the museum, there would be hell to pay from Nathan. Rafe wasn't worried about his own neck, but he didn't want to consider what might happen to Devony now that she had made herself his accomplice in a mission that was supposed to be covert and solo. He wasn't sure how he could reverse that very lethal problem without punching a hole in his entire operation.

He strode inside the garage with fangs bared and murder radiating from his eyes.

"Cruz. You fucking asshole." He yanked the gang leader out of his chair and shoved him hard, driving the human's back into the drywall of Ocho's office. "The next time you think about screwing me over, you'd better think again."

Liquor splashed from Cruz's dropped shot glass. He looked scared, which meant he wasn't as stupid as Rafe thought. "Hold up, man. Hold up!"

The pleading barely registered through the haze of Rafe's animosity. "You could've gotten a lot of people killed tonight. Give me one good reason why I shouldn't return the favor to you right fucking now."

"Wasn't personal," Cruz uttered, his words strangled. "I just . . . needed to know if I could count on you."

Rafe snarled. "Did you know anyone would be working at the museum tonight?"

"No! Jesus, I swear it. No."

Rafe wanted the asshole to lie to him. It wouldn't take much more than that to push him over the edge.

One dead gangbanger wouldn't derail his entire hunt for a lead on Opus Nostrum.

And right now, crushing Cruz's throat in his fist would feel damn good.

"Rafe." Devony's voice broke through his haze of anger.

He had told her on the way back to let him handle the situation and to trust that he knew what he was doing. At the moment, he wasn't sure he could uphold that promise.

"*Rafe.*"

Her hand came to rest on his shoulder. He glanced at her, his eyes still ablaze with amber fire and his fangs enormous in his mouth. She gave a faint shake of her head, her warm eyes wide and imploring.

As soon as he let Cruz go, the gang leader straightened, tugging at his leather jacket. He spat on the floor, then glanced around Rafe and motioned to Ocho. The other man came over carrying two thick stacks of banded hundred-dollar bills. Cruz gestured for Rafe to take them.

He scowled. "What's this?"

"Your share of tonight's proceeds."

Damn. Apparently, they hadn't wasted any time delivering the stolen artwork to their contact. Rafe figured they must have made the drop to Judah LaSalle not long after they'd cut and run on Devony and him at the museum.

Now that he was freed from Rafe's punishing hold, some of his bravado returned. "I told you, it was a test tonight. Congrats, you crazy motherfucker, you passed." Cruz smirked, self-satisfied, as Rafe took the money and put it in his jacket. "You need a reason why I'm the last person you want to kill, vampire? There's fifty-thousand of 'em. Keep proving your worth like you did tonight, and that's only the start."

He brushed past him without another word to accept a fresh drink from Axel.

Devony stepped away too, walking over to where the men had divvied up the rest of the night's take into similar stacks. She tucked hers into the inside pocket of her leather jacket, then with a murmured goodbye to the gang she started heading for the back door.

Rafe strode up to her before she reached the exit. "Where are you going?"

"What does it look like? I'm going home."

He shouldn't be surprised by her curt response. Although they had reached some kind of understanding with each other tonight, it hadn't come on the friendliest of terms. He had pushed her into a corner and that was obviously not a place Devony was accustomed to staying.

She was tenacious and bold. Fearless, as he witnessed tonight.

He had to admire that about her.

He admired a lot about her, including a host of things that he shouldn't. Not if he wanted to keep his head in the game and his focus on his mission. A beautiful, headstrong woman like Devony was only going to be a liability to him in the end.

He'd known that even before he put his hands on her to heal her tonight.

He hadn't even directly touched her skin, yet feeling her beneath his palms had taken on an intimacy he wasn't prepared for. Her heat, her strength, the softness of her curves combined with the preternatural, uniquely

Breed power that simmered beneath the surface of everything that was so unmistakably feminine about her.

He had been awed by her unique psychic ability, but it was the woman who intrigued him more. Far more than he should be willing to allow.

And when Devony had placed her hand over his while he healed her in the park, he'd nearly gone up in flames. If he hadn't pulled away, his desire for her would have incinerated the last shred of his control.

Even now, his fingertips vibrated with the indelible sensory memory of how she felt beneath his hands.

Inside, he smoldered with the need to touch her again.

To do much more than that.

"Hey, Brinks." Fish jogged over holding a shot of whisky. He held it out for her. "You can't leave without a little toast."

"Sure." She took the glass and wanly clinked it against his before taking a small sip.

Fish glanced at Rafe. "What about you, my man? Care to partake?"

"I never touch that shit."

The human chuckled. "No worries, I got you covered. We're heading out to one of the strip joints up the street. I'm sure you'll find something to wet your whistle over there."

With a cackle, he swaggered back to the rest of the gang.

Devony set her glass down without taking another sip. "Enjoy the show. I'm out of here."

She walked out to the parking lot without a backward glance. A moment later, the low rumble of her motorcycle sounded as she sped away.

Shit.

Rafe knew he ought to just let her go.

His interests would be better served spending time with the gang, making sure they all got good and drunk so he could prod them for details about Judah LaSalle or anyone else who might be orchestrating their activities. Hell, this might be his first real opportunity to get close enough to trance each one of the humans and extract the information he needed directly from their minds.

But not while Devony was out there in the city alone.

She might be a daywalking Breed female, but that didn't mean Rafe wanted to imagine her being confronted by his old friend Nathan's wrath.

If something happened to her now he would never forgive himself.

That feeling had nothing to do with gratitude for what she did for him in the museum, either. It went deeper than that, which disturbed him all the way to his marrow.

Devony wasn't his to worry about or protect. Caring about her wasn't part of his mission, and there was no place for compassion when his quest to destroy Opus Nostrum demanded only cold, lethal focus.

One misstep, one careless miscalculation, could cost him everything.

Like letting his concern for her ignite a reckless rage inside him tonight with Cruz.

The ferocity of his anger shocked him. It had shocked Devony too. He saw that in her stricken expression when he'd leapt on Cruz. When her voice had been the only thing that reeled him back from the edge.

Fuck.

It was obvious to him what he needed to do, before

he let things get more complicated than he already had.

He could not risk his mission by bringing her into the equation. Not in any form.

Which meant he had to remove her, the sooner the better.

While he considered the unpleasant task ahead of him, Cruz walked over with the rest of the gang. "We're getting ready to roll out in a few. You coming along, or what?"

"Another time."

He didn't offer any further excuse before heading out to his bike. The rain had finally stopped, and the storm had thinned the nighttime traffic. He didn't know where Devony lived, but he knew the distinctive purr of her Triumph. His Breed hearing was acute enough to zero in on that sound amid the rest of the vehicles moving through the streets.

He followed his ears until he spotted her taillight heading north toward the affluent neighborhood of Back Bay.

Rafe stayed about a mile behind her, watching in curiosity as she made one stop along the way. Parking outside one of the city's homeless shelters, she jogged up to the donation box and dropped all fifty grand in cash into the slot.

What the hell?

After risking her life to earn it, she just gave her entire share of the theft away.

Rafe hadn't imagined she was participating in Cruz's gang out of personal greed, but this was a revelation all on its own. It was an unexpectedly tender side to the tough-as-nails Breed female.

That she was harboring other well-guarded secrets as

well, he had no doubt.

Tonight, he intended to unwrap them all.

CHAPTER 9

Devony felt eyes on her.

The prickle of awareness had settled at her nape on the drive home to her brownstone and hadn't let up in the ten minutes since she had arrived.

Which is why she hadn't yet changed out of her lug-soled boots, fine-gauge turtleneck and stretchy, form-fitting black tactical pants.

The semiautomatic pistol she'd carried with her into the museum job tonight was still holstered on the belt around her hips, too, although she doubted the weapon would be much use against the intruder she knew was currently inside her house.

Breed.

She stepped out of her father's study and found Rafe standing in her foyer.

He had slipped past the deadbolts and security system in silence, and now had the audacity to give her a wry smile. "I was in the neighborhood. Sorry I didn't knock."

Outrage burst through her veins. "What the hell do you think you're doing?" She couldn't believe the arrogant male had actually found where she lived and barged in as if he owned the place. "Get out of here right now. Or I'll throw you out."

There was no need to pretend she wasn't fully capable of doing exactly that. Or at least willing to try.

"We need to talk, Devony."

Was he serious? She glared at him, her vision snapping with amber sparks. "We already did that earlier tonight, remember?"

He slowly shook his head. "No. You haven't told me anything yet. I need to know what you're doing in Cruz's gang. I mean what you're really doing."

So, he had followed her all the way from Ocho's garage. Tailed her. Spied on her. Right before he broke into her house.

"I don't think you're actually with them at all. You're only playing a role, using them for some reason. So, what are you after? Not money. I saw you leave yours in a charity box in town."

She swallowed as he took a step toward her. "I said you need to leave, Rafe. I'm not going to ask again."

He didn't look like he had any intention of complying. He scanned the opulent entryway of the old brownstone, taking in the dark mahogany millwork and stairs, the glittering chandelier overhead, and the sumptuous antique rug beneath his heavy boots.

"Whose Darkhaven is this?"

"It's mine." That wasn't a lie, even though it felt like one as she used it to evade his real question.

He glanced into the spacious family room to his left, with its polished grand piano and the delicate Louis XVI furnishings her mother had loved so well. On the other side of the foyer was the cozy library where she and her brother had spent countless hours as children devouring all of the stories and biographies and thought-provoking philosophical texts that lined the floor-to-ceiling shelves.

That was before. Before her parents moved the family back to London for their work with the government.

And long before the heinous and cowardly terror act that stole them all away from her earlier this year.

Instead of leaving as she'd told him to, Rafe stepped further inside her home.

"Do you live with someone?" He frowned. "Are you mated to someone, Devony?"

"No. Not that it's any of your business. This is my family's home."

"Your family lives very well. Where are they now?"

She shook her head. She hadn't spoken the words to anyone in all this time. She wasn't even sure she could say them now.

Not without breaking down in front of him—or worse, revealing some of the burning hatred that had lived inside her ever since their murders by Opus Nostrum.

"I want you to go, Rafe. Please."

Part of her worried that he would take his knowledge of her Darkhaven, and his questions about it, immediately back to Cruz. But a bigger part of her worried that his reason for coming here right now had nothing to do with the gang.

He was here for his own personal reasons. For his

own personal gain somehow.

"I need you to tell me what's really going on, Devony. I promise, everything will go a lot easier for you if you do."

He sounded so reasonable, even concerned about her. But there was a dark resolve in his eyes that was pure warrior.

She fisted her hands on her hips, her feet braced beneath her. "Easier for me? What's that supposed to mean?"

"I tried to explain that to you earlier tonight. You're in over your head. You're dealing with some very dangerous people—"

"Yes, I remember. Dangerous people like you and your old friends in the Order."

"And others," he added grimly. "I don't mean only Cruz and his ilk. I'm talking about people you never want to meet."

She shrugged. "I'm not afraid of anything anyone can do to me."

He gave her a dubious look. "Because you're a daywalker who was born with a hell of a powerful gift?"

"No. Because there's nothing anyone can take from me anymore," she answered evenly. "I've already lost everything I care about."

"What do you mean?"

She held his searching stare. "You need to leave now. This conversation is over."

To drive home her point, she mentally threw open the front door behind him. Night air rushed inside, cold and damp.

Without as much as a blink of reaction, Rafe slammed the heavy oak panel shut with the power of his own mind.

"What have you lost, Devony?" He walked toward her, studying her face. "I want to understand. I need to understand before I can help you."

"Help me?" She scoffed. "I don't need anyone's help, especially yours. I work alone. I *am* alone, dammit."

He frowned, processing the small admission she'd so carelessly let slip.

And he was still approaching her, moving closer to where she stood outside her father's study. Her pulse kicked into a harder tempo as he ate up the space between them. He was close enough to reach out to her, but he kept his hands loosely fisted at his sides.

"Something happened to your family," he said, not a question at all. "They're dead?"

She swallowed. Hearing him say it reinforced the awful reality of her loss. "Rafe, please. Just go. Leave me alone."

"Someone killed them. Is that what happened?" When she only stared at him, his gaze narrowed on her, zeroing in on the pain she couldn't keep from showing on her face. "Does Cruz have anything to do with their deaths? Or is it someone else, someone the gang is connected to?"

Oh, God. He was getting too close to the truth.

She saw him attack Cruz tonight—partially on her behalf—but that didn't mean she could trust him to keep this secret too. She had already given him one weapon to use against her. She couldn't hand him another.

Most certainly not this one.

"I said I want you to leave. *Now.*" She punctuated the demand with a mental shove against his muscular bulk. He skated backward a pace on his heels.

At twice her size and girded in masculine sinew, Rafe was a formidable Breed male. But as a daywalking female, she was nearly an equal match for him. If he thought he could come in here and make her cower, he was going to be in for a fight.

One dark blond brow arched and he stepped forward, closing even more distance between them. "Devony, all you have to do is talk to me. Trust me."

She pushed him back again, less gently this time.

Her heart hammered, and not only from the anger that was coursing through her veins. It was all she could do not to lick her lips as he calmly, boldly, took a step closer, unfazed by her attack.

"It doesn't have to be like this between us," he said, his deep voice vibrating through her and making the rapid beat of her pulse throb with a heavy anticipation. "We're not enemies, remember?"

"We're sure as hell not friends," she shot back.

Her breast heaved as the air between her and this dangerous Breed male seemed to electrify. That unbearable tension only mounted as he closed the distance even more.

"We're not anything else, either. Isn't that what you said tonight, Rafe? Isn't that what you want?"

He exhaled a short breath. A look of regret swept over his handsome face, and something even more unsettling to her.

Desire.

There was no mistaking it, even with her limited experience.

And what terrified her now was just how intensely he aroused her too.

In a wave of stark panic, she tried to shove him back

again, this time with her hands.

He caught them in his grasp, his reflexes lightning-fast, unerring. His hold on her was impossibly strong.

Infinitely tender.

His gaze pierced her, intense and smoldering. Slowly, he lowered her fisted hands between them. Then he reached up and caressed her cheek.

Before she took another breath, he bent his head toward hers and kissed her. Not the swift, aggressive claiming of his first kiss back at Ocho's garage, but a gentle coaxing that wrung a helpless moan from somewhere deep inside her. She couldn't fight the sweet onslaught of arousal that spiraled through her. She didn't want to fight it.

His tongue slid along the seam of her mouth and she opened to him, inhaling his spice-and-leather scent and melting into the blaze of heat that was igniting between them.

She wanted more.

She wanted it so badly she trembled with need for him.

He drew back on a muttered curse. "Christ. You're right, I shouldn't be here. This was a mistake. I should've known that and yet—"

He stopped mid-sentence, his molten gaze drawn to a point somewhere over her shoulder. To something inside her father's old study.

Rafe's brow furrowed. "That family photograph on the desk. The man in the picture with you . . . that's Roland Winters." He swung a hard look at her now, suspicious. "I was introduced to him at a peace summit in D.C. with the Order earlier this year. He was an administrative director with JUSTIS in the London office going on two decades, as I recall."

Devony shrank back, shifting so that she blocked the open entrance to the room. But it was too late to prevent Rafe from seeing more than he should have. Too late to keep him from understanding her pain and loss now too.

His frown deepened as his gaze returned to her. "Roland Winters died in that city five months ago. He, along with upwards of a hundred other JUSTIS agents and officials who were in the London headquarters when it was attacked. Jesus, Devony. You lost your father in that bombing?"

"I lost everyone." She could hardly swallow past the grief that had maintained a stranglehold on her ever since that awful night. "My father. My mother. My brother. They all worked for JUSTIS. My mom and Harrison were both in the undercover units. Everyone had been called in for a meeting at the London office when it was leveled by the explosion."

His breath left him on a slow, heavy sigh. "Shit. And where were you?" he asked gently.

"Here in Boston. I had been attending arts university for the last two years. When the news broke, I was in the middle of a piano recital at the concert hall, auditioning for a seat in the symphony. Those plans were over in an instant. Everything normal in my life just . . . ended that night."

"I'm sorry. I mean that, Devony. Unfortunately, it wasn't long ago that I came close to losing my family too. I don't know what I would've done if I had." The depth of pain in his deep voice surprised her. There was anger there too, and she couldn't help thinking that some of it might be self-directed. "What have you been doing in the time since the attack?"

"Adjusting."

He couldn't know just how true that statement was. Still, he studied her skeptically. "Why not go back to London? Why stay here in this empty Darkhaven by yourself? For fuck's sake, why not get as far away from here as you can and start over?"

"I can't go back to London. Maybe not ever. And I can't start over anywhere until I know the monsters responsible for my family's murders will be made to pay. I won't rest until it's done."

Rafe gave her a stark, questioning look. "A terrorist group claimed credit publicly for that attack, among others. You're talking about going after Opus Nostrum?"

"That's right."

"Tell me you're joking."

"Do I look like I'm joking?"

He swore again, more vividly this time. "And you think Cruz or someone he knows is going to lead you to them?"

She didn't want to tell him about her suspicions, or the steps she'd taken to pursue them in the months since her family's slayings. Just because he claimed he'd shaken hands with her father at one time didn't mean she could trust him.

But it was obvious Rafe was on to her ulterior motives where the gang was concerned. He'd been on to her almost from the start. "If Cruz doesn't lead me to Opus, then I'll keep looking. Eventually, I'll find a connection."

"You're insane, you know that? All you're going to do is get yourself killed, Devony. You may think you're strong—"

"I *am* strong," she countered grimly. "You've seen that for yourself."

"Yes," he admitted, looking none-too-pleased about it. "You'd be impressive even without your ability, but you have no idea what Opus is capable of."

"I think I do. I saw the images from London. I saw the pyre and the rubble. It doesn't get much clearer than that."

"You think that's the worst they can do?" He barked out a caustic laugh. "That's only the warmup, sweetheart. Nothing is beneath this cabal. They are everywhere. They will use anyone, exploit any weakness they can find. And they have. Christ, they've even tried to use me."

"Use you? What are you talking about?"

"Shit." He raked a hand over his head and pivoted away from her. "Why didn't I just stay the fuck away from you tonight?"

It wasn't a question she had an answer for. Right now, there was only one answer she needed to hear.

"Tell me," she said to his broad back. "Rafe, please . . . I need to know. What did Opus do to you? Did they hurt you too?"

"Hurt me?" He swung back and grimly shook his head. "I was only a pawn they used to hurt a lot of other people. They sent a mole into the Order's protection— a beautiful, treacherous one. She played me. You think your gift is powerful? This bitch had a siren's ability. She tricked me into thinking I was in love with her. All the while she was working against me. She fed Opus the Order's every move, waiting for the chance to strike at us from within. She almost got it, too. If it wasn't for some of my teammates in the Order, we'd all be dead."

"Oh, my God. Rafe, I'm sorry."

He shrugged. "I fucked up. I let everyone down. I allowed myself to be manipulated, and nearly got everyone I care about killed. My friends, my parents. Not to mention Lucan Thorne and several other Order elders."

"That's why you're not a warrior anymore? If this woman held that kind of power over you, how can the Order blame you? It hardly seems fair for them to kick you out for something that was out of your control."

He didn't answer. His dark expression shuttered at her probing questions, then he glanced away from her. "You think you have good reason to go after Opus? I've got more than a dozen of them. And if I have to tear through Cruz or anyone else to get my hands on even one of Opus's inner circle, I am damn well going to do it."

Devony couldn't help but sympathize with what he'd been through. Their lives had both been irrevocably altered because of Opus Nostrum's evil. Now, she understood they also shared a similar goal.

Maybe they would both stand a better chance of seeing those goals through to fruition if they joined forces.

"I need to show you something, Rafe."

She moved past him and entered the study.

Running her hand under her father's desk, she found the hidden button and pressed it. The bookcase silently unlatched, and Devony opened it wider, revealing all of the dossiers, photographs, maps, and scribbled notes of the private war she'd been waging alone for the past five months.

Rafe stared for a long moment. When he finally turned his head to look at her, his handsome face was slack with incredulity and awe.

"Holy shit," he said, a slight grin tugging at his lips.

Then he walked inside.

CHAPTER 10

R afe didn't know whether to feel impressed or a bit occupationally threatened by the depth and quality of Devony's work.

It had been more than a couple of hours since she showed him her private war room. With each passing minute he had only become more fascinated with what he saw. Not only the notes and photographs and handwritten theories she had shared with him, but with the woman herself.

Especially her.

"Ah. Here it is," she said, pulling a photograph out of a file folder stuffed with other images and documents. "This is the one I wanted to show you. I took it during a party on LaSalle's yacht a couple of weeks ago."

Rafe sat on the floor of the large study with her, surrounded by other piles of intelligence Devony had amassed in the handful of months since she set out on her quest to avenge her family by bringing down Opus Nostrum. It would take him days to study it all. Maybe a lot longer than that, if he allowed himself to be continually distracted by the incredible woman responsible for putting it together.

She had gone upstairs a while ago and changed clothes, trading her museum heist attire for a loose, gray V-neck sweater and black yoga pants. Her long brown hair was twisted haphazardly into a knot on top of her head. A few escaped tendrils curled at her nape, repeatedly drawing his eye to the delicate *dermaglyphs* that tracked onto her shoulders and neck.

He couldn't keep from imagining what the rest of her Breed skin markings might look like beneath her clothes. Rafe could barely stifle the urge to reach out and trace the intricate swirls and arches of her *glyphs* with his fingers . . . or with his mouth.

As a daywalker female, she would also have the Breedmate mark somewhere on her luscious body. Against his will, he imagined slowly peeling away the soft knit top and pants until he uncovered the tiny scarlet birthmark's hiding place.

Fuck.

Kissing her for a second time was just about the worst thing he could have done, because now all he could think about was doing it again. The way he'd felt after the first time should have been warning enough. All he'd done now was pour gasoline on the fire.

Devony wouldn't need to ash him for overstepping his bounds. He was burning up just fine on his own.

He had used the spare moments while she was changing clothes to send a message to the Order, alerting them to corral Nathan until Rafe had a chance to report in and explain the situation. He wasn't entirely sure how he was going to explain Devony Winters to his commanders.

But that was a problem he would have to deal with later.

Right now, it was all he could do to deal with the more immediate problem—namely, his intense, inconvenient attraction to her and his want to know more about her. He wanted to know everything, and not just because his mission could benefit from it.

Handing the printed photograph to him, she leaned against his shoulder and looked at the image along with him.

"It's too blurry to make everyone out," she said, apparently unaware of the effect her nearness was having on him. "It was the best I could manage without getting caught taking it."

Steeling himself to the warmth of her body, he scanned the snapshot of dozens of well-dressed, obviously wealthy people who had gathered in the salon of LaSalle's enormous boat.

When he spoke, his voice sounded rusty and thick. "Do you have the digital file too?"

"Of course."

"Good. I'd like a copy, if that's all right. I'm sure I can find a way to enhance the quality."

By "find a way," he meant to turn the image over to Gideon in D.C.

The Order would be interested in all of her gathered intel, although he doubted she would surrender it easily. And attempting to persuade her would be a problem all its own since he wasn't authorized to divulge the fact that he was still working for Lucan Thorne.

She had brought him into her personal crusade, primarily because he left her no other choice. But he was still in play as a solo operative. Seeing her private war room didn't change the parameters of his mission. Neither had kissing her.

Guilt rode him when he recalled her confusion over the reason for his ejection from the Order. She'd been more than confused.

She'd been outraged and defensive . . . for him.

"Do you think I'm crazy to be doing this, Rafe?"

"Crazy?" He scoffed lightly and shook his head. "I think you're amazing."

He couldn't help but marvel over the fact that until a few months ago, she had simply been living as a civilian—a music student studying away from home, for crissake. Now, no one could argue that she was a formidable operative.

She had pulled together an array of intelligence that exceeded even what the Order had collected thus far on Cruz and his associates. Hell, she had put Judah LaSalle in her sights weeks ago when Rafe and his comrades had only heard his name for the first time the other night.

He shook his head as he set the photograph down. "How have you managed to put this kind of operation together all by yourself?"

She gave him a cautious look. "Someone gave me a headstart."

"What do you mean? Does someone else know about any of this?"

God, he hoped not. It was already bad enough that she was involved. He didn't want to have to report back to Lucan or Commander Chase that he would be bringing in more than one problem for them to contain.

Devony got up and walked over to the painting of her mother that hung on the wall. She removed the framed portrait, revealing the steel front of a safe built into the wall.

"Apparently, my father had been working on a lot of this information the last time he was here in Boston. I discovered it . . . after," she said, opening the door and retrieving more files from inside. She came back and passed them to Rafe. "I don't think he told anyone what he was working on. He wrote all of his notes by hand, which means he didn't trust that it would be secure anywhere in electronic form."

"Not even on JUSTIS computers?"

"Maybe especially not there."

Rafe leafed through the pages of boldly scrawled notes and sketched diagrams Roland Winters had left behind when he died. Among the papers were handwritten logs of container shipments arriving and leaving from various Boston ports. A number of new and unfamiliar names made appearances in the notes, along with that of Judah LaSalle.

And on the port logs was more than one reference to a company called Crowe Industries.

Rafe's blood seethed when he saw it. He knew that name well. The business tycoon who owned the firm, Reginald Crowe, had been ubiquitous around the globe for decades, his name on everything from lavish international hotels to major corporations.

Earlier this year, Crowe had shocked the world when he'd masterminded what would have been a mass murder of epic proportions at a gathering of countless Breed and human dignitaries. If Crowe had had his way, the peace summit would have been the match that lit a horrific war.

The Order had killed Crowe that night, but not before he had announced to the public at large that he was part of a terrorist cabal calling themselves Opus Nostrum.

The Order had been chasing the elusive organization ever since.

Not to mention another powerful adversary who had arisen in recent months as well.

"Some of your father's notes are dated almost two years ago," Rafe said as Devony sat down beside him once more. "If he had his eyes on Crowe Industries at that time, then whether he realized it or not, he must have been getting damn close to Opus too."

She nodded, but there was a sorrow behind her eyes. "All my father ever wanted was a lasting peace in the world. My entire family was committed to that cause. They pledged their lives to it when they joined JUSTIS."

Rafe frowned, reflecting on the fact that she had lost not only her father in the London headquarters bombing, but her mother and brother as well. Although Devony was obviously a natural in covert fieldwork and intelligence gathering, he knew a sense of profound relief that she hadn't followed in the family's footsteps or she might have also been among the casualties that night.

"I take it you didn't share their interest in law enforcement?"

She gave him a disagreeing look. "Yes, I did. I wanted to join JUSTIS more than anything. My parents refused to consider it. To make them happy, I agreed to pursue music instead."

Rafe couldn't stop himself from reaching up to touch her cheek. "I'm very glad you did."

She blinked and bit her bottom lip. His gaze followed that sweetly innocent reaction, arousal gripping him in an even firmer hold. A growl built deep in the back of his throat, a warning not only to himself but to her.

He drew his hand away, his molars clenched tight to combat the swelling of his fangs. "I don't think your father or anyone else in your family would be happy to know you've picked up the torch he left behind. You should go back to music, Devony."

And he should go back to focusing on his own personal mission to bring down Opus and everyone loyal to their cause.

"I can't go back to my old life. It never really suited me to begin with. This is my life now."

Rafe exhaled sharply. "Subterfuge and killing? Risking your life and God knows what else by embedding yourself with scum like Cruz?"

"If that's what it takes, then yes."

"What will you do if you succeed in finding a link to Opus or any of its members?"

"I will kill them." No hesitation in her clear voice. Only cold and steady resolve. "I will finish this for my father. For my mother and Harrison, too. I need to finish this for myself."

Shit. Rafe stared at her, knowing there was nothing he could say to dissuade her. Then again, he didn't need to dissuade her. All it would take was one call to the Order and she would be removed to someplace safe until this was over.

And she would despise him for the rest of her eternal life.

It shouldn't matter to him. Until a few days ago, he

didn't have any idea she existed.

But now he did, and that simple fact changed everything.

Nothing could be the same after coming here tonight. Now he knew what she had endured because of Opus's evil. He understood her desire to make someone pay.

However, knowing that and allowing her to continue on this path were two different things.

She was interfering with Order objectives. She was interfering with his own as well. As righteous as her need to avenge her family might be, he had his own need for retribution too.

"You need to give this up." He shook his head. "You're going to get hurt, Devony. I don't want to see that happen."

"I'm not worried about me."

"Damn it, you should be." His reply came out harsher than intended.

She flinched, but didn't retreat. She didn't lose a scintilla of the stubborn resolve in her beautiful eyes or the upward jut of her chin. "Have you ever been alone, Rafe? I mean really, truly, alone?"

"No," he admitted soberly.

"Then don't talk to me about getting hurt. Don't tell me I need to give up when I have nothing else. This hurt," she said, clenching her fist at her breast as her voice choked. "This rage, is the reason I get out of bed every day. I can't stop until it stops. Can't you understand that?"

He did. As much as he wanted to deny it to her, he couldn't pretend he didn't know something of how she felt.

His family and friends might have all perished if Opus and their mole had succeeded.

If he had lost everyone that day?

Just the thought of that emptiness carved a hollow in his chest.

Devony had been living that pain every second of every day for five long months.

She sat beside him in a rigid silence that nearly broke him. Her grief was profound, even all this time later. When he first saw her in Asylum, she had seemed so closed-off and brittle. So angry. Now he knew why.

He cupped her lovely face, stroking her velvety skin with the pad of his thumb. "I'm sorry for what you've endured. No one should have to experience that kind of loss, Devony."

"I'm still hurting," she murmured thickly. "And I'm so tired of being alone."

Her naked vulnerability in that moment nearly killed him. He gathered her close, even though everything logical and reasonable inside him pleaded for him to keep his distance. He couldn't let her bear her pain alone.

Especially when he had been born with the ability to heal, to restore.

He spoke into the fragrant silk of her hair. "Do you want me to take it away for a little while? I will, if you want me to."

She swallowed hard, then slowly, firmly, shook her head. "No. I need to carry it. I need to keep them alive inside me, even if it hurts."

Christ, she was an incredible woman.

As attractive as he found her physically, her courage turned him on even more.

Her strength and resilience left his control in tatters.

If she had agreed to let him heal her grief, he would have done it gladly. And then he would have left immediately afterward and made the call to the Order to find a safe sanctuary for her, somewhere far away from this business with Opus Nostrum and from him.

But she hadn't caved to her pain.

No, Devony Winters was made of stronger stuff than that.

And he had never known anything sexier.

What he ought to do was leave.

Not only for the integrity of his mission for the Order, but for his own sanity too.

Hell, for what remained of his honor, if nothing else. No matter how thin that claim was now.

"It's getting late." His voice was gravel, his mouth filled with the presence of his fangs. "I should go."

"Don't." She met his gaze, her irises simmering with flecks of glowing amber. As he drank in the beauty of her face, her pupils began to narrow, transforming with the intensity of her arousal.

He felt the same need erupting inside him. All the desire he'd been trying to push down was quickly reaching the breaking point. Heat licked through his veins, his pulse drumming, all of his blood rushing toward the rigid and aching length of his erection.

"Devony—"

She didn't give him a chance to say anything more.

Her mouth crushed against his, her kiss a force of nature.

He caught her in his arms and tumbled back onto the rug with her.

CHAPTER 11

All night she had been burning to feel his kiss on her again.

She didn't know how to describe the profound sense of gratitude she felt when Rafe had offered to take away her grief with his healing ability. She hadn't expected kindness like that from the dangerous Breed male. He had healed her after the museum job, but that had been out of obligation for a comrade.

His offer to ease her pain tonight had been born of something different, something deeper. Something that seemed like true concern, even affection.

God forgive her, but she'd wanted to lean into that feeling so badly she had to force herself to deny him. She yearned to feel some kind of connection to someone . . .

No, not just someone. To him. Her longing for Rafe's care had been nearly overwhelming, but it paled compared to the driving hunger she had to know the heat of his lips on hers.

The hunger had burst out of her, and only intensified as he took her down onto the floor with him. He held her face in gentle hands, plundering her mouth with a savage need that seemed to exceed even her own.

"Ah, fuck," he uttered raggedly against her lips. "This wasn't supposed to happen. *You* weren't supposed to happen, Devony."

She hadn't been prepared for him, either.

All of the emptiness she had stuffed deep down inside her had opened up with him tonight. That bleak loneliness had been swallowing her whole for so long, but she'd never registered how fathomless and dark it had grown until she was sitting in this room with Rafe, sharing the details of her pain, and her plans for passing the hurt along to the monsters who had caused it.

But all of those dark realities were nothing but ashes now, incinerated under the heat of her need for this man.

A moan tore loose from her throat, sounding animal and raw.

She didn't care if she seemed desperate for him.

She *couldn't* care.

"Don't stop kissing me, Rafe." Her breath was reduced to ragged panting, her fangs surging out of her gums. "I ache," she gasped brokenly. "Oh, God, I need . . ."

He answered with a low groan and a hard thrust of his pelvis beneath hers. Even separated by their clothing, the rigid length of his erection seared her where it bit into her abdomen. She pressed down, thinking the friction might alleviate some of that heat, but it only intensified as she ground against him.

Rafe's arms wrapped around her like warm iron bands. Then, in a fluid roll he sent her over onto her back, pinning her under him as his kiss deepened into something wild and hot and uncontrolled.

Every vein and artery in her body throbbed as he covered her with his body and moved against her in an erotic rhythm. His tongue invaded her mouth, pushing past her teeth and fangs to stroke deep inside while his hips rocked heavily between her parted thighs.

The hard throb of her pulse kicked into an urgent drumbeat, making the pool of need in her core twist and coil, spiraling into a desire she could hardly contain.

Her skin felt too tight, too hot. Beneath her loose knit top and soft pants, her *dermaglyphs* felt more alive than ever before, as if the otherworldly skin markings were lit up and churning, licking her with fire.

She had felt desire before, but so infrequently she scarcely remembered when. None of the fumbling schoolboy kisses or clumsy hands that chanced to touch her in the past could compare to what she was feeling now. Rafe's touch obliterated everything that came before. His kiss ignited a fire in her that could not be contained.

When his hand slipped under the hem of her sweater to skim over her bare stomach, she arched into him on a shivery gasp. She writhed under him, pleasure swamping her as his palm moved higher, caressing her over the thin lace of her bra. The front clasp popped open a second later, and Devony moaned as he cupped her naked breast in his hand.

"Christ, you're soft," he murmured. "And I can feel your *glyphs* coming to life under my fingertips."

She could feel it too. Each brush of his hand sent

pleasure dancing across her skin, and turned the ache in her core into a molten yearning.

His kiss moved onto her throat. "I need to see you."

He didn't wait for permission. It was just as well. She could hardly find her voice to give it to him as the hunger in her mounted. Pushing her shirt up from the waist, his hands skated along her torso, bunching the fabric beneath her chin. He stopped kissing her for a moment, and removed her top and bra completely. Then he tilted his head down to look at her.

"You are so fucking beautiful." His deep voice carried a coarse edge, thickened from his desire and from the fangs that filled his mouth. The heat of his amber gaze bathed her in warm light as he lifted up and slowly drank in the sight of her. "I knew you would be gorgeous, Devony. All of these pretty *glyphs* on your soft, creamy skin. But you're beyond anything I imagined."

He touched her with the same reverence she saw in his eyes. When he bent forward and traced his tongue along the curves of one of her markings, she shuddered with sensation. He lavished kisses on every bared inch of her, moving from one breast to the other, then down to her navel. Her *glyphs* responded as if he commanded them, their colors surging and undulating under his lips, under his fingers, as he explored them all.

"I wonder where this one leads," he murmured, lowering himself over her body and licking one of the flourishes that disappeared below the waistband of her yoga pants. He tugged them down her hips, taking off her panties along with them. The breath he inhaled sounded ragged as his glowing gaze followed the path of a *glyph* that ran across her hip bone and onto the mound of her sex. His eyes flicked up to meet hers, a wicked tilt to his lips. "I think I found my favorite."

Spreading her legs to afford himself better access, he sank between her parted thighs and dropped a line of kisses from one end of the *dermaglyph* to the other. His short beard delivered a delicious abrasion, making Devony's arousal ratchet impossibly tighter. Lord, she thought she might explode from desire for him.

She nearly did in that next moment, when he pressed his mouth to the drenched seam of her body. His tongue cleaved between her folds and she sucked in a gulp of air. It left her on a shuddery sigh as he suckled her clit with ruthless demand.

Her response seemed to spur his own. He moaned and dragged her closer, his palms cupping her backside, holding her steady when she could hardly keep from writhing in hot, pleasurable agony.

She wasn't prepared for the sudden, overwhelming tide of sensation that rolled up on her.

The wave crested, then crashed, flooding every fiber of her being with a shimmery, quicksilver bliss. She cried out, his name ragged on her tongue as her release left her shaking in Rafe's hands, her body convulsing against his whiskered face.

When she finally dragged her eyelids open, she found him staring at her, studying her with pure male appreciation. Her vision was soaked in amber, her fangs feeling as long and sharp as daggers as she panted heavily through her parted lips.

Rafe grinned. "Holy hell, Devony. I wish you could see yourself right now. You're the sexiest woman I've ever laid eyes on."

All she could do was moan in reply. Even that wordless sound was rough and inhuman. She'd never made a noise like that before. Never felt this alive.

And as overcome as he seemed looking at her, Devony could not begin to describe what the sight of Rafe did to her now, with her body thrumming from the pleasure he'd just given her.

Handsome and golden, his immense body wrapped in muscle, he was magnificent simply by existing. But now, with his aquamarine eyes engulfed in amber fire, his face stark with desire, and his sharp fangs gleaming, he was nothing short of awesome.

A fierce possessiveness washed over her as she gazed at him. It came from a place in her that had already claimed him as hers, even before tonight. It was an untamed part of her, one that had been sleeping until tonight. Until Rafe's kiss in that parking lot woke her up.

Devony lifted up off the floor, one palm planted in the center of his chest.

He looked surprised at first, but an eager, approving light smoldered in his amber eyes as she urged him into a sitting position and rose onto her knees in front of him.

She pulled off his black T-shirt and let her gaze roam greedily over the tangles of *glyphs* covering his strong chest and arms. He didn't have as many as her. Thanks to her mother's laboratory-manipulated genetics, Devony had been born with an abundance of the skin markings, plus the diminutive teardrop-and-crescent-moon stamp of a Breedmate.

To anyone inside or outside of the Breed, she was unique. But to her, Rafe was a singular fascination.

One she simply could not resist.

She ran her hands over his smooth skin, watching the colors rush and churn along his *glyphs*. Dark wine, indigo and gold. Her own skin seethed with the same deep hues. All the colors of desire.

Rafe shuddered under her questing hands, his gaze molten. When she leaned forward and used her tongue to taste him the way he had done with her, his muscles flexed under her lips. The enormous bulge that filled the front of his black jeans grew even more pronounced.

His hands played in her hair, loosening it from the messy bun. "Have you ever been with a male of your own kind before?"

She licked her lips. "I've never been with anyone."

He drew back and seized her hands, stilling them on a low curse. "No one at all?" When she shook her head, his expression hardened. "Ah, fuck. Devony . . . you should've told me."

"Why? Would you want me less if you knew?"

His furrowed brow darkened even more. It took him a long moment to answer. "No. I don't think anything could make me want you less. Not now. Not at any time."

"Good." She kissed him, no gentle tangle of their lips and tongues, but a melding, a claiming.

She didn't want his tender care right now. She didn't want gentle.

She simply wanted him.

Without releasing him from her kiss, she reached down to unfasten the button and zipper of his jeans. She fumbled a little, but then Rafe's hands were there, too, as impatient and determined as hers.

When he was freed, she couldn't resist the urge to touch him . . . to taste him.

His cock stood thick and proud, as glorious as the rest of him.

She took his length in both hands, marveling at his

girth and heft. He hissed tightly as she stroked him, then released a strangled groan when she lowered her mouth over him and took him deep into her throat.

It seemed she was just finding her pace when he took hold of her shoulders and set her away from him on a raw, vivid curse.

"I shouldn't be doing this with you." His gaze scorched her, his handsome face filled with an awful torment. "You should make me leave, Devony."

"That's not what I want."

He scoffed low at her reply. "This has already gone too far." His words were uttered like a warning, though whether meant for her or himself, she couldn't be sure. "Daylight will be here soon enough. If I don't get back to my place, I won't be going anywhere for a long while."

"I know," she said. "And I'm still asking you to stay."

She wrapped her hand around his shaft and kissed him again, a scorching mating of their mouths. He didn't resist it. He didn't reject her.

No, far from it.

On a growl, he tunneled his fingers into her hair and returned her kiss with a savage claiming. The next thing she knew, she was on her back beneath him, his big body wedged between her parted thighs.

His kiss left her mouth and traveled down the length of her body. He spread her wide and devoured her sex, penetrating her with one finger until she thought she would go mad with arousal. He kept going, adding a second digit once her body grew accustomed to the first.

It wasn't enough. She craved something more than this. More of him. Still, he didn't stop, not until she was screaming with the onslaught of a shattering climax.

He shifted atop her, and then his hard length was a

rigid demand against her slick folds. He rocked there for a moment, teasing her body with the promise of what was to come.

She thought she was ready.

She thought she had already felt the full spectrum of ecstasy.

Oh, God, she was wrong.

Rafe's mouth found hers again, and then he gave a thrust of his hips and the blunt head of his cock pierced her. She cried out with the sharpness of it, with the overwhelming sensation of him filling her, stretching her, leaving space for nothing but the intensity of their joining.

She couldn't hold back her cry as the pain and pleasure merged, becoming something wild and unhinged. She rode it out, her fingernails raking his shoulders as wave after wave crashed into her.

"You feel too damn good," he murmured, glowering down at her as he watched her come. "You should have ashed me when you had the chance."

~ ~ ~

He wanted to go slowly.

He wanted to take care, be gentle with her, but Devony permitted none of that.

She was Breed, and she was fearless.

And holy hell, was she exquisite.

The tightness of her sheath gripped him, her virgin flesh giving way under the battering force of his invasion. He could scent the faint fragrance of blood mingling with the silky juices that bathed his cock as he thrust inside her. It should have rattled what little sense of honor he believed he still had. Instead, the beast in him responded with a roar of pure possession.

Her fingernails scored his shoulders, the lean muscles of her thighs wrapped around his hips as she rode the length and depth of every hard crash of their bodies. Her climax broke like a storm beneath him. He'd never felt anything so powerful and electric, so fucking hot.

And her lovely face. Ah, Christ. Her face was even more beautiful transformed by passion and release.

A wave of self-loathing buffeted him as he reveled in her uninhibited response. He had no right to be the one to witness her like this, nor to be the man she allowed to take her pleasure for the first time.

He had no right to any part of her. No claim on her body, and certainly not on her heart.

Yet the idea that any other male might touch Devony lit a cold fire in his veins.

No one would be good enough—least of all, him.

That didn't stop him from savoring each soft moan that fell from her lips as he pumped into her. Every welcoming arch of her hips to meet his. All of the powerful shudders that swept her strong body as he drove her mercilessly from one orgasm to the next.

He was the worst kind of bastard for being her first, especially when a minefield of half-truths lay between them.

But this was no lie—his desire for her. He hadn't been able to hide that truth from her. Not from the beginning, and certainly not ever again after tonight.

He couldn't hold back that need as he rocked into her with intensifying fury, powering into the warm, wet fist of her core.

Her eyes stayed open and fixed on him, no shyness in her fevered gaze as he thrust deeper with every stroke. A jagged sigh sawed from between her parted lips, her fangs gleaming.

Rafe growled, tumbling toward the edge of a steep abyss. He wouldn't be content to go there alone. Leaning down, he took her mouth in a savage kiss as he sank to the hilt and began a deeper claiming of her body.

"Oh, God," she moaned into his mouth. "Rafe, I can't take it."

He knew she didn't mean pain. A strangled cry tore from her. Her body jolted beneath him, her hands still clenched like talons on his shoulders.

Rafe kept moving within her, even as her throat erupted with a scream of hard release. He was lost to the erotic pressure of her core wrapped so tightly around him, the rippling contractions milking him. The feel of her was more than he could take too. It wrenched a raw curse from between his teeth and fangs.

Now, his own need demanded to be sated.

Bracing himself on one forearm, he drove deeper and harder into her heat, mesmerized by the look of hunger and ecstasy burning in her eyes.

Her pulse throbbed in the base of her throat, repeatedly drawing his gaze to that hammering beat. Hunger lashed him along with the rolling wave of the release he'd been struggling to prolong.

His blood thirst had been dealt with a couple of nights ago at LaSalle's party, but the sight of Devony's vein drumming so near to his mouth was a temptation that rocked him to his marrow.

"Fuck," he snarled, unprepared for the impulse rising up in him like a tidal wave.

He told himself it was only sex. He'd gone too long without it—not once since he'd been played for a fool by the Opus female who'd mesmerized him like a siren.

He'd denied himself out of punishment, but tonight he was paying the price. Devony was paying an even bigger price. Because as intense as this desire between them was, Rafe couldn't allow it to be anything more.

His mission was all that mattered to him.

His vengeance against Opus Nostrum, and the redemption he hoped he would finally seize once the smoke was cleared and the battle had been won.

Until then, everything else was simply an obstacle he needed to avoid. Including Devony Winters.

He tried to persuade himself that tonight was a mistake he would need to correct, and what he felt for her now was only a momentary weakness, one that would fade under the harsh light of day. He needed to believe that, because the alternative was unacceptable.

Devony Winters was a temptation he had no time for, and no right to indulge.

But yet he continued to bury himself in the perfect bliss of her body, powerless to stop. He savored every nuance of her response while his own body quickened and a roar exploded from him along with the rush of his staggering release.

And while everything male in him—everything Breed—roared with the need to possess her.

To claim her as his.

CHAPTER 12

Soft footsteps and the faint floral scent of Devony's shampooed hair alerted Rafe to her presence moments before she came into the open war room of her father's study the next morning.

Rafe had been awake for hours, already showered and dressed while she slept. As one of the Breed, he didn't require much sleep. Devony surely didn't either, but when he left her bedside not long before daybreak, she hadn't so much as stirred.

He should have left her Darkhaven as soon as he woke.

In truth, what he should have done was pack up her father's files and her collected intel too, and brought it all directly to the Order. He still should, right after making his overdue call to headquarters to advise them to come and pluck Devony Winters off the dangerous path she was on and place her immediately under the

Order's protection.

Not to mention out of his reach.

Especially after his spectacular dereliction of duty last night.

"Good morning." She walked up behind where he stood perusing the wall of photos and notes and diagrams. Her breasts pressed against his spine as she wrapped her arms around his waist and rested her chin on his shoulder. "How long have you been down here?"

He gave a slight shrug. "Not that long."

He pivoted around to face her, if only to extricate himself from the enticing warmth of her embrace. Big mistake. She was even more tempting now that he was looking at her. Evidently fresh from a shower, she wore pink silk pajama shorts and a plain white cotton camisole.

The innocent combination did little to conceal her perky breasts and the sexy *dermaglyphs* that decorated so much of her gorgeous limbs and curves. Last night he'd tasted nearly every square inch of those limbs and curves.

Today, instead of feeling sated from the hours he'd spent buried deep inside her, he was having a damn hard time pretending he didn't want to start all over again. Fresh guilt racked him over his disturbing lack of control, then and now.

He scowled. "How are you feeling?"

"Amazing." Her satisfied smile should have made him feel anything but remorse. "And a little embarrassed, if you want to know the truth. I've never thrown myself at a man before. Good thing I didn't realize what I was missing until last night."

Rafe grunted, a grin tugging at his mouth against his

will. As much as he wanted to regret making love with Devony, it was hard to get there when she was looking at him with a sultry gleam in her eyes. His cock stirred with instant, renewed interest, and his pulse kicked into a stronger tempo.

"I've never been someone's first time before," he muttered. "I'm sure I could've done a lot better by you."

"That sounds intriguing. What do you have in mind?"

He chuckled. "Don't ask. You might be shocked to know."

"Really?" Her bourbon-hued eyes widened in interest. "Try me."

Fuck. How the hell had they gone from "good morning" to talking about having sex again?

Rafe took a step back and cleared his throat. The document he held in his hand when she came into the room was now crushed in his fist.

Devony noticed it. "Is that one of my activity logs on Cruz's gang?"

"Yeah." He'd been combing through her files for the past couple of hours, absorbing every detail he could, and snapping photos of the items that were too extensive to commit to memory.

He learned that she had been embedded with Ricardo Cruz and his gang for nearly two months. Before that, she had infiltrated a different area gang, and still another before that. She had been dogged in her pursuit of information, and during that time had managed to keep a journal of each group's various criminal jobs, relevant conversations, even minutiae that might otherwise be overlooked.

To say she was thorough was an understatement.

And fearless.

He didn't want to consider how great the loss would be to his mission once he arranged for the Order to come in and remove her from the field.

Rafe set the log down on a worktable in the war room, then strode up to the four walls of intel that reminded him of a general's plan for a sweeping war campaign. "How long do you believe Cruz has been associating with Judah LaSalle?"

"More than a year, I would say." She walked up next to him to look at the dossiers and the red strings connecting one individual to another on the wall. "Not long after I met Fish, he told me about one of the first jobs LaSalle hired them to do. It was a break-in at some energy sciences lab in the Berkshires."

Rafe nodded without commenting that he likely knew the company in question. He would be willing to wager his right arm that the product being developed there was one of several ultraviolet technologies that fell into Opus Nostrum's hands earlier this year.

"Did Fish say what they were supposed to steal for LaSalle?"

"No. And they weren't successful, anyway. Security was too tight, so they had to abort."

"But LaSalle kept hiring them for other jobs?"

"He needs people like Cruz and his men."

"Expendable men," Rafe said.

"Right. Men who will do almost anything—risk almost anything—so long as it comes with a large enough payout. From what I've observed, they're simply boots on the ground for LaSalle, and he's untouchable so far. Besides, there's no clear evidence yet that he's connected to Opus."

Rafe wasn't so sure about that. The Berkshires break-in gave him hope that he was on the right track. He was already months ahead in terms of reconnaissance, all thanks to her.

Devony retrieved another one of her logs and handed it to him. "Here's a list of their most recent jobs for him."

Rafe scanned the record of random pickups and drops of unstated merchandise, assorted robberies, even a few instances of money laundering.

She pivoted to face him as he reviewed the document, leaning her back against the wall of intel. "I heard Ocho and Axel talking about a big job Cruz has been promising recently. I don't know what it is yet, but Cruz hasn't mentioned it to me at all."

Rafe stared at her, his mind calculating the fastest way to fix that problem. "I need to get one of the guys alone somewhere. I'd only need a few minutes, just long enough to interrogate the son of a bitch under a trance."

She was shaking her head even before he finished talking. "I've done that."

"You have?" He couldn't pretend he wasn't surprised—and impressed. "Which one did you question?"

"All of them, including Cruz." She arched a brow. "What do you think I've been doing with them all these months, just beating them at pool and pretending I don't despise drinking rot-gut whisky with them?"

He chuckled. "You're incredible, you know that?"

She smiled. "That's what you kept telling me last night."

Yes, it was. He'd meant every word too.

And he had to be some kind of asshole for the way

he still craved her, even considering that this time tomorrow she would be in Order custody and wishing she'd never met him.

She was so confident and fearless in normal situations, it was hard for him to reconcile the fact that she had been untouched until a few hours ago.

Until him.

"You are an incredible woman, Devony." He approached her and gently cupped her face in his hands. "Last night was incredible."

She nodded, and he couldn't deny himself the pleasure of one more kiss, even though he cursed himself for taking it from her with a clearer head than he had a few hours ago. And still the feeling of her lips brushing softly against his sent a torrent of jagged desire through his veins.

He groaned and pulled away.

"This isn't a good idea. I promised myself I wouldn't do this to you again."

"Do it to me? I kind of thought we did it together, Rafe. I mean, I may not have a lot of experience in this area, but I thought we did it together really well."

She came toward him now, her eyes glittering with sparks of amber and the determination he was swiftly finding irresistible.

"I think you and I do a lot of things really well. Too well to keep doing them on our own."

"What are you talking about?"

"This." She gestured to the walls around her, all of her work over the past five months. All of the heartache and loss she had channeled into her pursuit of the ones who hurt her. "We want the same thing, don't we? To see the end of Opus Nostrum. Neither one of us is going to rest until those bastards are no more. So, why don't we do it together?"

He glanced between them, where she now extended her hand to him. "Together?"

"As a team. As partners. What do you say, Rafe?"

He knew damn well what he should say. That his loyalty was already spoken for. He had a team of partners counting on him back in D.C., as well as the brethren he hoped to rejoin as soon as possible at the Boston Command Center. Until his mission was completed, he didn't have room for anything, or anyone, else.

He should have told her all of that last night, before he let the situation with her get so far out of his control.

As much as she deserved to know the truth, until he spoke to Lucan Thorne and Sterling Chase, he couldn't breach the Order's faith in him by divulging his continued role as a warrior.

And there was a selfish part of him that didn't want Devony to hate him.

Not last night, and not right now, when she was looking at him with such open trust and affection.

"I'll have your back and you have mine," she said, still waiting for his answer. "Do we have a deal?"

Rafe looked at her, swamped by respect and admiration, and something deeper that he didn't want to name. Of all the things he owed her in the short time since they'd met, this was the one promise he could give her. That regardless of his obligation to the Order, he would do whatever it took to keep her safe. That much he could commit to without reservation, and with full honesty.

"Okay," he said, the word like sandpaper in his throat as he took her hand in his. "We have a deal,

Devony."

The Order wasn't going to like it.

He wasn't convinced that he did, either.

CHAPTER 13

☾

They spent the majority of the day reviewing every piece of information Devony and her father had collected. She loved seeing the way Rafe's sharp mind worked, his indefatigable thirst for knowledge. He was focused and methodical, and she marveled at his keen ability to spot patterns and connections among even the most obscure bit of data.

He was a gorgeous male, to be sure, but his sexy brain was wreaking havoc on her senses too.

If she thought poring over her work together would help take her mind off all of the other things she wanted to be doing with him, she couldn't have been more wrong.

Every time he reached past her to pick up a photo or arranged a set of documents on their shared worktable, she struggled to resist the urge to lick the tangle of *glyphs* that tracked down his muscled forearm.

When he asked questions or shared his theories about Opus and the individuals who might have ties to them, she hung on every word, captivated by the sensual cut of his lips and her very vivid memories of all the wicked things his mouth had done to her body.

It was nearly impossible to ignore the steady drum of his pulse when he was seated so close to her. Her Breed senses locked on to that strong beat and the liquid rush of his blood pounding through his veins. Her fangs prickled in her gums, and she couldn't decide what she wanted more, to have Rafe inside her again, or to sink her sharp canines into the side of his neck.

That latter craving was the last thing she should be thinking about.

Blood bonds were sacred. They were eternal, and not to be entered into on impulse. She could feed all she wanted on human Hosts, but one sip of Rafe's blood would irrevocably seal her to him for as long as either of them lived.

Why that notion didn't freeze her in her tracks, she didn't want to know.

She had never been some starry-eyed girl mooning over the idea of happily-ever-after. God, was that what she was doing now with Rafe? She couldn't possibly be that foolish. Apparently, losing her virginity had also robbed her of some good sense.

"Where'd we put your father's cargo traffic log for Conley Terminal?" Rafe asked, jarring her out of her troubled thoughts.

Frowning, he sifted through an open file of handwritten notes.

Since it appeared she was alone in her distraction around him, she really needed to find something else to focus on. Especially since he seemed to have no trouble keeping a professional line drawn between them today.

"This one?" She slid one of the dozens of entries toward him.

He glanced at it only briefly, then shook his head. "I'm looking for the logs from February."

"Here you go." Devony retrieved the document in question and handed it to him, watching as he intently studied it.

Her fascination with him unsettled her, especially when it seemed markedly one-sided today. She was getting in over her head with him; she realized that. It wasn't just the incredible sex that had her stomach doing flips and her veins feeling as if they had absorbed a prolonged jolt of electricity.

It was simply being with Rafe that did that to her. Talking with him. Strategizing with him. Being close enough to feel the warmth and strength of his body, and to see the kindling embers in his aquamarine eyes when he looked at her.

She couldn't believe she had let herself get entangled so quickly and deeply with a male she knew so precious little about. He was dangerous; she'd seen that firsthand. He could be kind and caring; she had experienced that in the park when he healed her, and again last night when he had treated her with such gentleness—right before he had shown her the true meaning of passion.

But Rafe was also a tormented and angry man, fixated on vengeance against Opus.

Not that she could blame him.

As for the Order turning him out, their loss had become her gain. She had set out on her quest alone after losing her family, never imagining she'd find an ally along the way. There was a part of her that wanted to think she may have found something even more than that in Rafe.

As she watched him, she realized there was so much she wanted to know about him, so much she wanted to understand. She didn't even know his last name.

Propping her elbow on the table, she watched him leaf through the records. "I just realized there's something very important you haven't told me yet."

His head lifted sharply and he swung a bland, yet oddly guarded look at her. "What's that?"

"Is Rafe your full name, or is it short for something?"

He exhaled a wry laugh. "My given name's Xander, actually." That peculiar expression on his face relaxed into a knee-melting, crooked grin. "Xander Raphael Malebranche."

"It's beautiful."

He chuckled. "I'll tell my parents you said so next time I see them."

"How often is that?" she asked. "You haven't spoken much about them."

Other than his confession that he'd almost gotten his parents killed on account of his involvement with Opus Nostrum's mole, Devony might have assumed he had no family in his life either.

Looking at him, he seemed as alone as she was. Whether his solitude was self-imposed or a result of the shame he obviously carried for having been duped by an Opus operative, she wasn't sure.

All she did know was that he was hurting underneath the tough face he showed the world.

"It's been a while since I've seen them," he said. "A couple of months, maybe longer."

"So, not since you left the Order?"

He drew in a long breath, turning away from her to page absently through the files in front of him. "Yeah, I guess so. Around that time."

"Your last name," she said, realizing it was familiar to her. "Are you telling me you're related to Dante Malebranche?"

"He's my father."

"Seriously?" Devony sat back in her chair, astonished. "I don't think there's anyone in or around JUSTIS who doesn't know the names of Lucan Thorne and his warrior commanders. Wasn't your father one of the founding members of the original compound here in Boston?"

"Not quite," Rafe said, pivoting to look at her again. "There are others who go further back with Lucan than my father. But yes, he's been an Order warrior for a long time. He's one of the district commanders now, heading up the operation center and patrol team in Seattle."

"You sound very proud of him."

He nodded. "I am. My father is an extraordinary man, not only because of his long role in the Order. He's one of my best friends. And he casts a long shadow. My mother, Tess, as well."

Devony knew the feeling of pride he described. Her family didn't have the high profiles that Rafe's and some of the other Order's founding members had, but she had been immensely proud of her parents too. She had longed to prove herself to them somehow.

Instead, they coddled her under lock and key growing up, sheltered her. When she was old enough, they pushed her toward safe pursuits like music and dance. As if they expected her to disappoint them somehow. As if she already had.

"What does your father think about you no longer being part of the Order, Rafe?"

He shrugged, deflecting. "I haven't asked him."

"And your mother?"

He folded his muscled arms over his chest and held her in a narrowed stare. "Why are you asking so many questions about this?"

His defensiveness took her aback. She shook her head. "I'm sorry. I was just curious. I'm just trying to understand."

"Understand what?"

"You."

"What for?"

"Because I want to know more about you. Because I care . . . about you."

She looked away from him and shook her head again. "And because I don't have parents to talk to anymore, to ask what they think about my choices or anything else in this world. I'm just curious what it's like to have parents who are a constant in your life."

Rafe reached out to her, drawing her gaze back to him with his fingers resting gently beneath her chin. "What are you talking about? I know you've been grieving over your family these past few months, but it sounds like they've been gone for much longer than that."

She hadn't intended to carve into her own psychic wounds. Rafe's coaxing, solemn stare drew the words out of her as easily as his caress on the side of her face. "I was alone even before my family was killed in the London bombing. My parents lived for JUSTIS. So did my brother. Their work sent them all over the world, which meant I was raised by strangers most of my childhood. Nannies, governesses, boarding schools here in the States. I felt so lonely back then. I didn't realize it could be possible to feel even emptier, like I do now that they're really gone. Now that I truly have no one left."

"No," Rafe said. "That's not right. You're mistaken about having no family left. You're a daywalker, Devony. That means your mother was unique too."

"Yes. She was born Breed, a Gen One who could also walk in daylight. Her early years were hideous. Brutal. She told me a madman raised her as part of a program for genetically designed Breed females."

Rafe nodded as if he knew. "She was one of Dragos's experiments. Your mother, along with the half-sisters who were also part of that program before the Order put a stop to it."

"Half-sisters?" Devony murmured, her heart lurching to think that others had been subjected to the same awful torture her mother had endured.

"You didn't know there were others?"

"No. I didn't even consider there could be. Neither did my mother, I'm certain of that. She rarely spoke of that period in her life, and never that she knew of others like her." Devony swallowed, a strange kind of hope coming to life in her breast. "How many do you think there might be?"

"I know of several personally. And the Order is working toward finding the rest. Tavia Chase is leading that effort, along with Brynne Kirkland. Until the time of the attack in London, Brynne was actually working in that city for JUSTIS."

Devony gaped, but she couldn't help it. "My mother had a half-sister in JUSTIS? In the London office? My

God." She sat back, feeling as if a train had just slammed into her. "She never knew. My mom was covert her entire career, rarely home. All that time, she had a sister living in the same city, working in the same organization?"

Rafe nodded. "Which means you have two aunts—one of them right here in Boston. You also have a pair of daywalker cousins, Carys and Aric Chase. They're both working with the Order now."

"My cousins." She could hardly contain the bubble of excitement that swelled in her. Or the sudden flood of uncertainty. "Do you think . . . do you think they would ever want to meet me?"

He chuckled. "I have no doubt about that whatsoever."

"Will you help? I know that's asking a lot, especially considering the way things are between you and the Order—"

"I'll make it happen for you, Devony. Whatever it takes, as soon as you're ready to."

His reply was so sincere, so resolute, she couldn't resist wrapping her arms around him in a fierce embrace. "Thank you."

"Don't thank me yet. I haven't done anything."

She drew back and drank in his handsome, solemn face. "Thank you for telling me about them. That's more than enough right now. It's everything."

He tipped his head and pressed a kiss to her mouth. "You're not alone, Devony."

"Oh, God, I want to believe that so badly." She stared into his penetrating eyes, watching their oceanic color begin to smolder with fire. His gaze felt like a promise, one she was afraid to trust, no matter how desperately she wanted it.

"You're not alone anymore," he uttered, his deep voice raw with tenderness . . . and desire.

"Make me believe it, Rafe."

She kissed him back, letting her lips linger against his. On a growl, he dragged her off her seat and onto his lap, capturing her mouth in a deep, fevered kiss.

In the next second, he lifted her, his hands sliding beneath her backside as he pivoted and swung her up onto the worktable. They undressed each other with impatient hands, eager to be skin-on-skin. Some of the papers and stacks of files tumbled to the floor, instantly disregarded.

She hardly noticed or cared.

There was no room for thoughts of vengeance or loss or pain when Rafe had her in his arms.

There was only this moment. Only this man.

And the craving for him that seemed to be growing more demanding, more insatiable, each moment they were together.

CHAPTER 14

Rafe returned to his apartment in Southie as soon as night fell.

He needed a shower and a fresh change of clothes. Even more than that, he needed space to think and put his head back on straight, because the hours he'd spent with Devony were beginning to scramble his ability to focus.

As he soaked under the showerhead in his studio's bathroom tub, he realized it wasn't only his physical interest in Devony that disturbed him—although that was more than enough cause for alarm—it was his interest in her happiness that was the greater problem.

What the hell had gotten into him, promising he'd make introductions for her with Tavia Chase and the twins? Bad enough if he'd stopped there, but he'd also dragged in former JUSTIS agent Brynne Kirkland, divulging her relationship with the Order.

All for what? To see Devony smile? To give her some illusion of family after hearing her confess she felt unseen or abandoned by her own?

Her childhood scars weren't his to mend. He didn't need to assuage her sadness, especially not with information that wasn't his to reveal, and promises he wasn't certain how he could keep.

Not without dropping his cover.

He was treading too damn close to that line already. Sharing his thoughts about Cruz's gang and Opus. Agreeing to partner with her, for fuck's sake.

He must be out of his mind.

That wasn't even the worst of the trouble he was getting himself into where the gorgeous daywalker was concerned.

He'd just been inside her for hours already today and all he could think about was how long before he could have her again.

If he didn't know better, he'd wonder if Devony Winters didn't also have some amount of the seductive gift that Opus's mole had used on him in Montreal. But where he had been blinded by Iona Lynch's mesmerizing, her psychic manipulation of his feelings and his attraction to her, the hold Devony had on him was something deeper.

It was far more powerful because it was real.

She was real.

Not perfect. Not capitulating and meek, but bold, even combative at times. Devony wasn't the helpless waif he needed to coddle and protect, like the siren who had persuaded him into thinking that was what he wanted.

She was strong and capable, which made the rare

glimpses of her vulnerability all the more authentic. Her emotional confessions were all the more impactful because she trusted him enough to let him see there were hidden cracks in her armor.

It made him feel even more protective of her, and that was dangerous territory when his feelings toward her were soft enough.

A shame his feelings were the only thing soft about him when he was near her.

He had tried his damnedest most of the day to keep a healthy distance. Trapped inside her Darkhaven during the daylight hours had been torture when it also meant no escape from his arousal. Sitting beside her, hunkered over notes and reconnaissance files, had proved an exercise in self-control, one he had barely passed.

While he worked diligently to study and analyze the intel that would aid him in his mission, his senses had been trained exclusively on her. The tempting heat of her body next to him. The intoxicating scent of her skin. The sexy, soft rasp of her voice. The curious, searching way her bourbon gaze seemed to peer straight into his soul.

She had wanted him too.

He'd felt the quickening of her pulse as they worked together in her war room. He'd heard the rapid throb of her heartbeat next to him at the table and it was all he could do to block out the enticing sound.

Each time he ventured a glance at her, his gaze was drawn to the pretty hollow below her throat where that steady pound ticked so close to the surface of her skin.

His fangs responded even now, the points digging into his tongue.

It hadn't been long since he last fed, so he knew he

couldn't blame his thirst on simple lack of sustenance.

He couldn't blame any of what he was feeling for her on basic biology. Not even the way his cock roused at the thought of her now, despite the fact that he'd barely given it a rest since he stepped into Devony's house the night before.

On a frustrated groan, he cranked the spigot as far as it would go into the cold zone and let the icy water douse him.

It hadn't really helped. When he finally stepped out to towel off, all he'd done was add freezing and irritated to his foul mood.

He didn't expect his check-in with the Order was going to be any improvement on that front, but he needed to bring them up to speed. He could only imagine what his commanders were thinking now that they'd had a chance to talk to Nathan and hear about the near-disaster at the museum.

Throwing on a pair of jeans, Rafe headed out to the computer workstation and initiated the video link. He expected to find Gideon at the other end of the call.

Instead, it was Lucan.

"Sir," Rafe greeted with a nod of respect.

"I hope you're calling with some good news."

He didn't think getting naked with Devony Winters was going to qualify as that to the Order's leader. Then again, it wasn't exactly good news that he'd participated in a vault robbery of millions' worth of priceless art, either.

He probably ought to begin with the least fucked-up aspect of his mission so far.

"I'm in with the gang. Cruz and I aren't going to be best friends, but I think he trusts me. There's been talk of something big coming down the pike soon. I'll make sure I'm in on it. I'm confident we've found a solid link in LaSalle, one that's going to eventually lead us to someone in Opus."

Lucan grunted. "Glad to hear it. After that shit-show over at the MFA, I had my doubts."

"Yeah, about that," Rafe hedged. "How's Jordana?"

"She's fine. A little shaken, but that's understandable considering the circumstances."

"And Nathan?"

Lucan arched a black brow. "Fit to be tied, and I mean that almost literally. He was ready to kill you even after Chase informed him that you're covert and operating with the Order's full support."

"So, he knows now." Rafe nodded. "How'd he take that news?"

"You know your team captain, he's an emotionless machine most of the time. No shock, given the way he was raised in the Hunter program. Nathan may not have said as much, but I know he's got to be relieved. That's not to say you won't have to answer to him about what happened in that museum vault."

Rafe frowned. "I didn't know Jordana was going to be there. Hell, I didn't even know about the heist until I was in the van and rolling with Cruz and the rest of the gang."

Lucan nodded. "They had to test you."

"That's right. If I'd thought there was any chance Jordana or Carys might end up in harm's way, I would've aborted the mission."

"I know, son. When all of this is over, you'll have to work on convincing Nathan of that."

Rafe welcomed the chance. He had a lot of bridges

to rebuild on the other side of his mission. Now, he had to add Devony's name to that list too.

"Are you going to tell me about the woman?" Lucan's gray gaze bore into him. "Nathan and Jordana told quite a story in their debriefing. They said she's Breed. This daywalker, is she the female you reported on the other day, the one you said they call Brinks?"

"Her name is Devony," Rafe said. "Devony Winters. Her father is—"

"Ah, Christ. Roland Winters," Lucan muttered, his scowl deepening. "Why am I just now hearing from you that a goddamn JUSTIS director's daughter is involved in this?"

"I only discovered her name last night, sir."

"She fucking Cruz?"

"Hell, no." Rafe's reply came out sharper and more defensive than he intended. "Devony's not actually part of Cruz's gang. She's working her own mission, been embedded with them for a couple of months."

"Embedded," he said, suspicion rankling his forehead. "You mean as a JUSTIS covert agent?"

"No. She's a civilian, Lucan. Actually, up until the bombing in London killed her parents and brother, Devony was a music student studying here in Boston. She's been trying to track down the ones responsible for the attack on the JUSTIS office. She's looking for Opus, same as we are. She wants to see them destroyed because of what they did to her family."

"Son of a bitch." On the other end of the video feed, the Order's leader sat back in his big desk chair. He slowly shook his head. "We can't have this, Rafe. She's going to get in our way. Hell, she already is. We need to contain her. I'll have Chase take care of—"

"Lucan." Rafe didn't know what he could say, how to explain that Devony had actually proven to be a help, not a hindrance, to his mission. There wasn't anything he could say. He had to show him. "Hold on for a minute. I'm going to upload some information."

He grabbed his phone and sent some of the photos he took of Devony's war room and the handwritten notes her father had left behind. Then he waited, watching as Lucan reviewed the intel in unreadable silence.

"That's just the start of the information she's collected these past few months. The logs were assembled by Roland Winters over about a year's time. He kept them hidden in a safe at the family's Darkhaven in Back Bay. Devony doesn't think he told anyone about them, including his colleagues at JUSTIS."

"She volunteered all of this information to you?"

"Yes, sir."

"Was this before or after she drained Jordana of her power and knocked one of our most lethal warriors on his ass for more than an hour inside that museum?"

Rafe cleared his throat. "After. Devony's got the ability to siphon another's ability and use it herself. But it costs her. She was weak and in a lot of pain afterward. I helped her. I followed her home later, and she eventually told me everything."

As far as field reports went, his was light on details about that night. He didn't think the blow-by-blow was going to make Lucan any happier. Not that the shrewd Gen One needed him to color everything in. From the grim look on his face, it was obvious he understood exactly what Rafe wasn't saying.

"Does she know about your mission for the Order?"

"No. That part of my cover is intact. As far as she knows, I want to take Opus out for my own personal reasons."

Lucan grunted. "I don't think that's all too far from the truth."

"No, sir. You know I want to redeem myself. I've never made a secret of that. But my loyalty is with the Order. I'm not going to let you down again."

"You didn't let us down in Montreal, Rafe. That's a burden you placed on your own shoulders." Lucan studied him for a long moment, his brows flat over his measuring gaze. "This is your mission, Rafe. As long as you don't compromise your cover with her, I'm going to let you call the shots where this female is concerned. But understand, that means you'll live with the results."

"Yes, sir."

"So, what do you recommend we do about Devony Winters?"

Rafe knew all it would take was a word and Lucan would ensure she was placed under Order protection somewhere out of the blast range of Opus or anyone in their circle. She would be safe. She would be out of his way, somewhere he didn't have to think about the prospect of her getting hurt or distracting him from his goal.

But all of those things would come at a price.

And as much as he wanted to think their partnership wasn't real, the warrior in him recognized he wasn't going to find a stronger ally in this quest.

"Devony stays. She's mine to look after."

Lucan gave him a grave nod. "All right, son. She's yours."

As he spoke, a chime went off on one of the devices

on his desk. He glanced at it and scowled, a look of true concern on his face. His low, whispered curse spoke volumes.

"Is something wrong, sir?"

He started to shake his head, then slowly exhaled and met Rafe's stare through the monitor. "We've been dealing with an issue in Europe for the past few days. It concerns the team doing some black ops work near Budapest."

"Micah's team," Rafe said. He recalled that another of the Order's elders, Tegan, had only recently come back from that region where his son had been deployed. "What's going on?"

Lucan gave him a sober look. "Micah's team went dark the other day."

Holy hell. Rafe felt a jab of worry, even dread, for one of his closest friends. "Do you mean they're MIA?"

"We're not ready to call it that yet."

But he didn't have to. Rafe could see the truth in Lucan's shadowed expression. No wonder he and Chase and Gideon had barked at him the other night for reporting in late. It wasn't often the Order had to deal with the loss of one of their own, never mind an entire team that included a family member.

"Go take of your business, son. As soon as you have something solid to move on, you let me know. We're going to get this done. I'll be damned before I accept the alternative."

CHAPTER 15

Rafe strode into Asylum around nine o'clock that night and headed to the pool tables in back where Cruz's text had directed him to go.

The gang looked like they'd been there for a while, already settled in at one of the far banquettes with a round of beers half-consumed between them and a game of eight-ball nearing its completion on the billiards table.

Devony was with them, too, dressed in that hot-as-fuck black leather motorcycle jacket and a pair of dark jeans and high-heeled boots that made her legs look like they went on for days. Now, the sight of her in her long-sleeved turtleneck made him as hard as he would be if he saw her standing there in lacy lingerie. Mainly because he had no need to imagine what she was hiding under all of her concealing clothes.

He had touched every inch of her.

Had tasted every sweet curve and crevice.

She met his gaze across the tavern and he felt it as powerfully as if she'd wrapped her hand around his cock.

A private smile tilted her lips before she abruptly glanced away from him—and not before he glimpsed the faint flicker of amber sparks dancing in her eyes.

His own gaze crackled with heat too. He masked it with bravado, swaggering past the tables of bar patrons and ignoring the flirty feminine stares and whispers that followed in his wake. He didn't give a shit about any of the would-be blood Hosts or other women who tried to catch his attention.

There was only one female in the place who stirred his interest. The one doing her best to pretend he didn't exist as he walked up and knocked fists with the guys standing around the pool table.

Fish was sporting a flashy new watch on his wrist. Ocho and Axel were both garbed in gaudy designer shirts that Rafe guessed must have come from the Fall Collection for douchebags. Cruz had opted for a less overt display of his recent windfall, but Rafe didn't miss the diamond pinky ring sparkling on his left hand.

"Someone's been doing a little shopping, I see."

Fish grinned, holding his arm up to show off the new hardware. "Set me back twenty-five large, but ain't it sharp?"

Rafe played along, nodding as if he were impressed. "Nice."

"Already got my eye on an upgrade once we collect on our next job."

"Yeah?" His curiosity piqued, he glanced at Cruz. "Sounds like something big."

"It is," Fish further volunteered, keeping his voice to a conspiratorial level in spite of the music drowning out most of the conversation in the place. "We've been sitting on this one for weeks, just waiting on a go-time. Right, Cruz?"

Rafe had hoped it wouldn't take long to hear something about the job Devony had alerted him to. Based on the gang leader's cautious gaze as it cut away from Fish, it seemed he was in luck.

"I'm intrigued," he told Cruz. "However you can use me on this, count me in."

A tight nod. "We gonna finish this game, or what?"

They returned to their places around the pool table. Rafe hung back, watching as Axel took his shot. He sank a couple of stripes for Fish and himself before losing his turn to Devony on the opposing team with Ocho.

Thank fuck for loud sound systems and poor human hearing, because there was no curbing the low, possessive animal growl that boiled out of Rafe's throat as he watched her grip the long cue and bend over the edge of the table in front of him to take her shot.

She was all business about the game, not doing anything designed to make him squirm, but damn if he could keep his cock from standing at attention. Behind the flat line of his lips, he clenched his molars together and struggled to keep his fangs from erupting out of his gums. Sparks danced in his field of vision as she shifted her stance on those spike-heeled boots, then struck with her cue.

Balls nicked against each other, followed by the clean thump of the red solid dropping into the pocket she'd called. Axel and Fish groaned, realizing they were all but beaten now that she had control of the table.

"Impressive," Rafe murmured as she walked past him on her way to set up her next move. And he wasn't talking about her precision-perfect shot.

She gave him a private little smile. "You game to try me? Once I clean up here, I'll be happy to take a turn running you around the table too."

He arched a brow. "That could be interesting."

"Very." She kept walking, smoothly heading to the other side of the table.

With his erection straining behind his zipper, Rafe tugged his jacket down, and leaned his back against the wall to watch the final rounds of play.

Cruz flagged a waitress and ordered another round of beer for the group. Then he sauntered over with his near-empty mug in hand. He glanced toward the pool table for a moment before settling in beside Rafe.

"Looks like Brinks is starting to warm up to you."

"Think so?" Rafe shrugged. He knew their conversation had been well out of earshot of the man, but he couldn't feign indifference when it came to a knockout like Devony and expect to be believed. "She's not hard to look at, is she? I mean, despite all the razor-wire in her attitude."

Cruz chuckled. "When a bitch looks as good as her, who cares about attitude? In the end, they all fuck the same. Some like her just need to be slapped around awhile first, show them who's really in charge."

Rafe felt his lip curl back from his teeth, a smile that was far from friendly.

Not that the gang leader noticed the difference. He relaxed next to him and drained the last of his beer. "So, you asked about the gig we've got coming up."

Rafe gave a curt nod, still incapable of a reply when disdain for the man had his fangs cutting into his tongue. It took Herculean effort to bring his Breed nature to heel and keep his fists away from Cruz's ugly face while the guy kept talking.

"Like Fish said, we've known it was in the pipeline for some time. I've got it on good authority that everything's almost in place."

"Good authority, meaning LaSalle?" Hardly a need to ask, and Cruz's flat stare was confirmation enough. "What kind of job are we talking about?"

"Merchandise pickup," he said. "The goods are on the move as we speak, heading for Conley Terminal from overseas. They're expected to arrive tomorrow night. Customs agents will have already been paid off and turning a blind eye, so all we need to do is be there to intercept the merchandise and reroute it to our client."

"Intercept and reroute. Meaning we're going to steal it." Rafe frowned. "Steal it from who? What is the merchandise we're grabbing?"

"You don't need to worry about that. You don't need to worry about where we get our orders, either. You're getting paid for your muscle and your other Breed skills, that's all."

Rafe grunted, about two seconds away from punching the dirtbag in his sneering face. "How much are we talking about on this job?"

"Three-quarters of a mil. Split five ways."

"Don't you mean six ways?"

He shook his head. "I mean five. We don't need Brinks on this one." The gang leader's thin lips flattened in a cold smile within his goatee. "Now that we've got you to break us into anyplace we need to go, we don't need her at all anymore."

Shit. He didn't like the idea of Devony being mixed

up with lowlife criminals like these, but he wasn't ready to lose his sole ally. She wasn't going to like any of this, either.

"We'll meet at Ocho's tomorrow night and go from there," Cruz said. "I'll message you as soon as I get word that we're on."

Rafe nodded, but his attention was somewhere else. He surreptitiously glanced Devony's way, just in time to see her slam the eight-ball into the corner pocket for the win. With Ocho hooting over their victory while Fish and Axel hurried to rack up another game for a rematch, Devony murmured that she was done playing and was going to the bar for something stronger than beer.

Rafe watched her cross the tavern. Her stride was swift and purposeful, but he knew her well enough to recognize when she was upset. No, she was flat-out furious. He had no doubt she heard every word Cruz said.

Bypassing the bar, she headed into the short hallway toward the restrooms.

Fresh beers arrived for the gang as Cruz moved over to the pool table to team up with Ocho against the other pair.

Rafe clapped Cruz on the shoulder as if they were old friends. "I'll be back in a few. All this drinking is making me thirsty, and there's a hot little blonde at that far table over there who looks like she's eager to help me out."

The gang chortled. Rafe left them behind and swaggered over to one of the human females who'd been undressing him with her eyes since he walked in. She couldn't get off her chair fast enough when he curled his finger at her in invitation.

Wrapping his arm around her bony shoulders, he ushered her past the bar and into the hallway where Devony had disappeared a moment ago.

A small pack of women stood chattering and applying their makeup in the cramped ladies' room when Rafe stepped inside.

"Out," he commanded in a growl, his fangs bared. They fled at once. He mentally locked the door behind them and held it there.

Then he turned to the woman staring up at him with lust-filled eyes under his arm. He put his hand on her forehead. "Sleep."

She slumped into an immediate trance that wouldn't lift until he willed it to.

Rafe brought her into the largest of the three empty stalls and seated her ragdoll body on the toilet.

Only one stall had its door closed. Devony opened it from inside. She stood there, fully clothed and fuming, her booted feet planted wide, arms crossed over her breasts and her eyes blazing amber in her outrage.

"He thinks he can screw me over?" The tips of her fangs glinted with each word. "He called me a bitch who might need to get slapped around a little? He has no idea what I could do to him. I want to kill that slimy bastard with my bare hands right now."

No wonder she practically ran for the restroom. She was so pissed off, there was no way she could have hidden her true nature in public.

And damn if she wasn't even more beautiful when she was snarling like a Valkyrie.

Outside the restroom door came the sound of tittering female voices. Someone tried the door, but it didn't give. Rafe was still holding it closed with his mind.

"Out of order," he growled, and the unwanted interruption went away.

He went back to the more immediate problem of Devony's righteous anger. "Cruz is an asshole. You think I don't want to park my fist in his chest cavity right now? Unfortunately, we need him. We need both him and Judah LaSalle alive and well until we can establish if there's a link between them and Opus. We're getting close. This big job could be the thing that gets us there."

Nothing he said seemed to cool her fury. Her fangs filled her mouth, razor tips as bright and sharp as diamonds. Her pupils were slender vertical slits, surrounded by molten light. Rafe couldn't see her *dermaglyphs*, but he knew the skin markings would be livid with color beneath her turtleneck and jeans.

Since he was a Breed male with red blood flowing in his veins, it was impossible for him not to take a moment to appreciate the otherworldly glory of Devony's transformation. As a woman, she was stunning. As an outraged, indomitable Breed female, she was magnificent.

Ah, Christ. She was hot as fucking hell and what he wanted to do more than anything else right now was to feel her body crushed against his. He wanted to cool her anger by stoking a different kind of fire in her.

But then she narrowed her seething glare on him.

"I'll bet you're glad Cruz wants me gone, aren't you?" She took a step forward, coming out of the stall and closing the short distance between them. "You've wanted me out of your way from the minute you showed up. Now, you've got it. Congratulations."

"That's not true."

Over her searing stare, one brow lifted in challenge.

Rafe cursed and tried again. "All right, it *was* true. Everything's different now. We're a team, Devony."

"Okay, then go back out there and tell Cruz you want me on that job tomorrow night."

"If I do that, it's only going to make him suspicious. You know that. He thinks you're human. We need him to continue believing that until this is over. If we give him any reason to get skittish, he'll tip off LaSalle and we'll be starting all over again." Rafe caressed the side of her face. "The job tomorrow isn't as important as the intel we might take away from it. And I promise to share it with you. Partners, remember?"

Her breathing slowed from its furious gallop of a moment ago. She held his gaze, her forehead still furrowed as she considered everything he said.

Rafe couldn't resist brushing his lips over hers. "Do you have any idea how gorgeous you are? I've been standing around out there with a raging hard-on ever since I walked in and saw you again. But right now?" He blew out a low breath and shook his head. "Right now, I don't think I could keep my hands off you if Cruz and everyone else in the whole fucking place tried to knock down that door."

"Would it hold?"

Her saucy question went straight to his erection. "I'll make damn sure it does."

Moving closer to him, Devony gestured toward the stall where the tranced blonde was snoring quietly. "What about her?"

"The guys assume I'm somewhere tapping her vein. She's out until I wake her."

Devony made a purring sound as her hands waded into his hair. "Want to hear a secret? I was hoping you'd follow me back here. Because ever since you walked into this bar tonight, all I can think about is how long I'd have to wait before I could feel you inside me again."

"Ah, fuck." Rafe's breath sawed out of him, raw and rasping. "I'm not going to let either one of us wait another goddamn second."

He crushed his mouth against hers. Gathering her into his arms, he pivoted around with her, pulling her clear of the stalls and moving them both into the center of the small space in front of the sinks. Their hands moved greedily, frantically. Zippers rasped open. Jeans abraded skin as they were hastily pushed down off each other's hips.

Rafe was hard as stone in Devony's fevered grasp. On a groan, he slid his fingers into the cleft of her sex. Hot, liquid silk drenched her delicate flesh, slickening her folds. His hips pumped in reflex to the feel of all of that velvety wetness, his erection surging and rampant in the vise of her stroking hand.

He slipped a finger inside the tightness of her body. "You're so soft here, baby. So ready for me."

"Yes." The word boiled from between her parted lips. She dropped her head back on a hiss, the tendons in her graceful neck pulled taut as she ground against his hand. Tiny muscles rippled along his fingers as he stroked into her. "Oh God, Rafe. I need you. I need this. Right now."

His answer was a feral-sounding snarl. He needed her too. He needed everything with her.

"Turn around," he uttered, his voice rough and raw.

He swiveled her in front of him, bending her forward with his palm against her clothed back. She held on to the sink, her sweet ass thrust toward him in invitation.

He caressed the round swells, using both hands to spread her wide. Her body glistened, flushed dark pink and so pretty.

He teased her silky seam with the head of his cock, then sank inside on a long, slow thrust that had his molars clenched so tight it was a wonder they didn't shatter.

She moaned and moved against him, spurring him into a wilder tempo. They crashed together, surrendered to the heat and force of their desire. Rafe needed his hands on her skin, needed to see the play of color in her *glyphs* as he drove into her. He smoothed his palms under the back of her turtleneck, baring her pretty back to his glowing gaze. Her skin undulated with living colors. He traced his fingers over the flourishes, then up to the diminutive teardrop-and-crescent-moon birthmark that rode her right shoulder blade.

His fangs throbbed with the need to take hold of her as she rocked beneath him. He wanted to mark her, claim her, bind her to him as his.

Fuck.

The thought alone should have shaken him. It damn well shouldn't have made his blood race faster, harder through his veins. It shouldn't have intensified his want of her. Shouldn't have made him hunger for something he didn't deserve—and wouldn't—so long as his life belonged to his mission for the Order.

Rafe met her molten gaze in the dingy mirror. God help him, but he saw some of the same forbidden hunger in her eyes. Her fangs were long and sharp behind her parted lips, her eyes flicking to where his own pulse hammered visibly in his throat.

He hardly recognized the possessive snarl that

vibrated through him in that moment. He didn't want to acknowledge what he was feeling.

Not simply lust and overwhelming pleasure, although he felt that all the way to his marrow. No, what he felt was even more powerful than that as he watched Devony's beautiful face and felt her body shatter around him in a fierce orgasm.

Mine.

The word slammed through him as he exploded deep inside her.

Mine.

It was a dangerous word. One that stayed with him, as constant as his own heartbeat, even after they hastily put themselves back together and he sent Devony out ahead of him.

With the tranced woman awakened and her pliable human mind filled with the suggestion that he'd just shown her the time of her life, Rafe returned to the crowded tavern and dropped the blonde at the table with her giggling friends.

Then he headed for the back of Asylum where the gang, and the reality of his mission, awaited.

CHAPTER 16

The private warehouse near Conley Terminal looked like it had been a relic about twenty years ago. Rust-streaked, dilapidated, the steel-and-brick structure might have seemed abandoned among its neighbors if not for the obvious security presence just inside the front door.

Rafe and the rest of the gang sat a couple of blocks away in an unmarked delivery truck Ocho had obtained from one of his many questionable colleagues. Fish and Axel were dressed in stolen port authority uniforms. All of the gang were armed with semiautomatics, Rafe included.

Cruz held a pair of compact binoculars in front of his face as he peered out at the warehouse. "There's the midnight shift reporting for duty. You all know what to do. As soon as the other guards are gone, we're going in."

They had reviewed the plan earlier tonight at Ocho's.

According to Cruz, LaSalle had assured him the job was expected to be a simple one. Gain access to the warehouse. Grab the crates of newly arrived merchandise from overseas. Deliver them to the drop location. Collect the fat payout.

Rafe had run enough cleanup patrols with his Order teammates to know that greedy criminals like these tended to get sloppy when someone waved enough dollar signs in front of them. He didn't expect the job tonight to be as simple as Cruz claimed. And although Devony was still angry to be excluded, he was glad he didn't have to dread anything happening to her during this sketchy undertaking.

They had agreed to keep their distance after their restroom rendezvous at Asylum last night. Rafe went home to his place in Southie and stayed there until meeting up with the gang. She had agreed to stay put at her Darkhaven and await word from him once the job was over.

As promised, he'd sent her what details he knew, including the warehouse location and the drop site. If things went as he planned, he hoped to get close enough to Judah LaSalle to trance the bastard and squeeze him for everything he might know about Opus Nostrum.

The sooner he had that intel, the sooner he could get on with the task of wiping the organization off the map.

Then he would have time to consider what Devony Winters was coming to mean to him, and whether those feelings stood any chance of being reciprocated.

"Okay," Cruz announced. "New guards are inside . . . and there go the old ones around the corner. Time to move. Hit it, Ocho."

The truck lurched into gear. Ocho drove it in front

of the warehouse, and Rafe hopped out behind Fish and Axel. As they had done at the MFA, the two men provided a momentary distraction while Rafe leapt to action putting the lights out on the guards.

Cruz and Ocho moved in behind them, crowbars in hand. They located the sealed crates they were after and made quick work cracking them open. One by one, the men began unloading smaller crates onto a wheeled dolly.

Rafe hadn't been tasked with handling the merchandise, not that he cared. Tonight, he'd been relegated to lookout and problem-solver. He stood watch as the men alternated between loading the dolly and moving it out to the waiting truck.

"Faster," Cruz ordered the others, patrolling around like a general. "Come on, let's go! Look alive."

Rafe caught up with Fish on the side. "Hey, talk to me. Whose shit are we stealing tonight?"

"I don't know, man," Fish answered in a low whisper. "Some kinda arms dealer, according to Ocho. LaSalle's got friends who're willing to pay about anything to get their hands on whatever's in those crates."

Cruz eyed Rafe cautiously, a strangely smug look in his eyes as Fish and Axel came back for another load. Rafe didn't like the look the gang leader had on his face. He didn't like the feeling that he was somehow the brunt of an unspoken joke.

"Something funny, Cruz?"

He shrugged. "I'm not laughing, man."

"Neither am I," Rafe said. "What the fuck's going on? What are we hauling out of he—"

The sound of a vehicle approaching outside the

warehouse snagged his attention. A car door opened. A pair of boots slapped against concrete.

The guards who'd left a few minutes ago had circled back unexpectedly. One of them double-timed it inside the warehouse. "Yo, Jansen. It's just me. Forgot that damn birthday card for my wife."

He walked in farther. "Hey, you know there's a rental truck sitting outside? Meeks and I just texted the boss to see if he might'a sent someone over for that new shipment. . . . Jansen?"

Rafe stood in front of him now, moving through the warehouse in the blink of an eye. Palming the man's balding forehead before he had a chance to voice his surprise, Rafe dropped the guard into an immediate trance.

But he wasn't the last of their problems.

The guard's partner had circled around to the back of the warehouse for a sneak attack. His command to Cruz and the other men to freeze was answered by a hail of gunshots from the gang. He howled sharply and returned fire. The scent of blood filled the air.

Son of a bitch.

Rafe flashed into the fray and found Axel dead on the floor of the warehouse, the back of his skull blown out. The guard was dead too. He lay in a growing pool of blood a few yards from where Cruz continued to bark orders to his men.

"Forget about loading the dolly. No time now." The gang leader grabbed one of the crates and started to hurry away with it. "All of you grab what you can and let's get the fuck out of here!"

Rafe wheeled on him, blocking his path. His eyes burned like coals, glowing against the blanched whiteness of Cruz's face. The spilled blood would have been enough to bring Rafe's fangs out, but it was fury and suspicion for this man that made the sharp points erupt from his gums.

"What the hell are you and LaSalle up to here? What the fuck is in these crates? Tell me before I decide to tear out your damn throat."

Cruz didn't look scared. He looked . . . triumphant.

He let go of the crate he was holding.

It hit the floor between them, the crash echoing like cannon fire. Rafe felt a sudden heat gathering beneath him. He glanced down, shocked to see luminescent, milky blue rivulets leaking out of the broken slats.

Holy hell.

Liquidized ultraviolet light.

He'd known the advanced technology existed. It was one of Opus's favorite new developments—and something they had been attempting to weaponize on a large scale for some time. In the past few months, the Order had destroyed other caches of the Breed-killing rounds of UV light. Evidently, not all of them.

And Rafe had never seen the shit up close and personal like this before.

It seared his eyes. He staggered back, shielding his face with his arm.

It wasn't enough to stop the burn that washed over him as the streams of pure light surrounded him.

He reached for Cruz on a bellowed roar, but the gang leader danced out of his reach on a low chuckle.

"Get your asses moving," he shouted to Fish and Ocho. "LaSalle is waiting for us at the drop."

CHAPTER 17

S he couldn't stand the waiting.

After pacing in her brownstone Darkhaven for the past couple of hours, Devony had finally given in to her impatience and hopped on her motorcycle. Rafe's promise to update her once the job was over should have been reassurance enough, but she couldn't shake the feeling that something was wrong.

She headed past the drop location near Atlantic Wharf, but saw no sign of the men anywhere near the marina. They were late, which only deepened her sense of dread.

Gunning her bike, she sped for the industrial park near the shipping terminal. The sick feeling in her stomach eased a bit when she spotted the gang's vehicle parked out front, Ocho jogging around from the back to hop into the driver's seat. Cruz and Fish each carried a bulky crate out from the warehouse and loaded them into the truck.

Thank God. It appeared they were preparing to roll out right now.

Maybe that visual confirmation should have been enough to appease her. After all, she wasn't even supposed to know about the gig tonight, let alone be there.

But one thing she didn't see was Rafe.

The stench of gunfire hung in the air. And the closer she got to the warehouse, the more certain she was that she smelled blood.

Human blood, not Breed.

Yet that did nothing for the gnawing alarm that was building inside her chest.

She sped for the idling truck, practically leaping off her motorcycle once she reached it. Cruz was still at the rear of the vehicle with Fish. He rolled the door down and slammed the lock tight as Devony ran up to them.

"What the fuck are you doing here?"

"Tell me what happened," she said, panic climbing up her throat. "Where's Rafe? Is he here with you?"

Cruz didn't answer. He jerked his goateed chin at Fish. "Get your ass in the cab. Now!"

Fish hesitated only for a second, his face uncertain as he glanced at Devony. Then he hurried away as ordered.

On a snarl, Devony grabbed a fistful of the gang leader's shirt. She didn't have the patience to pretend she wasn't prepared to do him serious harm. "Damn you, Cruz. Tell me what the hell is going—"

He shoved her hard, tearing out of her grasp. As she staggered back, he darted around to the other side of the open cab. "Ocho! Let's go!"

The truck lurched forward in a scream of spinning tires and smoking rubber.

Devony's vision flooded with fire. Every particle of her being that was otherworldly, ferociously Breed, exploded to life inside her.

She leapt into the air, landing like a cat on the roof of the speeding truck.

Another leap and an airborne twist brought her boots down onto the hood of the vehicle, facing Ocho and Cruz's stunned expressions on the other side of the windshield.

She smashed her fist through the glass and grabbed Cruz by the throat. "Where. The. Fuck. Is. Rafe?"

Cruz sputtered and choked, clawing at her fingers. "Fuck you, bitch!"

"Holy shit!" Ocho's eyes nearly popped out of his skull behind the wheel. "She's a damn Breed!"

The truck swerved, but Devony rode it out. As she held Cruz in her punishing grip, she noticed something odd about his clothes. Bright blue, strangely illuminated paint splattered the front of his shirt and jeans. He had some on his hands too.

No, not paint.

What the fuck?

In the midst of the jostling and chaos up front, Fish crept forward from the back of the truck. "He's in the warehouse, Brinks." He swallowed hard, gave a halting shake of his head. "The liquid UV from the crates . . ."

Oh, shit.

Oh, no.

Devony bellowed her fury. She wanted nothing more than to unleash hell on Cruz, but concern for Rafe overruled everything else.

She vaulted off the vehicle. It careened away into the night while she all but flew back to the warehouse.

An unconscious security guard lay in a slump inside the entrance. Two more had been tranced nearby. They were all starting to rouse. Which meant Rafe's hold on their minds was beginning to slip away.

"Rafe!"

Devony ran farther inside, her senses overcome with the scent of spilled blood. So much blood. Death, too. Axel's body lay not far from another guard's bullet-riddled corpse.

And there was Rafe.

Writhing on the floor next to a broken crate that was still oozing shimmery, luminescent blue liquid from inside it. Rafe lay in a growing pool of the stuff. Everywhere the concentrated, ultraviolet material touched his bare skin was hideous with burns. Even his handsome face.

"Oh, my God. Rafe."

The sound of her voice seemed to rouse him. He lifted his head but his swollen eyelids didn't, or couldn't, open. "Devony," he rasped. "What the hell are you doing? Go. Cruz and the others—"

"They're gone," she told him, already crouched at his side. "They drove off in the truck."

"Liquid UV."

"I know. Fish told me." Her boots slipped in the mercury-like puddles as she struggled to pull Rafe out of the spill. "We need to get you out of here."

He groaned in agony as she dragged him up onto his feet, wedging her shoulder beneath his arm to support him. She didn't know where he got the strength to move in his horrific condition, but he staggered out of the warehouse with her into the cool night.

"We can't take my bike. You won't be able to ride."

"The guards' car." Rafe pointed to the unmarked sedan parked in the side lot.

Devony started the engine with her mind while they hurried toward the vehicle. She carefully helped Rafe into the passenger seat, wincing at the agonizing pain he clearly suffered.

"I'm good," he said. "Just drive, baby."

"Okay." She jumped in behind the wheel and hit the gas.

She drove deeper into the city, unsure where she was going. Her gaze strayed repeatedly to Rafe, her heart squeezing with deepening concern. He was in worse condition than she first realized. His lungs wheezed. His hands were blistered, pulpy masses. UV burns scorched his forehead, eyelids, and cheeks. Even his lips were singed. The peeling, white skin cracked and bled with the slightest movement of his mouth.

He needed help desperately.

What he needed was healing, and from the look of him, there was no time to waste.

She spotted a bridge underpass ahead. The exit ramp beneath it was partially blocked by construction cones and barriers, the entire area cordoned off for repairs. It looked quiet and pitch dark, the nearest place she could see where they could pull over for a while and catch their breath.

"What are you doing?" he rasped from beside her. "We're slowing down. Why?"

"It's all right." God, she hated to let him hear the jagged sound of her voice. She wanted to be strong, but she could hardly contain the emotion that had been lodged in her throat from the moment she saw him back in that warehouse. "I'm pulling over somewhere safe that you can rest."

"No. Can't slow down." Agitated, he shifted abruptly. His wounded hands moved aimlessly in front of him because he couldn't see. He groaned, a sound of frustration and agony. "I need to stop Cruz. Those crates . . . gotta be stealing that shit for Opus."

"You're not going anywhere right now. You need rest. You need healing."

Against his growled protest, she parked the sedan under the flapping plastic sheet that draped down from the top of the repaired bridge. Swiveling toward him, she drew in a shallow, worry-filled breath. His pain terrified her. It shattered her.

But if she lost him now, because of Cruz and LaSalle?

If she lost him because of Opus Nostrum . . .

No. She refused to think it.

She refused to allow even the possibility that they could take him from her too.

"Let me help you." She reached over to him, laying her hands gingerly on his chest.

She had barely begun to pull his healing ability into herself when she realized it wasn't going to work. His body was depleted, rallying all of its energy into combatting the damage from the ultraviolet exposure. He was fading in and out of consciousness already. She could siphon his psychic ability, but it would mean draining him of the last of his strength. She wasn't sure she could push it back into him fast enough to save him.

And failure wasn't an option she was willing to risk.

She severed the connection, drawing her hands away.

"You need blood, Rafe."

She glanced out the windows, seeing nothing but deserted roadway and construction around them. Not a single human anywhere to be found, and no time to race around searching for a blood Host for him. Not that she wanted to see him feed from someone else. Not even under these circumstances.

Especially not then.

Human blood was an inferior solution, anyway. His body would need something far more powerful to boost its recovery.

Her blood.

There was hardly anything purer.

There was nothing in this world that would heal him faster.

But if she gave it to him, she could never take it back. The bond would remain long after he healed. It would be unbreakable. If she fed him even one sip, he would be fused to her forever through that bond—a gift he might view as a curse.

She didn't take that understanding lightly.

He might come to hate her for it, but at least he would be alive.

Devony brought her wrist to her mouth and bit into the veins that pulsed there. Blood dripped onto Rafe's scorched skin and into his beard as she lowered her hand to his parted, blistered lips.

He moaned at the first drop that slid onto his tongue. His big body twitched as the steady patter continued to flow. He licked at it, then his mouth fastened over the punctures and he drew deep from her. As he swallowed, a low rumble built in his chest.

Abruptly, his eyes peeled open. Fire blazed in the

tormented pools of aquamarine.

"Devony." Her name was a threatening snarl.

"Drink," she whispered.

And he did.

CHAPTER 18

He was burning up.
Lightning in his veins. In his muscles and bones.

In every depleted, thirsting cell in his body.

And he couldn't get enough.

The full-body, overwhelming agony that had dropped him on the floor of the warehouse and nearly scorched the life out of him now gave way to something infinitely more humbling.

Devony Winters.

Her essence rushed into him with every hungry gulp he took from her veins. Bold, intense, sweet . . . intoxicating. Unforgettable.

Life-altering.

She had been all of those things to him even before this moment, but now she lived inside him through his link to her. He felt her strength and power feeding his ravaged body, restoring the damage that surely would have killed him if she hadn't defied his instructions and come looking for him tonight.

His extraordinary partner.

He owed her his life.

God, he owed Devony so much more than that.

And he still owed her the truth.

He lifted his eyelids and found her watching him with tender relief as he fed from her. "It's working, Rafe. Keep drinking. Your skin is healing. The burns . . . they're starting to fade."

He groaned against her wrist, feeling like the worst kind of bastard as all of her emotions flooded into him at once. Her fear over the gravity of his injuries fading now, replaced by a bright, rising joy over seeing him on the mend.

The astonishing depth of her care for him.

It was too much. He had taken too much from her, not just at her wrist tonight, but from the moment he first met her.

Now this. The connection he would have to her for as long as either of them lived.

Fuck.

Angrily, he forced himself to release her, sweeping his tongue over the twin punctures and sealing them closed.

He sat up, taking a quick inventory of himself. Beneath the healing light of Devony's blood, he still hurt like hell. His skin still felt as if it were being stripped off him with a hot knife, but he was breathing. He was alive.

Thanks to Devony, he was alive.

Remorse clawed at him. Not because he didn't want her gift, but because of the regret she would bear once she realized he didn't deserve it.

Scowling, he glanced at her. "You shouldn't have done that."

Her expression faltered a bit. Some of the bright intensity of her emotions dimmed in the face of his stony response.

He couldn't help it. Guilt sank its talons into him as she stared at him in the silence of the vehicle.

The best way he knew how to ensure her gift wasn't wasted on him was to do everything in his power to see her family avenged and Opus Nostrum destroyed. He wasn't going to rest until it was done.

"Slide over," he said, already opening the passenger door. "I'll drive now."

He hoofed it around to the other side and climbed in. They were a few miles out from the center of Boston. Rafe sped back toward the drop location.

He was all but certain the few minutes' detour while he came back online had probably given Cruz ample time to transfer the crates to LaSalle or whoever was actually at the other end of the supply-and-demand chain. So, he couldn't have been more pleased to see the delivery truck still parked at Atlantic Wharf.

Except . . . something wasn't right.

"Rafe," Devony murmured from beside him.

"Yeah. I know." There was no activity near the truck. When he saw the massive hole punched through the windshield, he arched a brow at Devony.

She gave him a flat look. "I should've killed Cruz while I had his throat in my fist."

Rafe parked the sedan in front of the other vehicle. "I'll be right back," he said. "Stay here."

"Like hell I will."

She jumped out with him and together they approached the truck. They both smelled blood long before they saw the bodies of Cruz, Fish, and Ocho. All three had been shot execution-style.

The corpses were cold. Whoever had done the killings had been gone for some time.

And all of the crates of liquid UV were missing.

"Oh, my God," Devony murmured. "Do you think LaSalle double-crossed them?"

Rafe shook his head. "I don't know. Fish said the crates belonged to an arms dealer. Apparently, LaSalle's contact needed someone to play middleman."

"Expendables," Devony guessed.

Rafe nodded. "Yeah, but this seems more professional than payback from a local gun runner. I've seen this kind of carnage before. A few months ago in Montreal, after an Opus death squad took out a pharmaceutical tycoon and his entire estate."

"There's LaSalle's yacht," she said, pointing toward the marina. Light glowed from the windows of the massive white vessel docked at the end of a long pier. "He's still here."

Rafe didn't like the look of it. Or the smell. If the area around the truck reeked of death, LaSalle's yacht carried the stench of a slaughterhouse.

"Opus's assassins have been here too," he muttered.

He didn't like the idea of Devony approaching the yacht alongside him, but she'd already demonstrated that she wasn't the type of partner to take a backseat when faced with danger.

And thank God for that earlier tonight.

His skin still felt like hell, but it didn't slow him down as they crept up on LaSalle's vessel and cautiously boarded it.

The place was silent except for the chatter of a sports telecast blaring from somewhere in the main cabin. Armed bodyguards had been shot at point-blank range in the head. Crew members had suffered similar fates, some with their throats slashed. Rafe moved quickly through the cabin, his ear trained to the faint rasp of fading breaths and the slowing tick of a dying heart.

"It's LaSalle," Devony said.

The man lay in the main salon of the yacht with several other of his crew. Blood painted everything, including the large-screen TV on the other side of the luxurious living space.

Rafe hunkered down next to Judah LaSalle. "Tell me who you're working for."

All he got was a wet wheeze in reply. The human was too far gone to talk. He had seconds left, maybe less.

"What's wrong, LaSalle? Opus decide you outlived your usefulness?" Rafe demanded. He grabbed hold of LaSalle, giving him a jolt of healing—just enough to extract a little sound from his drowning lungs. "Goddamn it, tell me who your contact is."

"I don't . . . don't know." Blood bubbled in the corners of the dying man's mouth. "I don't have . . . don't have a contact. I just . . . just do what they ask me. Then money shows up in my . . . in my bank account."

"Do you think he's telling the truth?"

Rafe glanced up at Devony. "There's one way to find out."

Placing his palm over the human's clammy brow, he tranced him and asked the question again. LaSalle told him the same thing. He never had direct contact with anyone—at least, until tonight.

"Who was it that did this?" Rafe asked.

LaSalle weakly shook his head. "I swear . . . don't know. They said I . . . said I fucked up. They said . . . said you and the girl . . . said you both had to go."

Rafe swung a look at Devony. "We need to get out of here."

She wasn't paying attention to him anymore. Her gaze was riveted to the blood-splattered TV screen. Rafe felt her shock in his own bloodstream, as cold as ice water.

The game had been pre-empted by a local news bulletin—a report of a massive explosion in a residential area of Back Bay. In the background behind the reporter, an inferno roared, ash and smoke billowing into the night sky as firefighters struggled to contain it.

Rafe let go of LaSalle. The man's last breath rattled out of him as his body slumped to the floor again.

Rafe moved next to Devony. "Holy shit."

She slowly turned her head toward him now. "That's my block, Rafe. That building . . . that's my house."

CHAPTER 19

Devony sat beside him in silence in the warehouse guards' stolen sedan as he drove.

Rafe glanced at her shell-shocked face, illuminated by the dim light of the dashboard. "Are you all right?"

She nodded once, but it was merely a reflex response. She didn't look at him. She'd hardly said two words since they left all the carnage behind at the marina.

She was a strong, courageous woman, but not even a seasoned Order warrior would be expected to witness that kind of slaughter and come out of it unaffected. And now, according to LaSalle, Opus's death squad had orders to come for the two of them.

Rafe wasn't overly concerned that he was in their crosshairs. Just being associated with Lucan Thorne and the Order had put an Opus Nostrum target on his back. He lived with that truth every day. For Devony, the threat was new.

And tonight it had become starkly, dangerously, real. "They firebombed my home, Rafe."

"Yeah." He winced inwardly at her wooden tone and reached over to her, placing his hand over her cool fingers. "But you're okay. You're safe. That's all that matters."

She mutely shook her head. "But everything else . . . All my work, my father's research and notes. We've lost all of it now. We're going to have to start all over, Rafe."

He clamped his jaw closed, struggling to hold the secret that he had passed nearly every piece of intel she had over to the Order. Gideon had probably data mined every photo and note a dozen times each by now.

The Order hadn't lost anything tonight, but he couldn't divulge that to Devony without clearing it with his commanders.

Rafe's answering curse came out brittle. "I'm sorry you've gotten mixed up in any of this. I'm just damn glad you weren't anywhere near your Darkhaven when those Opus killers got there."

Now, it wouldn't be safe for her anywhere else in the city, either.

With the exception of one location.

There was only one place he knew of where he could rest confidently knowing neither Opus nor anyone loyal to them could touch her.

He headed there now, despite the understanding that his arrival could blow everything up in his face. His covert mission. His commanders' faith in him. Hell, his entire future as a warrior could be lost by bringing an unauthorized civilian—one with JUSTIS ties and a price on her head—into the Order's domain.

But all of those things paled compared to the

possibility of losing Devony's trust at the same time.

The fact that he hadn't told her about any of that—the fact that he *couldn't* tell her without breaching his duty to the Order—ate at him as the highly secured command center and surrounding grounds came into view up ahead.

When he turned in to the property, Devony finally snapped out of her daze. "Where are we?"

"The only place we can go right now."

He touched the security panel, holding his palm in front of the reader as he waited for a response. It didn't take long.

"The fuck are you doing here?" Elijah's low drawl over the speaker was anything but welcoming. With only a couple of hours left before daybreak, the patrol team must have only just reported back to base.

"I need to see the commander."

"So call and make an appointment." His comrade's attitude was to be expected, especially considering their last conversation at Asylum.

"It's urgent, Eli. I'm not leaving until I talk to Chase."

The warrior snorted. "Then it'll be your funeral, man."

When the gate opened, Rafe drove inside. He felt Devony's apprehension as they approached the sprawling mansion. According to the elder warriors, the Order's original compound in this city had been impressive. This newer one was a fortress, constructed twenty years ago, after the first was compromised by an enemy and had to be destroyed.

Devony turned a worried glance at him. "Rafe, are you sure about this?"

"It'll be all right." He killed the engine and faced her. He couldn't resist reaching out to stroke the side of her wary face. "You'll be safe here, I promise."

To his surprise, as they walked from the vehicle to the front door of the imposing mansion, Devony slipped her hand in his. He didn't know if the gesture was meant to reassure him or herself. Nor did he care.

After the night they had just endured, he was glad to hold on to her. He was more than glad to feel her at his side; he was proud.

He wouldn't even be standing there if not for the life-saving gift of her blood.

Through his bond to her, he felt the knot of worry tighten inside her as the door swung open and Eli stood in front of them. He was flanked by Jax, both warriors still in patrol gear, right down to the weapons that bristled at the ready in their hands.

"I'll be damned," Jax muttered to Eli. "I thought you had to be joking when you said he was waiting outside."

For what wasn't the first time, Rafe wished his teammates understood the truth. That he wasn't the turncoat loser he still had to pretend he was. Their suspicion burned, even though he had worked hard for the past few weeks to make sure he'd earned it.

Seeing that mistrust leveled on Devony, too, put a sharper edge to his voice. "I need to talk to the commander."

Neither one of them moved out of the way.

Elijah's gaze narrowed on Devony for a moment before sliding back to Rafe. He let out a caustic laugh. "Who's the stray? Didn't I see her hanging with that gang of losers when we ran into you at Asylum the other night?"

Rafe lowered his head on a warning growl. "She's mine. That's all you need to know."

The protective, possessive part of him rose to Devony's defense. His response would be the same no matter if he were staring down a friend or a bona fide enemy.

To his credit, Eli stood down. Just a little.

Jax crossed his arms, still in battle stance at the threshold. "You've got some kind of balls, man. The commander's not going to like this. Neither will Nathan, once he finds out you're here and you brought her with you."

Rafe didn't have the patience for reprimands or questions, especially when he couldn't tell his teammates a damn thing. And not while he was standing outside with Devony knowing Opus's death squad was likely combing the city for her.

"I'm not here to talk to either of you, damn it." He took a step forward, ready to forcibly enter the mansion if he had to. "I'm only going to talk to Chase."

"Let him in."

From behind the pair of hulking warriors, Commander Sterling Chase appeared. Eli and Jax parted, making way for the immense Breed male. Chase was always an imposing figure with his broad shoulders, muscled bulk, and piercing blue eyes beneath his crown of golden hair. Tonight, there was a gravity to his demeanor that Rafe had rarely seen.

His displeased gaze moved from Rafe to Devony, lingering for a moment on their joined hands. He turned away from them without comment. "Come inside, both of you. Rafe, my office."

Rafe stepped forward, leading Devony. On Chase's

dismissal, Eli and Jax went back to whatever they'd been doing before Rafe's arrival. And from within another room on the main floor of the mansion, Chase's mate, Tavia, appeared along with Carys and her mate, Rune.

Carys gaped, a hopeful smile spreading over her beautiful face. "Rafe? Oh, my God!"

When she would have run to him in greeting, the dark-haired behemoth who was her blood-bonded mate held her back, his thick arm wrapped firmly, yet tenderly, around her midsection.

Although Carys was as unaware as anyone that his exile wasn't permanent, it felt good to see she hadn't lost faith in him. He only hoped her brother Aric and the rest of the warriors would be equally forgiving if and when he was able to return to the fold.

Of those in the room now, only Commander Chase and his mate Tavia were privy to the truth. Tavia strode up to Devony and him.

"Hello, Rafe." Her soft gaze lit on Devony. "Hi. I'm Tavia Chase."

"This is Devony Winters," Rafe said when she seemed incapable of words. "Her parents and brother both worked for JUSTIS in London, at the headquarters."

"Oh, I see," Tavia said, a look of tender sympathy in her eyes.

"Devony's Breed," Rafe added. "She's a daywalker."

Carys's eyes went wide. "Are you serious? That means we're related."

Tavia seemed less surprised, which indicated that Lucan had shared the information Rafe provided in his last report. Chase had obviously made his mate aware of the half-sister she had lost in the JUSTIS bombing, and the niece who had unexpectedly ended up in the middle of Rafe's mission.

Through his bond with Devony, Rafe felt her jolt of elation as she looked at the older woman who shared her extraordinary bloodline. A small breath leaked out of her as she let go of his hand to accept Tavia's in greeting. "I'm so pleased to meet you both."

"Likewise, Devony."

Chase nodded to his mate. "Tavia, would you and Carys like to chat with Devony while I talk privately with Rafe?"

"Of course. It would be our pleasure."

"I'll be right here," Rafe told Devony when she glanced at him in question. Although the way Chase's displeased gaze bore into him, he wasn't sure he would have any of his ass left once the commander was through chewing it out.

He motioned toward his office. They moved inside and Rafe stood at attention on the other side of the desk while Chase dropped into his leather chair behind it.

"Go ahead and sit, son. We could be here a while." As Rafe took the offered seat, Chase stared at him over steepled fingers. "I'm going to assume you've got a damn good reason for showing up here unannounced tonight, with a civilian female under your arm, no less. Let me go all the way out on a limb and suggest it might have something to do with the fact that you're apparently fucking an Order asset. When Lucan gave you permission to keep the female in play if you needed to, I doubt this is what he had in mind."

Shit. The accusation rankled, but it was the commander's crude assessment of Devony that really put an edge in Rafe's tone. "She is not just some asset, sir."

Chase grunted. "I guess that answers the first part of my question."

Rafe forged on, knowing there was no sense in trying to hide that he and Devony were involved. "She's in danger. I wouldn't have brought her here for anything less."

"Am I supposed to be relieved to hear that?" Chase swore under his breath. "From what I understand, Lucan specifically told you to hold your cover with her. He's not going to want to hear you defied an order by getting tangled up with her."

"My cover is still intact," Rafe muttered, feeling sick about that now. It had eaten at him nearly from the beginning, but especially now. "She doesn't know I'm still a part of the Order. Coming here tonight and running up against Eli and Jax only confirmed my cover."

"You care about this female."

Rafe couldn't deny it. Chase's look of sober understanding said he didn't need the confirmation, anyway.

"Tell me what happened tonight."

Rafe gave him a rundown of the chain of disasters, from the stolen—and now missing—crates of liquid UV to the wholesale assassination of Cruz and his gang along with Judah LaSalle, the Order's current best lead in their hunt for members of Opus Nostrum's inner circle.

Chase listened to all of the bad news in grim silence, as if he had already lived through a thousand similar catastrophes in his tenure as a warrior, and, like Lucan, had the broad shoulders to carry them all.

As bad as his problems had gotten tonight, Rafe

could handle them too.

Except for the one that had placed Devony in the line of fire.

"They burned down her brownstone tonight." Just saying the words put a chill in his veins. Just thinking about the danger she was in made his blood seethe with murderous intent. "I tranced LaSalle before he died. He told me that the death squad said they were coming after both Devony and me. While I was squeezing him for the information, we saw the news bulletin on his TV. Reporters and fire trucks were all over her block in Back Bay. I brought Devony straight here."

"Jesus, that inferno raging across town is her Darkhaven?"

"Was," Rafe corrected. "She's got nowhere else to go, Chase."

"That's not quite true. She can go back home to London. Mathias Rowan has been here in Boston on other business. I'm sure he'll be willing to get her home safely when he heads back tomorrow. His unit in London can provide her round-the-clock protection while we deal with this situation with Opus."

"What? No. No fucking way." Rafe wanted to think his vehement rejection of that idea had more to do with concerns for her wellbeing than his want to keep her close to him. That's not what his heart was saying, though.

"She doesn't have a home in London anymore. Not since her family was killed. She won't want to return there. Even if she did, you and I both know she'll be safer here, with us."

With him.

Just because he didn't say the words out loud didn't

mean they weren't thrumming through every fiber of his being.

He wanted her. Not just to ensure she was safe and secure. Not merely as a valuable partner in his goal to see Opus destroyed.

He just wanted . . . her.

Chase considered him for a moment before exhaling a long sigh. He leaned forward, elbows resting on the desk. "Listen, Rafe, Lucan told me about her situation. It's rough, what she went through. Losing her parents and her brother in one fell swoop. Anyone would want a little payback for that. But this is our fight with Opus, not hers."

"No." Rafe shook his head. "Tonight, by threatening her, they made it my fight."

It was true. As much as he craved retribution after being played for a fool by Opus in Montreal, this resolve to obliterate the cabal was something different. It went deeper, ran infinitely colder.

His own humiliation was nothing compared to the very real threat to Devony's life.

"She stays with me."

Chase's brows rose in challenge. "As commander of this operation center, I might have something to say about that. And I can assure you, Lucan will—"

"I drank from her."

"Ah, fuck. Tell me you're joking."

Rafe held the bleak stare of his commander. "Earlier tonight, after Cruz smashed a crate of liquid UV in front of me. The burns were . . . bad. Devony wasn't supposed to take part in the robbery, but she came looking for me anyway. If she hadn't found me when she did—if she hadn't given me her blood . . ." Rafe slowly shook his head. "I owe her my life."

"I see." Chase studied him, then shook his head. "I'll put a call in to D.C. I know Lucan will want to hear all of this directly from you. He's going to want to decide where this goes from here. In the meantime, I need to get boots on the ground to go try to contain what's left of that UV supply at the warehouse. Aric and his new team arrived earlier tonight," Chase added. "Looks like they just got their first assignment."

Damn. His best friend's daywalker team was already put together. They were here in Boston, and Rafe wouldn't even have known if he hadn't shown up tonight.

Although he hadn't actually been ousted from the Order weeks ago, it still took him aback to realize how life had moved on as if he were gone for good. Until now, he hadn't realized how much he truly missed being back in the fold, an active part of operations.

Chase got up from his chair. "I can't say I like what I've heard tonight, Rafe, or where things stand with you and Devony Winters. But I'm not going to act like you're the first warrior to fuck things up six ways from Sunday on account of a woman."

The sardonic remark gave him more hope than it probably should, but right now he'd take it.

Rafe rose to his feet as well. "Thank you, sir."

"Go on, get out of here." The Order elder gave him a frown and a dismissive wave. "Go make sure your female is all right. Be ready to meet me in the compound war room in one hour."

"Yes, sir."

CHAPTER 20

D evony couldn't stop staring.

Tavia Chase was stunningly beautiful. Tall and elegant in her basic black outfit of tailored pants and a fine-gauge knit sweater, she exuded a calm confidence that immediately put Devony at ease. Her face was a study in classic beauty, high cheekbones, smooth skin, and a generous mouth—all of it framed by a luxurious mane of caramel-brown hair.

Carys shared many of her mother's features and her remarkable beauty, but where Tavia conveyed a steady strength, her daughter practically vibrated with wild, magnetic energy.

For many reasons, Devony was awestruck by both daywalker females, not the least of which being that they were her own relatives.

After introductions in the foyer, the two women had taken her to a lovely guestroom suite in a quiet part of the mansion. They were seated together in a comfortable conversation area of the room, Devony on an oversized upholstered chair, Tavia and Carys perched across from her on a silk-covered sofa.

"Are you sure you're all right?" Tavia asked gently. "I can only imagine how you must be feeling after your ordeal tonight."

Devony had explained to them about her brownstone being attacked, but even after assuring the two women she was fine, it hadn't seemed to lessen their concern. They fussed over her, offering food and drink and the full use of the sumptuous guestroom. Carys had even brought her sleepwear and a change of clothes from her own wardrobe. The silk robe and pajamas were as much a temptation as the oversized soaking tub in the adjacent bath.

But it was difficult to think of her own comfort knowing Rafe was somewhere else in the mansion being confronted by another of the Chases, one of the Order's most formidable members.

Sterling Chase, his former commander.

"I can't believe you've been right under our noses here in Boston," Carys said. She had also been avidly studying Devony from the moment they sat down. "How did you and Rafe meet?"

"It's ah . . . kind of a long story."

"And one for another time," Tavia said. "I'm sure Devony would like to rest."

Carys's expression slumped. "All right, until then. I'm sorry, I just have so many questions for you."

Devony could hardly hide her curiosity, either. There was so much she wanted to ask these two women, so much she wanted to know about their lives. But she hadn't come there on a social call. She wasn't even sure she and Rafe would be allowed to stay.

"I'd like that, Carys."

"Good. You'll even have a chance to meet my brother, Aric. He and his mate, Kaya, are here now from Montreal," she said, her blue eyes sparkling. "They've come with a few other daywalkers who've joined the Order as part of a special unit with him. You'll have to meet them all while you're here."

Tavia gently cleared her throat, more than likely to curtail her daughter from divulging Order business to a stranger. She rose, indicating for Carys to join her. "Please, make yourself at home, Devony. As I said, we're going to let you relax now. If you need anything at all, consider it yours."

She followed the pair to the door. Carys stepped out with a bright smile and a friendly wave, but Tavia paused there. She pulled Devony into a brief hug.

"I know these are terrible circumstances for our first meeting, but I'm very glad you're here." Her fingers were cool and soothing as she smoothed some of Devony's hair off her face. "I'm only sorry I didn't get the chance to meet your mother . . . my sister. I'm sure she was a very special woman."

"She was," Devony said. "She was the bravest woman I knew."

Tavia nodded. "I have a feeling she would say the same thing about you, if she were here to see you now."

Devony swallowed, emotion jamming in her throat at the sentiment, however unwarranted. She wasn't brave. She was angry. She was hurting. She wanted to deliver pain—not only as retribution for her family now, but for how close she'd come to losing Rafe.

And if Opus thought they could scare her away by torching her home tonight, all they had done was galvanize her need for vengeance into something stronger, steelier.

And now, she had a partner in that battle.

If it had to be the two of them against the rest of the world—even against the Order, if it should come down to that—she was ready for that fight. She was ready for anything, so long as Rafe was at her side.

Breaking into her grim thoughts, Tavia leaned in and kissed her cheek. "We'll have time to talk some more after you've had a chance to settle in."

Devony managed a smile. "I hope so."

She closed the door behind the women, realizing just now how exhausted she truly was. And she smelled awful, too. All the death and violence she and Rafe had left behind in the city still clung to her jacket, turtleneck, and jeans. A bath and a fresh change of clothes were more than a temptation; they were a necessity.

She turned on the water to the large soaking tub and traded her clothing for the white silk robe Carys had given her. The cool, glossy fabric was pure decadence against her bare skin. With the warm water slowly gathering in the tub, she checked out the tall bottles of bath oil, settling on a rose-infused vanilla fragrance that smelled almost good enough to eat.

A quiet rap sounded on the door in the other room.

She hurried out, expecting to find Carys or Tavia waiting on the other side.

"Rafe."

She flew to him. She couldn't have stayed out of his arms if her life depended on it. He stepped inside with her wrapped in his arms, and shut the door behind them, turning the lock with his mind.

They had only been apart less than an hour since arriving at the Order's mansion, but to her it felt like an eternity. After the night they had endured, she never wanted to be separated from him again.

"I've been worried," she whispered against his lips. "How did it go?"

"I'm handling it." He shrugged, dismissive of her concern as he continued to kiss her. "You look gorgeous in this. Smell like vanilla."

"Carys lent me a few things. I was just about to take a bath." Her words were all but lost amid the fevered brush of his lips over hers.

"I feel like I've been away from you for days." He tipped her face up to his, a look of torment and wonder in his glittering aquamarine eyes. "Do you have any idea how much I need to feel you in my arms right now?"

Breathless with desire, she shook her head. "Show me."

He frowned. "I'm covered in grit and grime. Christ, I smell like death."

"Do I look like I care?"

She pulled him down for her kiss. Her fingers tangled in his hair as her tongue sought his, their hot breaths mingling, bodies crushed together, held there by his strong arms.

Devony whimpered, overcome by the flood of emotions that rushed up on her as Rafe kissed her senseless. She couldn't explain her desperation for him. Somehow, the moment she saw him in the open doorway just now had felt so fragile—an illusion that could shatter with a single breath.

Maybe it was the havoc of the past few hours that

made her feel so breakable. All of the death. So much ugliness and violence, topped off by a brutal demonstration of what it meant to make an enemy out of Opus Nostrum. And, then, the destruction of her home.

But worst of all was the stark understanding that tonight she had likely been only minutes away from losing Rafe forever, if the liquid UV had been allowed to do its worst on him.

God help her, she would never forget that awful feeling as long as she lived.

The anguish swelled inside her, a black tide of dread.

"Hey." Rafe pulled back from their kiss, his brows knit. He gave a tight shake of his head. "Don't think about what happened tonight."

He knew how bleak her thoughts had gone. Of course, he knew. He could feel her strongest emotions through the blood she had given him. Now, he always would.

"Hey, look at me." He stroked her brow, her cheek, her lips. Sparks danced and smoldered in his eyes. "I'm here. You're safe, Devony. As long as I'm breathing, you will be safe. I promise you that. Tonight, we're together . . . because of you."

"Rafe." His name was a sigh through her teeth and emerging fangs. That shivery breath melted into a moan as he lowered his mouth to hers again.

All of the trauma and worries incinerated under the heat of his kiss. But where their need for each other was so often an explosive one, tonight there was as much unhurried tenderness as there was unbearable desire.

On a harsh groan, his lips moved away from hers, trailing down over the edge of her jaw and onto the sensitive column of her neck. Devony sucked in her breath, arousal spiraling through her. It twined with the powerful craving to feel his fangs sink into her bare flesh.

He growled in response to the hot coil of her need. "Fuck, you're killing me. I can feel everything."

She couldn't help it. Couldn't curb all the sensations he stoked within her. They climbed higher with every flick of his tongue and graze of his sharp fangs. Each caress of his hands over the silk covering her naked body licked through her like an open flame.

"Jesus, Devony . . . you are amazing. So fucking beautiful."

He opened the robe and slid his hand onto her breast, kneading and stroking, pinching the pebbled nipple. His palm skimmed the front of her, down onto her abdomen as his tongue swept inside her mouth. She squirmed under his sensual assault, desire swamping her, pooling hot and wet in her core.

And then he touched her there. His fingers delved into the cleft of her body, slipping through her juices, making the hard hammer of her pulse become a drumming roar. She pulled in a sharp breath as he teased her clit and the sensitive flesh surrounding it. When he stepped back from her, she couldn't hold back her protesting groan.

"I wish you could see yourself as I am right now," he rasped. He licked his lips as the heat of his glowing eyes raked every inch of her. Everywhere his amber-filled gaze touched her, she burned. He drank her in slowly, as if he had all night to savor every inch of her.

God help her, she would never last.

She took a step toward him and he shook his head,

a wicked tilt to his sexy mouth. He pulled his shirt off with impatient hands, tossing it aside. No trace of the UV burns remained on him anywhere now. Across his muscled chest and the ridges of his stomach, his *glyphs* roiled, alive with all the deep colors of desire.

Behind the zipper of his black jeans, his cock strained, thick and strong.

Devony's vision burned even hotter as she studied him. Need rolled through her, along with a surging wave of possessiveness. *Mine.*

She didn't know if she spoke the word out loud or merely thought it. Either way, it lived in her blood. It pounded through her veins and into all of her senses as he moved in close again and caught her face in his strong hands.

"Yes," he said, his blazing eyes locked on hers. "Mine."

He kissed her until she was breathless and quivering in his hands, then slowly sank down before her. "Open for me, baby."

His hand guided her thighs apart, his thumb flicking over the crest of her sex. Her clit was already engorged and aching for his touch. When he stroked his fingers over it, she nearly climaxed on the spot.

A low purr vibrated deep in his throat as he pressed his lips to her. "I could get drunk on the smell of you," he rasped, his hot breath skating over her sensitive flesh. "I already know how sweet you taste."

His head dipped between her legs. His mouth closed over her, his tongue delving into her folds. She cried out when he suckled the tight bundle of nerves nestled between them. The pleasure was searing, intense, wrenching a jagged moan from somewhere deep inside her.

And Rafe's mouth was relentless, merciless. She couldn't slow down the mounting wave of release that crashed into her. She shattered against his tongue, one gale after another buffeting her as he held her against his mouth and wrung every last gasp and shiver from her body.

She sagged forward as the tremors slowly began to ease.

"You should've warned me you were going to do that," she murmured, breathless as he rose to his feet. "I have a bath running. I should turn off the water before the tub overflows."

Rafe smirked. "I've got a better idea."

He scooped her up in his arms and carried her into the bathroom.

CHAPTER 21

Fragrant suds wreathed the spacious en suite, but the vanilla-and-roses oil Devony had put in the water had nothing on the intoxicating scent of her arousal. Or the taste of her release.

Rafe's veins pounded in response to her pleasure.

Every cell in his body echoed with her climax, as powerful as if it had been his own.

Fuck. He'd heard the blood bond was intense, but he hadn't been prepared. He hadn't been nearly prepared for the erotic pleasure of it, nor for the feeling of connection, completion.

He hadn't been prepared for Devony Winters, even before her blood was living inside him.

Rafe set her bare feet down on the cool tiles of the bathroom. He expected to hastily strip out of his jeans and boots so they could pick up where they left off, but her hands were right there with him, tugging down his zipper as he got rid of the rest of his clothes.

His cock was on the verge of exploding as she freed it from his pants and cupped the stiff shaft in her palms. His own hands shook as he shoved off his jeans and boxer briefs.

Her tongue met his flesh and he hissed. "Ah, Christ."

She guided him to the tub with her, his erection held in her caressing hands. She sat on the wide marble edge in front of him, which put her mouth at the perfect angle to take him deep.

And she did.

Holy hell, she took him so fully into her throat his vision spun behind his closed eyelids.

On a grunt, he grabbed a fistful of her dark hair, winding his hand in the silky ropes. Her fangs abraded his tender skin—not enough to break the surface, but to drive him mad with the erotic scrape of the sharp points and the velvety wetness of her stroking tongue.

At this rate, he wouldn't be able to hold out for long.

And he didn't want to make this night about his pleasure. He wanted it all to belong to her.

As a balm for everything she'd been through with him tonight.

As a pledge for all the better things he wanted to give her.

Mostly, as an apology for the honesty he'd withheld from her from the beginning, his devotion to duty even when his heart belonged to her.

"Come here," he growled, gathering her to him and lifting her off the edge of the large tub.

She gave him a sexy smile. "Turnaround is only fair."

"Not tonight."

He kissed her deeply, slowly, the taste of him on her

lips making his arousal spike like a jolt of electricity. He guided her into the tub and settled her on his lap, facing him.

"You are so lovely, Devony." He leaned in and kissed her, taking his time to explore every nuance of her sweet mouth.

He cupped her face in one hand, while his other stroked her soft skin. Her *glyphs* felt hot and alive under his fingertips, and he indulged in an unhurried exploration of every arch and flourish.

"So soft."

Her breast filled his hand, the nipple puckered and taut between his thumb and finger as he rolled it just enough to wring a heated, broken cry from her lips. Her spine arched, thrusting her forward like an offering. He bent down so he could kiss all the places his hand had been, teasing the rosy peaks of each breast while his fingers slid into the water to stroke between her legs.

Rafe had no restraint. Not with her. She made him crave too much. Things he didn't deserve. Things he didn't dare permit himself to consider.

Like another hot taste of her blood.

The first had been out of necessity. Now he craved more. God help him, he craved everything about her.

But this wasn't about taking right now. He wanted to give.

He wanted to give her everything she could possibly want or need or desire, and not just for tonight.

While that should scare him shitless, it didn't.

No, far from it.

Sliding his palms beneath her backside, he pulled her farther onto his lap. His cock jutted up out of the water and frothy suds. He lifted her, and together they settled her body over his.

"Ohh," she sighed, holding on to his shoulders as he pierced her. "So good."

Rafe had even fewer words than she did. He couldn't hold back his tight groan as she sank down onto his length, inch by glorious inch. Her sheath gripped him, the plush walls rippling with tiny tremors as they adjusted to accommodate his size.

Devony's lids slowly lifted, revealing the bright coals of her eyes. "Does it feel this perfect for you too?"

"Better." A growl curled up the back of his throat at her hungry look. He took a firmer hold of the curves of her ass, guiding her tempo as she began to rock against him.

He felt her pleasure coil and loosen with each long, hard slide of their bodies together.

He couldn't get close enough to her. Not even when he was impaled within her completely, their pelvises grinding against each other.

She moaned as their rhythm intensified. Rafe held her aloft in his palms, his arms doing the bulk of the work for both of them as she rode him. Her climax barreled up on her, spurring his own into a harder gallop. Lava roared into his veins. He couldn't hold it back. Devony's release hit at the same time his did, both of them crashing together, then splintering in a hot rush.

He lifted his head to watch her come and found her staring at him. Her fiery eyes were fixed on his throat, her fangs sharp and gleaming as she shuddered with the force of her orgasm. He could never get tired of seeing her like this, her true nature on full display for him, her passion surrendered to him with complete abandon.

But the fevered look in her pleasure-drenched gaze

was something else. Hunger. Blood thirst.

He felt the razor edge of it. The dangerous intensity of her need.

He felt the astonishing depth of her love . . . for him.

It was a revelation, one that hit him with the force of a freight train. He stared at her, scowling to feel the tenderness of her affection braided inseparably with the intensity of her craving for his bond.

She nodded, a sad smile tugging at her lips. "It's true. I've fallen in love with you, Rafe. There's no sense trying to pretend I don't when I know you can feel it."

He closed his eyes for a moment, shaking his head. "You shouldn't."

His own arousal twisted tighter, her vulnerability toward him stripping away his defenses. Not that he had many where this extraordinary woman was concerned.

Devony Winters owned him. And everything male in him—everything Breed—responded with a savage need to possess her in every way.

He lunged forward and took her in a hard kiss.

"Fuck." He pulled back on a hiss. His fingers came away from his mouth stained with blood. "Ah, Christ . . . Devony."

She'd bit his lip. And now she stared at him, unapologetic.

A warning blazed in her eyes. He knew he should heed it.

He should stop this now.

He should leave the room, before they went too far.

Too fucking late for that. What smoldered between them could not be undone even without a blood bond to lash them together for the rest of their lives.

Rafe knew it.

She understood that too. He couldn't pretend he didn't feel Devony's certitude coursing through his own veins with every hammering beat of his heart.

He knew he should be the stronger one.

For her, if not for himself and his future with the Order.

But tonight, he wanted this to be about her. About giving her comfort and pleasure. He wanted to give her whatever she needed to get through an awful night and the ugliness that had gotten too close to her.

He had come here tonight wanting to give her everything.

What she seemed to want most right now was the one thing he wanted too. Selfishly. Undeniably.

"Come here," he said, his voice gravel in his throat. He took her beautiful face in his hands and kissed her again, unable to resist. Unable to deny her anything.

And when her mouth pulled away from his to drift down toward his neck, all he could manage was a strangled growl as her lips settled over his carotid and the sharp points of her fangs sank into his skin.

His body arced violently, a raw curse tearing from his lips. The heat of her mouth at his vein, her tongue lapping hungrily at him, was the most erotic pleasure he'd ever known. His cock responded instantly, jolting back to life inside her. He moved beneath her, unable to keep his hips from thrusting in time with the greedy suction of her drinking.

She moaned against him, her spine undulating. Her sex gripped him like a fist. She slammed down hard on him, his blood fueling an even wilder sexual thirst in both of them now. One that demanded to be sated.

Devony's arousal hammered through him via their

fledgling blood bond, more vivid than ever.

Her love poured into him too. Bright and fierce and powerful.

Her trust in him burned.

As much as he wanted a life with her, it wasn't his to promise. Not when the Order owned his future and Opus Nostrum still had a stranglehold on his present. If his enemies ever learned how great a weakness Devony could be for him, he had no doubt they would use that knowledge against him. And if anything should happen to her because of him. . . .

Guilt stabbed him at the thought.

Ah, Christ. This was a mistake.

"Enough," he uttered. When she didn't immediately stop, he ground out a tight curse. "Enough."

Her tongue swept over the punctures she'd made, sealing them closed. "Rafe, did I—" She took a hesitant breath, still nuzzled beneath his chin. "I'm sorry . . ."

He snarled at the sound of her uncertain apology. "No," he said, stroking her hair. "Shit. It's not . . . it's nothing you did wrong. Don't think that."

"Then why do I feel like it is?" She pulled back and stared at him, confusion and pain swimming in her molten eyes.

He could hardly hold her wounded gaze. "Fuck."

Some pitiful part of him wanted nothing more than to get out of the tub and make his escape before he hurt her any more. But desire still beat through her veins, hot and uncontained. He couldn't heap more rejection on top of the regret he'd already caused them both.

She didn't resist when he drew her close and covered her mouth with his.

The blood bond had its tethers wrapped around

them both.

Rafe kissed her slowly, deeply. Her need coiled quickly, out of her control. The anguished sound she made nearly killed him. On a harsh curse, he flipped her over and onto her knees in the water and thrust into her from behind.

He couldn't look into her eyes while his remorse had him clenched in cold talons.

But he could give her pleasure.

She rocked against him, overcome by the intensity of their bond. That was the irony of it right now. No matter how unworthy he knew himself to be, their connection couldn't be denied.

When Devony let go a scream and convulsed with the explosion of a ferocious orgasm a few moments later, he collected her against him and followed her right into that fire.

CHAPTER 22

He felt like the worst sort of coward leaving Devony in the guestroom with a head full of doubts and a heart full of hurt.

The excuse that he was expected in a meeting with Sterling Chase was the truth, but it tasted as awful as a lie as he closed the guestroom door behind him and headed through the mansion on his way to the operations area of the command center. She hadn't pressed him to explain his abrupt withdrawal after she had drunk from him.

That's how he knew he had wounded her deeply.

The woman he'd first met only days ago would have confronted him head-on. She wouldn't have hesitated to lock horns and fearlessly demand he explain himself.

Tonight, she had retreated without a word of argument. Because she'd been afraid of what he might say.

She didn't have to tell him that; he felt her dread through their bond.

Dread he had caused by holding duty above his own heart.

Worse, by holding duty above hers.

Rafe stalked down the long hallway of the sprawling mansion's residential wing, his steps slowing on their own as he reached the chamber that had been his until the past few weeks.

He didn't know why he felt compelled to go inside. It wouldn't be his again until his mission was officially over. Maybe not even then, because he intended to end that mission tonight.

He was still committed to taking down Opus Nostrum. That would never change until he succeeded or took his last breath. But if the Order wanted him to fulfill that objective as one of them, he was going to tell Devony everything. With or without their blessing.

And he was going to inform Chase and Lucan of that fact right now.

He preferred not to do it wearing clothes that were stained with blood and death. After his bath with Devony, it had seemed almost sacrilege to put them on again, so he was glad to find his closet still stocked with street attire and combat gear just as he'd left it.

He changed into basic jeans and a black T-shirt, then laced up a pair of black leather boots. As he tied the last knot and stood up to leave, he found Tavia Chase standing in the open doorway.

"You kept my quarters for me."

His commander's mate smiled. "Of course, I did. I expected you'd be back eventually. Now, I'm not so sure."

Tavia had been aware from the beginning that his exile was all part of the operation. But she wasn't talking about him returning from his mission. She meant ever.

And he couldn't seem to tell her any different.

"Devony is a special young woman," she said. "I can see that right away. I can see why you love her."

Rafe scowled, but he couldn't deny it. Tavia was too astute to believe otherwise. He'd grown up in the Order from the time he was an infant. The elder warriors and their mates were his family, his fellow comrades were closer than any brother could be.

As for Tavia, she was a respected tactician and valued member of the Order's team, much like the rest of the warriors' mates. Right now, what Rafe needed was a confidante.

"I drank from her tonight. I was injured, and she helped me." He lowered his head and swore under his breath. Because taking her blood in a moment of weakness would be selfish enough, but then he'd gone and made it worse. "A little while ago, I let her drink from me. We're blood-bonded, Tavia."

"Congratulations."

"No." He shook his head. "No, I did it all wrong. I fucked this up. We're together because of a lie. Because I was on a mission and she was an asset I needed to win over. Then I discovered her secrets and I exploited them. I made her think she could trust me."

"Are you saying she can't?"

"No, that's not it. I'd do anything for her. I'd give my life for hers."

Tavia's gentle gaze held him. "Let's hope it doesn't come down to that."

"After what happened in Montreal, I told myself never again. I was never going to trust myself to believe what I was feeling because it might not be real. I never wanted to be blinded like that again."

"You were tricked, Rafe." Tavia shook her head. "That Opus spy could've chosen anyone. And from what I saw of Devony tonight, I don't think she could possibly be more different."

"I know that. It's not Devony I doubt."

"Then what?"

"It's this." He held his fist to his sternum, where it felt as if a hole were opening up.

It had only worsened after he allowed Devony to drink from his vein while she still had faith in him. Was this helpless feeling love?

"I must be crazy, right? I must be fucking nuts to feel like this about Devony when I've only known her for a handful of days."

Tavia smiled. "You'll have to ask someone other than me. In fact, you'll have to look further than this city. I don't think there's anyone under this roof, or any other Order command center around the world—including your parents—who needed more time than you and Devony have had to know in their hearts they'd met their mate."

As much as he wanted to take some solace in that, what it meant was he had a lot of explaining to do. And a lot of making up.

He only hoped Devony would give him that chance.

First, he needed to inform his commander and Lucan that starting now, they were going to have to trust her as he did.

On his way out the door, Tavia reached out and gave

his beard-grizzled cheek a reassuring caress. "I know Sterling isn't happy with you right now, but I can't thank you enough for looking after my niece. For loving her. The rest will fall into place as it should, you'll see."

He wasn't so sure about that, but he nodded. She accompanied him as he continued to the command center's war room.

He'd been expecting the meeting to be between Chase and him in Boston, with Lucan and Gideon on video from headquarters in D.C. That was the case, but in addition, all but two seats at the large conference table were filled. Tavia walked in and took the one immediately beside the commander.

Elijah and Jax sat with Nathan and Jordana on one side of Chase, the lone vacant chair situated between the commander and Rafe's captain. On the other side of the table from Chase was the team commander from London, Mathias Rowan. He hadn't brought his pregnant mate, Nova, but her brother, Rune, was seated beside his blood-bonded mate, Carys Chase.

And displayed on the large panel screens around the war room were all of the photographs, notes, and data files Rafe had collected while he was at Devony's brownstone a few nights ago.

Considering the originals were now nothing but cinders among the rubble of her home, he probably should be grateful to see the information now. Instead the guilt he'd felt upon leaving Devony in the guestroom a few minutes ago only settled more coldly in his gut.

Every bit of intel she had shared with him in confidence felt like a betrayal to see it here now.

Sick with the feeling, he hardly noticed all of the conversations had halted now that he had arrived.

Expectant, unreadable gazes watched him from all points of the room.

Chase indicated the empty chair. "Come in and have a seat, Rafe."

He walked in, the silence around him feeling as heavy as a shroud.

As he sat down, Nathan gave him a sober, sidelong glance. Right before a rare smirk twisted his stern mouth. "You asshole. Do you have any idea how close I came to killing you the other night?"

Rafe exhaled and looked at his commander for confirmation.

"I've told them," Chase said.

The war room erupted with a few chuckles and a lot of ball-busting. Rafe took it all, glad for every insult and good-natured jab they flung at him. The weight of the past few weeks—the months following his disgrace in Montreal—melted away in the space of a few seconds.

Jax and Eli got up from their seats at the table and walked up to him, both grinning and shaking their heads.

Eli punched him in the shoulder. "It's a damn relief to know you're not the fucked up maniac I thought you were."

"Don't be so sure about that," Rafe quipped, smiling at his teammate.

Jax held his hand out to him. "Welcome back, bro. Even if I still want to kick your ass right now."

Rafe cocked a grin. "I'd like to see you try."

Carys and Rune came over now too. The stern former cage fighter who was her mate gave Rafe's hand a hard pump. "Not a day's gone by that she hasn't worried about you."

He glanced at Carys, who'd been like a sister to him

his entire life. "I'm sorry. I couldn't say anything to anyone."

"I don't care," she said, throwing her arms around him. "You're back where you belong now, and that's all that matters to me."

Mathias Rowan approached as well. The London commander had been a part of the Order's inner circle for two decades, a stoic ally through numerous battles and catastrophes. Now, there was a sober, almost parental look in his gaze. No doubt, the father-to-be was thinking about his own son on the way, one who might eventually wish to follow in his footsteps as a warrior for the Order.

Mathias gripped Rafe's shoulder. "Chase told me what happened in that warehouse earlier tonight. The liquid UV." He shook his head on a low curse. "It's damn good to see you standing here with us tonight, Rafe."

He wouldn't be, if not for Devony.

He didn't have to tell Mathias that. Since Chase had told his good friend about Rafe's injuries, he would have also explained to the London commander that it was Breed blood that had saved him.

Devony's blood.

Her bond.

He wanted to tell everyone in the room what she meant to him, but the din of competing conversations was stilled by the buzzing of Chase's comm unit. He answered the call, frowning as he received the report.

"That was Aric and his team," he announced after setting the phone down on the table. He glanced at Rafe. "The warehouse at Conley Terminal had been cleaned out by the time our team arrived. No dead bodies. No crates of liquid UV. No trace of the spill, either."

"Opus moved quickly. They knew we'd come looking to grab the rest of that cargo."

Chase nodded. "I called the team back in. They'll be here within the hour."

"Any idea who owns the warehouse?" Mathias asked.

"Yeah," Gideon said via the video feed. "About five layers of shell corporations. I've been hacking my way through them for the past hour."

"One of the guys in Cruz's gang told me the shit we were stealing belonged to some kind of arms dealer," Rafe said. "And Cruz mentioned the cargo was arriving from overseas."

"Great. That helps." Gideon's reply was punctuated by the clacking of his keyboard on the other end. "Shouldn't take me long to find the bastard."

"We need that lead," Lucan said, his grim face filling another of the monitors that were linked in to the war room. "With Judah LaSalle dead, that dealer may be our next best lead. Anyone holding on to liquid UV is either in bed with Opus Nostrum or on their bad side. I don't give a shit which camp this son of a bitch is in. I just want him in our hands—yesterday."

"I'll put a team on it as soon as we have your go," Chase said.

Lucan nodded, glancing at Rafe. "Excellent work on all of this. I know it hasn't been easy for you, living like this these past weeks. Or more recently."

"No, sir." Rafe cleared his throat. "Ah . . . about that."

When he came down here with the intent to explain to his commander and the Order's leader what Devony meant to him, he hadn't expected an audience of his whole damn team and then some. But the words needed to be said and he couldn't wait another moment to put them out there.

He'd screwed things up with her, not only tonight, but from the beginning. He only hoped he would have the chance to make them right.

"It's about Devony," he said. "I've made a terrible mistake with her—"

He felt her presence through their blood bond . . . even before he heard her sharp intake of breath just outside the room.

He turned around and there she was.

All the breath left his lungs on a curse.

She stared at him, but only for a second. Her wounded gaze flicked to the other members of the Order gathered around the room alongside him. His friends, obviously.

Teammates he had never truly lost.

Then she glanced over at the screens that contained all the information she had opened up to him in the privacy of her Darkhaven. All of father's meticulous notes and theories. Her months of work in her quest to avenge her slain family.

All of the secrets she had shared with Rafe in the moments before he took her virginity on the floor of her father's study.

Christ.

He felt her stunned confusion like a blow to his chest. Her sharp feeling of betrayal pierced him.

"Devony."

She mutely backed away.

"Devony, wait."

She took a step into the corridor.
Then, in a flash of movement, she was gone.

CHAPTER 23

☾

She was an idiot.

He told her he was dangerous. He told her she was in over her head. That they wouldn't be friends or anything else.

She hadn't believed him.

She still didn't want to believe it, and yet she had just seen the evidence of his duplicity with her own eyes. She felt it. His guilt seeped into her through their blood bond, feeling as thick and black as oil.

He had betrayed her.

Lied to her.

Used her.

A choked sob caught in her throat as she moved through the Order's mansion as a flash of motion. She hurried back into the lovely guestroom Tavia Chase had provided for her, feeling on the verge of a hideous emotional breakdown.

She couldn't let herself fall apart. Not here. Not when Rafe and the rest of his comrades were likely down in the command center's meeting room roaring with laughter over her naïveté. Her blind stupidity.

Her foolishness over allowing herself to fall in love with him. To bind herself to him in blood.

Oh, God.

She needed to get out of there.

She slammed the door behind her and held it shut with her mind as she hastily changed out of Carys's borrowed clothing and back into the grime-caked black turtleneck and jeans she had arrived in. She didn't want anything she had been offered here. Not the comfort or the clothing, not the kindness, either. Not if it had never been real.

She especially didn't want a damn thing from Rafe.

"Devony." He stood on the other side of the closed door.

She heard him try the latch, heard him swear when he couldn't break through the mental hold she had on the lock.

She just wanted to get away from him.

"Leave me alone."

"I can't do that." He tried the lock again. Another vivid curse. "Damn it, Devony. I need to see you. I need to talk to you, and not through this door."

She didn't answer. Mostly because she didn't trust her voice. She could feel the sincerity of his plea. He was hurting too. He felt as terrible as she did. Maybe more, although how that could even be possible she didn't know.

Good. Let him hurt too.

"Go away, Rafe. Go back to your friends. I'm leav—

"

The thick wood panel burst off its hinges, exploding inward. Rafe stood in the ruined doorway, a look of pure anguish on his handsome face.

"Devony, I'm sorry."

"For which part? Pretending we were some kind of team when you were still part of the Order? Stealing weeks of my work and my father's, and then giving it to your comrades behind my back?" She shook her head. "I guess you learned a few tricks from that mole from Opus, didn't you?"

"That's not fair," he said calmly. "Even if I do deserve every bit of your anger."

She refused to be lulled by his sincerity now. Not when he'd left her in this same room only an hour ago with the ache of his guilt carving a hollow in her breast. He'd made a mistake with her. That's what he told everyone in that room just now.

She had made an even bigger one by trusting him.

By falling in love with him.

And now he knew all of that because he could feel her strongest emotions through their bond. The bond he had regretted almost from the instant he let her take the first sip from his vein.

"How far would you have gone to get what you wanted from me, Rafe? God, I didn't even make you work that hard. You didn't have to seduce me for the information. I was all too happy to throw myself at you."

His brow furrowed into a deep scowl. "It was never about that. Nothing we did together had anything to do with my wanting your intel. *We* have nothing to do with my work for the Order. Christ, it couldn't be further from the truth."

"Were you ever cut loose from the Order?"

"No. That was part of my cover." He went on without her asking for further explanation. "I began distancing myself from my teammates not long after I returned from Montreal. Then we manufactured some public displays of my insubordination, enough to get tongues wagging before Chase and Lucan fabricated my release from the Order. Very few people knew the truth. My commanders, my parents. It had to be solid. We needed Cruz and his associates to believe I'd been ousted so they'd give me a chance. So they'd trust me enough to let me in."

"I needed to believe it too. Right?"

He nodded, his expression grave.

"You could've told me, Rafe. I would've kept your secret. You could have trusted me." He had no answer for that, no reply. She knew she was asking him to choose her over his duty to the Order, but dammit, she wanted to think he might have at least considered it. His silence was killing her. "When did you give the Order my files and intel?"

"The night after we made love the first time." He exhaled a short sigh. "I didn't do it to hurt you. If anything, I wanted to help you."

"Help me." She scoffed, her throat raw with emotion. "And if we had actually gotten close to our goal together, if we'd closed in on Opus, would you have helped me destroy whoever killed my family?"

He said nothing for a long moment, then, finally, he shook his head. "No, Devony. I wouldn't have let you anywhere near that kind of danger. I still won't."

"You have nothing to say about that."

"Yes, I do." He took a step toward her, cautiously,

as if she were a wild animal about to bolt. "I have something to say about it because my blood lives in you now, and yours in me."

She groaned, desperate to get away from him now. "Don't talk to me about our bond. I felt your regret, Rafe. I felt how badly you wished we could take it back."

"Yes, I did," he said, a sharpness edging his deep voice. "I wanted to take it back because I knew I hadn't been honest with you."

"Well, now we have honesty," she shot back, on the verge of tears she refused to shed in front of him. "And now we're stuck with a blood bond neither one of wants anymore."

The sting of that statement crossed his features like a lash. "Goddamn it, Devony."

He reached for her and she dodged his touch. As soon as she cleared him, she flashed out of the guestroom and through the residential wing of the mansion.

But Rafe was Breed, too. He was faster, already standing in front of her when she slowed in the foyer and reached for the polished brass handle of the door. He blocked her way out, his eyes smoldering with amber sparks.

His sharp fangs glinted as he spoke. "What are you doing?"

"What does it look like? I'm leaving."

"Where?"

She didn't know. She would figure it out later. All she knew was she had to get away from him, away from this place. She couldn't think when her heart was cracking open in her breast.

"Get out of my way, Rafe."

He didn't so much as flinch. "Talk to me, please."

"We have nothing left to say."

"Not true," he said, giving a tight shake of his head. "I've got plenty to say. And I'll start by saying that I love you."

God, why was he determined to see her fall apart? Hadn't he already wounded her enough?

She felt his sincerity. She even felt his love, too. But it didn't ease the pain of his betrayal.

A sob hitched in her throat. "Please move, Rafe."

"I can't do that."

He wasn't going to let her go. He reached out for her, and instead of flying into his arms the way she wanted to do so desperately, she put her hands out in front of her. She pressed her palms to the solid warmth of his chest and held them there.

She saw the moment he realized what she was doing. His gaze went wide, but it was too late. She had already established the connection.

A cry wrenched from her throat as she put everything she had into her touch. In a burst of fury, she siphoned away his power . . . and all his strength.

With a stunned groan, he sagged to his knees on the thick rug.

She let go then, her hands shaking and her heart shattering.

He gasped her name as unconsciousness took him under.

Devony fumbled for the door's latch, barely holding herself together as she fled into the gathering light of daybreak.

CHAPTER 24

Ⓒ

When Rafe opened his eyes, it felt like someone stabbed heated daggers into them.

He shut his lids fast and let out a groan. Damn. Had someone strapped a vise around his rib cage while he was out cold? His throat tasted like ashes too.

He hurt everywhere. His limbs, his torso.

Fuck, even his hair hurt.

But he was alive.

He knew he was, because for all his bodily pain, it was his heart that ached the worst. And holy hell, that was saying something.

He lifted his eyelids again, battling through the agony of the light hitting his retinas. A large, blurry shadow in front of him slowly took shape.

"Have a good nap?" Nathan loomed over him, peering down at him from the side of an infirmary bed where Rafe lay. "How are you enjoying that full-body migraine? The real fun doesn't start until you try to sit up."

"Shit." Rafe attempted to raise his head and wave of nausea slammed into him.

Nathan's mouth twisted. "Yeah, there it is."

Rafe groaned as he dropped back onto the pillow. "Devony . . ."

"She's gone." As amused as his team captain seemed to be about Rafe's physical discomfort, his tone now was almost gentle. "She left the mansion right after she drained your power and dropped you in the foyer."

"How long?" The question scraped out of him, not only because his lungs felt constricted by the aftereffects of Devony's powerful punch. "How long since she left?"

"Couple of hours."

Ah, Christ. Two hours in the city by herself while Opus's kill squad could be out looking for her? The very idea sent a flood of cold fear slicing through his veins. He knew Devony was strong and smart. Tough as hell. She was a Breed female, for fuck's sake. He knew she was capable of fending for herself. After all, she'd plowed through him easily enough and he was a combat-tested warrior and twice her size.

She didn't need him to look after her, but he hated the idea that she was alone. She was also hurting and upset—all because of him.

If his careless actions had driven her into harm's way, he'd never be able to live with that.

Rafe heaved himself up from the thin mattress, pushing past the pain. "Need to go after her. I have to . . . find her."

"You're not in any shape to do that yet," Nathan said.

And damn it, he was right. The bed spun beneath him from just that small movement. The room wobbled in front of his face like a funhouse mirror.

"That female of yours packs a hell of a punch. Unfortunately, I speak from experience."

Rafe leaned into the agony, pushing himself up to a sitting position. His limbs felt like jelly, far from functional. "How long does it last?"

Nathan grunted. "It took about three hours before I could feel my feet under me again. Jordana recovered more quickly, so apparently the bigger the target, the harder we fall. She's not pissed at you, but part of me still wants to kill you for having a role in putting my mate through that."

"I'm sorry," Rafe said. "And I know Devony's sorry too. She didn't want to hurt either of you."

"She did it to protect you."

Rafe nodded, a movement that made his skull throb.

He would have done the same thing for her if he was able. He'd still do anything to protect her. And yet, he'd deceived her and broken her heart instead.

He had hurt her worse than anyone else possibly could. He'd felt that in the moments before she'd leveled him with her incredible power.

"She loves you," Nathan said. "I saw it in her face that night at the museum."

"Now she hates me."

"You really believe that?"

He shrugged. Carefully shook his pounding head. Even though she was gone, he could feel her through their bond.

She didn't hate him. He could still feel her love, and that gave him some small glimmer of hope that he could fix this.

But right now, her hurt was stronger than anything else she was feeling.

If she couldn't forgive him, he might lose her forever.

"I have to go." He swung his deadweight legs over the side of the infirmary cot. "I have to find her and bring her back."

A deep, sardonic voice answered from the open doorway. "Then you're going to need wings."

Rafe glanced around Nathan and watched Aric Chase stroll into the open room. He paused next to the bed and exhaled a snort. "You look like shit."

Rafe chuckled, and fuck, that hurt. Only his best friend could pull a smile out of him when his body was a feeble lump and his heart was shredded in his chest. "Good to see you too. What do you know about Devony? Where is she?"

"On her way to London, evidently. Gideon just sent word that she popped up on a commercial flight to Heathrow this morning. She should be on the ground there in about five hours."

London. She was going home, even though she hadn't wanted to go back there ever again after losing her family.

"I need to be there too. I need to make her listen to me." Rafe tried to get up, but dropped right back down onto the bed. "Damn it."

Aric gave him an assessing look. "This female really did a number on you, eh?"

He wasn't talking about the fact that she had knocked him on his ass today. And Rafe wasn't going to pretend with either one of his closest friends that he wasn't out of his head with misery over the fact that he had lost Devony's faith today.

That he might have lost it for good.

"We're bonded. I took her blood. Fuck, I took a hell of a lot more than that from her." He met the sober stares of both Breed males. "Then, last night after we arrived here, I let her drink from me too. I love her, and now she thinks I played her as an asset for my mission. She thinks I used her for intel. Shit. She thinks I chose the Order over her."

"Didn't you?" Nathan's logic, as usual, cut as cleanly and as coldly as a knife.

Rafe wanted to rage at his friend, but even his anger failed him.

Because what the former assassin said was true. He had chosen the Order over her.

Rafe regretted that now. He had regretted it from the beginning. And he was going to regret it for the rest of his eternal life.

Because Nathan was right. Devony was right.

He *had* chosen duty over her.

And there was no way for him to take that back now.

CHAPTER 25

Devony paid the taxi driver in cash as she got out at the curb in front of her family's Darkhaven in South Kensington.

After leaving the Order's mansion in Boston, she'd gone straight to the airport and to a small locker there, where she had stored her passport and a few thousand dollars in multiple currencies. She hadn't grown up in a family of spies and law enforcement officers without picking up a few professional tips along the way.

Using her real ID and traveling in public while Opus's goons might be on her trail had been a risk, but she'd had little choice. Now that she was away from Boston, she allowed herself to exhale some of the paranoia that had clung to her until now.

The lovely Onslow Square stucco and brick townhouses with their black wrought-iron fences and classic, white-columned entrances had always been a welcome, comforting sight to her. Across the street, as the sun's last rays set over the tranquil garden square, birds sang in the tree-filled park she used to play in as a child.

Now, the peace was merely a facade.

The familiarity provided no solace, because even though she'd fled to the only place she had left to go, she was coming here broken, with her heart in tatters. And with her family dead, this picture-perfect block in London would never be home for her again.

The Darkhaven had been vacant for months, everything just as her parents had left it. Their lives interrupted, all of the rooms and furnishings frozen in time.

Now that Devony was there, she wished she hadn't come. She had regretted leaving Boston as soon as she stepped foot on the plane.

And she had been sick with herself for what she'd done to Rafe in her desperation to preserve her pride—what little she had left where he was concerned.

It was fear that made her run when she wanted to stay.

That kind of cowardice had never been her style.

Now, Rafe was thousands of miles away, in physical agony these past few hours. She knew because she felt his pain too. Her bond to him gave her his anguish the same way it connected her to his pleasure.

She had hardly been able to endure it for the majority of her flight to London.

Feeling the depth of his love for her had only made the thought of his pain more unbearable.

She had hurt him, not just physically.

God, how they had hurt each other.

She'd thought Opus Nostrum had killed everything that mattered to her, but she had been wrong. Because Rafe Malebranche had killed her heart.

It didn't matter that she'd only known him for a handful of days. He'd stormed in and now her life would never be the same.

She loved him, even though he'd hurt her. She couldn't stop just because her heart was broken. Now, she would love him with all its shattered pieces.

Devony walked through every room in the Darkhaven, feeling like a ghost. Her bedroom was a relic of her childhood. Still the girly pink accents and sweet, fussy furnishings her mother had surrounded her in with the hopes that her headstrong daughter would gravitate toward a softer life than her own.

She glanced down at her dirty, battle-worn black clothing and biker boots. How disappointed her mother must have been with her.

Devony was never going to choose the safest, softest path. She'd tried, for them. The music studies, the university classes. Although she enjoyed those pursuits, they didn't fulfill her. She longed to make a difference in the world. She felt the need for a higher calling.

She hadn't dared to reach for it until after losing everyone she loved. She hadn't imagined there was a way for her to truly make a difference until she began working together with Rafe on their shared quest to destroy Opus Nostrum.

All a lie.

They had shared that common goal, but he'd never been working with her. He had been playing her for a fool, using her information to help his true teammates in the Order.

She was on her own in her quest now, and none of her determination to avenge her family had faded since she left Boston. Let the Order have all of her father's notes and research, along with her reconnaissance of the past few months. She could start over. Now that she had an Opus target on her back, she *would* have to begin all over.

New name. New appearance. New targets and plan of attack.

New life.

One that probably wouldn't include Rafe. That last part was the one she could hardly bear to imagine.

After a quick shower and change of clothes, Devony headed back downstairs to settle in and regroup. The spacious townhouse was cold and dark, dust collected on the furnishings and on the grand piano that sat in the spacious living room. In back of the house, her mother's small garden patio was overgrown and strewn with dried autumn leaves.

It broke something in her to see the place so forlorn and forgotten. And her piano. While music had been more her parents' dream for her than her own, she had always found a measure of solace in the feel of the cool keys beneath her fingertips. It drew her now, too.

She drifted into the living room and sat down on the cushioned bench. Her hands left prints in the fine layer of dust on the glossy black lid of the keyboard as she lifted it.

She played a few notes, her fingers moving from memory through one of the classical compositions her parents used to love hearing her play.

She frowned when one of the keys produced an odd, muffled chord. She hit the note again and heard something dislodge inside the instrument.

"What the hell?"

There had to be something blocking the strings under the old grand's cover. She stood up and carefully lifted the heavy black lid.

An envelope was tucked inside. She knew the vellum paper. It was from her father's personal supply.

Devony retrieved the envelope, then closed the piano cover and sat back down on the bench.

Her fingers trembled as she carefully tore open the seal. A single printed photograph was all the envelope contained.

Devony stared at the picture, her breath leaking out of her on a gasp. "Oh, my God."

CHAPTER 26

R afe knocked on the doorjamb of his commander's office.

Chase looked up from the scattered papers and photographs on his desk, an expression of mild surprise on his face. "You look a hell of a lot better than you did when I saw you a few hours ago."

"Yes, sir." Rafe stood at attention, dressed in his black patrol uniform, his face shaved clean and hair trimmed into some semblance of control.

He was steady on his feet now, all traces of the agony from Devony's parting shot subsided. All except the pain that had taken up residence in his heart. He didn't expect that would be dissipating anytime soon. As in, never.

Not as long as he and Devony were apart.

"Come in," Chase said. He had patrol team plans for tonight and other mission materials on his desk, along with some of the files and photos Rafe had taken from Devony's brownstone.

"I just got off a call with Lucan," Chase said. "The intel you and Devony supplied has given us multiple avenues to investigate, both from here in Boston and D.C. Gideon thinks it'll take days to unpack it all, but we've got a good start on several new leads as we speak."

Rafe inclined his head. "I'm glad it's proving useful. I can't take any of the credit for it, though. That belongs solely to Devony. And to her father as well."

Chase nodded. "We owe them both a debt, especially if any of these new leads prove out. Gideon says Roland Winters's handwritten notes seem to indicate he suspected his files may not be safe at JUSTIS."

"That's what Devony thought too. Her father kept his research at the Boston Darkhaven, not at home in London. I think he knew if anything happened to him, his work would be safest with her. I think he wanted her to be the one to find it, because he knew she would do something about it."

Rafe had the past several hours to consider everything that had happened during his time with Devony. She had told him that her family pushed her away from law enforcement, tried to shelter her, but it seemed to him that her father understood what she was capable of. He knew the kind of strong, competent, determined woman she was.

Roland Winters had to know that if he left a torch burning behind him, no matter how dim, Devony would be the best person—perhaps the only one—he trusted to pick it up and run with it to the end.

Chase's brows rose. "She's a special woman. Takes courage to go after men like Ricardo Cruz and Judah

LaSalle the way she did. And to think she meant to follow their trail all the way to Opus's inner circle if it took her there? She had no idea what she was up against."

"She didn't care what she was up against," Rafe said, unable to keep the pride out of his voice when he spoke about the woman he loved. "Devony wanted justice for what was done to her family. I don't expect she's changed her mind about that now. What happened here—the way I hurt her—isn't going to slow her down for a minute."

"She's tenacious," Chase remarked.

Rafe smiled and shook his head. "She is . . . extraordinary. She's the most incredible woman I know. And I let her go."

Chase grunted, a wry twist to his mouth. "Didn't look like she gave you much choice, the way she cut your legs out from under you."

"I deserved it. I hurt her, and I deserved every bit of the pain she left me with. Devony said I should've told her about my mission, that I was working covert for the Order. She said I could've trusted her to keep it a secret. But to do that, I would've had to break my trust with you. With Lucan and my teammates. I would've had to choose."

Sterling Chase leaned back in his chair, a solemnity in his face and in his tone. "That's a lot for anyone to ask of one of us."

"Yes, sir." Rafe exhaled a heavy sigh. "But it shouldn't have been for me."

He reached for the buckle on his weapons belt and unfastened it. Then he carefully laid it atop the patrol plans on his commander's desk.

"The Order has been my life from the time I was born. It's my family, as important to me as my mother and father. My teammates, my commanders, everyone in the Order. I would lay down my life for any one of you, any day of the week. But I'm in love with Devony Winters. She's my mate by blood." He swore softly and shook his head. "She's everything that matters to me."

It was the truth.

He'd come back from Montreal with vengeance burning a hole in his belly. He'd thought going after Opus Nostrum—destroying them single-handedly—was the one thing he wanted more than anything else. He thought retribution was all he was living for.

Now, he wanted something else even more.

Devony's forgiveness.

He wanted her future, with him at her side.

And he wasn't going to let another second pass without going after her.

"You know, you can't take back what you've done, son." Chase gave him a sympathetic look. "Someday, I'll tell you all the ways I fucked up with Tavia. I know my friend Dante's got plenty of similar stories where your mother, Tess, is concerned."

"But Tavia forgave you. My mother forgave my father," Rafe said, finding some hope in those truths. "That's all I want from Devony, too. I'll spend the rest of my life trying to make things right between us. But first I need to find out if she'll have me."

And to do that, he needed to get his ass on a flight to London as soon as possible.

The commander sat forward, his fingers steepled in front of him. "I had a feeling you were going to say that. And that's why I put Mathias Rowan's return trip to

London on standby this afternoon. He's waiting for you in the war room."

Rafe didn't even try to curb the grin that broke over his face. He reached for the elder warrior's hand and gave it a firm shake. "Thank you, sir."

Chase gave him a tight nod. Then he slid the weapons belt back toward Rafe. "You keep this. I'm not about to let one of my best warriors go that easily."

Rafe put the belt back around his hips and fastened it, giving his commander a nod of gratitude.

Then he left the room in a flash of motion to go catch his waiting ride to London.

CHAPTER 27

Propping her elbows on the desk in her father's office, Devony held the sides of her head in her splayed fingers and blew out a tired sigh.

Her temples throbbed. Her eyeballs felt seared to a crisp after several hours of obsessive—albeit fruitless—searching for answers about the photograph she'd found.

Or, rather, the photograph her father had left for her to find.

Because there could be no doubt about that. There was no other reason for him to secret something like that inside an instrument no one else would give a second look.

She picked up the printed picture and stared at it for what had to be the hundredth time since she took it out of the envelope. No matter how many times she stared at it, the image continued to confuse her.

It was a printed copy of a candid photograph, snapped at some type of social gathering. Within the crowd of people stood three men: her brother, Harrison; business tycoon Reginald Crowe; and another man snapped just as he'd begun to turn his face away from the camera.

Devony recognized Crowe. Anyone would. One of the wealthiest men in the world, he had also been one of the most dangerous, as it turned out. Earlier this year, he had led Opus Nostrum's effort to plant an ultraviolet bomb at a Global Nations Council peace summit. He would have gotten away with it, had it not been for the Order.

And now she recalled that among her father's research at the Back Bay brownstone were port logs dating back as far as two years ago concerning shipment activities for Crowe Industries. Her father had been scrutinizing Crowe more than a year before the incident at the peace summit.

Why was Harrison standing there chatting with Reginald Crowe like old chums in the photo? Had it been part of his covert work with JUSTIS?

Devony didn't recognize the third man. Evidently, her father hadn't, either. He'd drawn a circle around the man's semi-obscured profile and had jotted a question mark on the image.

She had spent the past six hours scouring the internet for information or other images, and running facial recognition apps to see if she could find anything out about the unknown man. She had even logged in to JUSTIS's secured site using her father's credentials she'd memorized—the ID and password she thought he'd carelessly left in his safe behind her mother's portrait in

Boston.

Now, she wondered if he'd wanted her to have that information too. Maybe he'd left all of his notes and research for her to pick up in his absence. For all the good it did.

She had lost everything to Opus's firebombing and to the Order. And tonight she had found exactly nothing on the mysterious third man.

If her father thought she could resolve the question for him after his death, he had given her too much credit. All the photograph had done was raise a lot of troubling questions in her mind.

As did the date he'd scrawled onto the envelope. The day before the bombing at JUSTIS's London headquarters.

Had he known about the danger? Had he some inkling of what was about to happen?

She dismissed both notions immediately. Her father never would have let his beloved wife and son get anywhere near that building if he feared it might be compromised. He would have sounded a swift and very vocal alarm within the organization the instant he suspected there might be trouble brewing.

So, no. He couldn't have known any of that.

But he had been concerned enough about his son and the two men in the photo to place it somewhere she would eventually discover it, should anything happen to him.

God, she hated to think that he might have feared for his own safety.

Or that he feared for her brother's and had been unable to protect him in the end.

Could the third man have had something to do with

the attack on JUSTIS? Had Harrison been the true target of a bombing that had killed so many?

Her mind swam with a thousand possible scenarios and tangled theories, each one seeming to give birth to many more.

Obviously, she had spent too much time sitting behind her father's workstation tonight. Her obsessive need for information and answers was beginning to wear on her body and her mind.

She got up from the desk and stretched, realizing she hadn't eaten or had anything to drink since she arrived. Being a daywalker, she didn't need nourishment the way humans did. She didn't need to consume blood every few days the way Rafe and other members of the Breed did, either.

She'd drunk from human blood Hosts before, but how she would ever do that again after she'd tasted Rafe's blood, she had no idea. She didn't want to think about that eventuality.

She didn't want to think about Rafe at all, but he'd been living in her thoughts all night, just as he lived in her blood through their bond.

Forever.

She didn't even have to concentrate to feel his presence inside her now. He felt almost close enough to touch, which was a particularly harsh cruelty when she knew she had closed the door on her relationship with him—literally and figuratively.

But, wishful thinking or not, the comforting buzz in her veins accompanied her as she headed into the kitchen to make some tea.

Her anger with Rafe had ebbed hours ago. Her hurt was still raw, her heart still frayed and aching, but she couldn't hate him. She hadn't ever hated him, not even a little.

She loved him.

And more than anything, she wanted to see him again.

As she put the kettle on and rummaged for the tea and a mug, she realized that it wasn't only her anger that had faded.

During the months following her family's deaths, she had been driven by grief and fury. Revenge was what she lived for, not doing what was right or just. Those noble principles that she'd admired growing up, even aspired to, had morphed into something ugly and reckless after the JUSTIS bombing.

She had lost her grounding once she set out to avenge her loved ones. It had been buried by her pain over her family's murders, turned into a poisonous hatred that had hardened her to the world around her. It had hardened her heart.

She still wanted Opus Nostrum to pay for her family's slaying and everyone else in the London office that awful night, but her personal vendetta had galvanized into something stronger, steelier.

A sense of purpose, not vigilantism.

Coming to know Rafe had done that for her. Partnering with him in a shared cause, opening herself up to him as a friend and confidante, as a lover.

He had made her realize she didn't want to be alone on her quest. She wanted to be part of something more.

With him.

The kettle whined on the stove. Devony poured hot water over the diffuser and breathed in the soothing, orange-and-spice fragrance of the loose tea leaves.

She felt an odd prickle at the back of her neck as she took the first careful sip.

Her head came up, and she listened for a moment to the utter silence of the empty Darkhaven.

She didn't hear anything, but she was certain she wasn't alone inside the house now.

A jolt of hopefulness arrowed through her. "Rafe?"

No one answered. Holding her steaming mug, she padded out of the kitchen to the short hallway that led out to the foyer.

If Rafe were close, shouldn't she feel his presence through their bond? She felt certain she would, but her hope was irrational as she stepped into the open area at the front entrance of the Darkhaven.

It wasn't Rafe.

The instant her gaze lit on who stood there, her tea slipped out of her grasp. She didn't even feel the hot liquid splashing against her bare feet and ankles as the mug crashed to the tiles in front of her. Her heart was too full, her mind too stunned, to feel anything except disbelief and a surge of overwhelming joy.

"Harrison?"

Her brother looked thinner than she recalled him, his handsome face a little gaunt against the bright copper-penny color of his brush-cut hair. Devony stepped around the spill on the floor, elation almost sending her racing forward to embrace him.

Almost.

Something halted her. She wasn't sure why she hesitated, but uncertainty stilled her footsteps. Her instincts seemed to freeze her limbs despite the desperate hope bubbling inside her.

"Harry." She wrapped her arms around herself

instead of him. "My God. Is it really you?"

His mouth curved. "It's me, Dovey."

His nickname for her from the time they were children. It should have comforted her, but somehow, paired with the odd look on his face, the endearment rang hollow now, his voice airless and strange.

"But . . . how are you here?" She shook her head, torn between confusion and astonishment. "Where have you been all this time? Why didn't you try to contact me? Does this also mean that Mum and Dad are—"

He shook his head. "They're gone."

"Gone." The word felt so cold, so inconsequential falling off his tongue. She knew it was simply a fact, however painful.

Yet she felt their deaths settle on her all over again now that she was looking at her brother, alive and well. Somehow, miraculously, unharmed.

"They're more than gone, Harrison. They're dead. You all were, at least that's what I've believed all this time. You, our parents, and a hundred other people who were also in that building when the bomb took it down. Yet here you are."

He tilted his head as she spoke. "I thought you'd be happy to see me."

"I am. You have no idea how many times I've wished to see you—all of you—again. But I'm . . . confused." God, she only wished she were confused. Because the most logical explanation for him to be standing in front of her right now was one that sent a chill into her veins. "How is it possible? There were no survivors. Opus left nothing but rubble behind that night. So, please explain to me how you were the only person to escape that blast?"

"We're at war, Dovey." He took a step toward her. "People get hurt in war. People die."

A feeling of nausea swept over her at his bland tone. "I'm not talking about war. I'm talking about cold-blooded murder. Opus Nostrum killed our parents. They killed your colleagues at JUSTIS. As of now, they also want to kill me." She exhaled a shaky breath as she stared into the face of this emotionless semblance of her brother. This stranger. "I don't suppose I need to tell you that, though. Do I?"

When he didn't deny it, something shattered inside her. The part of her that had loved her brother, admired him as a hero for his commitment to upholding the law. The part of her that had mourned him these past five months alongside her parents.

"How long, Harry? When did Opus get their hooks into you?"

He shrugged, approaching a couple more steps. "Does it matter?"

"It does to me. Were you already on their side when Reginald Crowe tried to detonate his bomb at the summit earlier this year?" He didn't answer, which was answer enough. Devony scoffed. "What happened? How did they brainwash you?"

"Brainwash?" He chuckled. "I'm seeing clearly for the first time because of Opus. They want peace—true and lasting peace. But they know it won't come to fruition without war. A big war, one that can reset the balance of power and put better minds in charge. Stronger minds."

"You mean, like Reginald Crowe? Things didn't work out so well for him, as I recall."

Anger flared in her brother's dark eyes. "Reginald

Crowe was a brilliant man. All the members of Opus's inner circle are the best minds this world has ever seen. I didn't realize that until Crowe took me into his confidence. I was working a covert op, assigned to help break up a corrupt network of government officials on the take. Instead, I met Crowe and a few of his associates. They showed me what could be, what we could create together."

Devony scoffed quietly. "And then the covert agent became the convert."

He smiled, and this time it was genuine. "The summit was only the beginning. The Order got in the way of that. They killed Reginald Crowe, but we've gotten stronger since then. The Order won't be in our way for long."

"What are you talking about?"

"Opus can't be stopped. We *will not* be stopped."

"You're crazy, Harrison. You're out of your mind."

"And you're always so fucking self-righteous," he hissed, the tips of his fangs glinting in the low light of the foyer. "You and our parents. Especially them, always preaching about higher purpose and duty. Trying to tell me about honor when my Opus brethren and I are doing the noblest work right under everyone's noses."

"Is that why you killed them that night at headquarters?" Her voice was wooden, her heart heavy with the understanding of what her brother must have done. "The reports after the bombing all speculated that it was an inside job. No one could've placed the explosives and executed their precision detonation without intimate knowledge of the building . . . and of who was likely to be there that night. It was you."

He released a beleaguered sigh. "Why couldn't you

just stick to your music, Dovey? What the hell were you thinking, going after LaSalle? Or fucking that warrior from the Order?" He practically spat the words, his face contorting with barely restrained rage. "You're an embarrassment to both of us. I'm so disappointed at what you've become."

She arched a brow, fury igniting in her blood. "Right back at you, brother."

"Opus wants you dead now," he announced blandly. "I don't want that. I knew you'd come running back home after they blew up the Boston Darkhaven. They've given me a chance to show you the way, Devony. I hope you'll be smart enough to take it."

"Smart enough to become one of Opus's pawns, like you? That's not smart, Harry. It's weak. And that's never going to be me."

He laughed as if she were the crazy one. "Do you understand what I'm offering you?" He held up his hands the way he would show off precious treasures. "With our power, you and I working together, we could be unstoppable. We could run Opus together one day."

Devony inched back on her bare feet as he began to approach once more. "You're out of your mind, Harrison." He was clearly, dangerously, insane. No longer the brother she grew up with, but a tool of Opus Nostrum. And their parents' killer. "Our father was getting close to the truth, wasn't he? I think sooner or later, he was going to figure out you were the enemy."

Harrison smiled, lifted his bulky shoulder. "Probably. I wasn't going to let that happen, you understand."

"Of course not," she said. "I think he knew that too. I think that's why he left behind months of research for me to find. I think that's also why he hid a photograph of you and Crowe and another man in the hopes that I would come across it after Dad was gone."

"What photograph? What other man?"

"That's what I want to know. I'm going to find out, Harry. I'm not going to rest until Opus is destroyed."

Rage burned in her brother's eyes. His lip curled back from his teeth and fangs. "You need to give me that photo, Devony. And all of our father's research. You need to give all of it to me. Right. Fucking. Now."

She shook her head, taking another cautious step away from him. "I don't have Dad's files anymore. Your brilliant friends at Opus blew it all up when they torched my house."

He smirked. "Your loss is my gain, then."

"Not quite. The Order has copies of everything."

A roar erupted from him. "You idiot!"

He lunged. In that same instant, she used her mind to hurl the sharpest chunk of her broken mug at her brother's head. She put all her strength behind it. The jagged shard connected with the bone over his right eye and tore the skin open. He staggered back, blood dripping down his face.

His growl was unearthly. "You bitch. Now you're going to suffer."

He grabbed hold of her before she could escape his reach. His hands bit into her arms like talons, his eyes throwing off rage like a furnace.

She felt his power lock on to hers, seeking the connection so he could siphon her. But the hold wouldn't take. "What the—? You drank from someone. You slut! You're fucking bonded to that Order scum?"

Devony wrenched loose and shoved her brother

backward with the full force of her strength. He crashed into one of her mother's antique tables. It exploded beneath him, splintering into pieces as he fell to the floor.

She had to get out of there. She had to escape so she could let Rafe and the Order know that Harrison was corrupt. More than that, she needed to make sure they had the photograph her father had left for her.

She flashed into the office and grabbed it, stuffing it into the back pocket of her jeans. Harrison was struggling to his feet as she zipped past him in the foyer.

But now it wasn't only him she had to contend with.

Two other Breed males stepped inside the front door. Cold eyes held her as they blocked her exit from the house. Unlike her brother, this pair was armed with guns and knives.

Harrison swiped angrily at the blood running into his eye and down the side of his face. "I told you they gave me one chance to show you the way." He spat a mouthful of blood onto the heirloom rug. "You're beyond my help now, Devony. Or my mercy."

"So, you're just going to let your death squad friends kill me?"

"Yes, Devony." He walked up to her, stared her squarely in the eyes. "I don't see anyone who's going to stop them. Do you?"

"I will," Rafe answered.

CHAPTER 28

Mathias Rowan had a car waiting for Rafe when the Order's private jet touched down at Heathrow. If Rafe had known Devony's terror was going to flood into his veins like a cold river halfway from the airport to Kensington, he would have enlisted Rowan and the whole damn warrior team in London to accompany him.

He wished like hell he had some backup now, as he'd entered the Darkhaven through the back door and found her trapped inside with a trio of menacing Breed thugs. The well-armed pair in suits just inside the front door posed the most immediate threat to her. Both grabbed for their guns the instant Rafe appeared in the kitchen archway.

Rafe didn't hesitate for a moment. He let one of his blades fly. It nailed the bigger of the two in the throat. His larynx impaled, the vampire sagged to his knees on a choked howl, clutching at the blade protruding out of the front of his neck.

The thug's suited partner opened fire at the same time, hitting Rafe in the stomach.

Devony screamed. "No!"

Fuck. Her cry hurt him worse than the gunshot wound.

Rafe could handle the injury and the pain. He'd taken a lot worse before and it hadn't slowed him down. But thanks to their blood bond, every hit he took would be echoed inside her. He was going to kill these three assholes tonight for that offense alone.

Devony launched herself at the shooter, eyes ablaze and fangs erupting behind her parted lips. The huge guy tried to shake her off his back, but he didn't go down. And, just like his Opus death squad partner, he had come here to kill.

"Devony!"

Rafe hardly got the chance to form the thought, let alone leap to her defense, before the third Breed male came at him with murder burning in his whisky-colored eyes.

Eyes that bore a striking resemblance to Devony's.

Holy hell. It couldn't be.

And yet it was.

He didn't know how it could be possible that her brother was alive and well after all these months, but since he'd stated his intent to harm Devony—Christ, to kill her in cold blood—his miraculous resurrection was going to end here and now.

On a crazed bellow, Harrison Winters plowed into Rafe's injured midsection, taking both of them down to the floor. Devony's not-so-dead brother pinned Rafe beneath him. Spittle gathered at the corners of his snarling mouth as he brought his hand up to Rafe's chest.

No fucking way.

Rafe dodged the other male's siphoning touch and threw him off. Winters came at him again, his bare hands curled like claws. He took a swipe at Rafe, trying to latch on to him.

Rafe was faster. And he had another dagger sheathed on his weapons belt. He pulled it free and flipped it around in his grasp, then brought the razor edge down between his attacker's third and middle fingers.

Winters roared. His left hand gushed blood, nearly split in half. "Now, you die, warrior."

Using his right, he slammed his fist into the side of Rafe's skull.

His vision spun as he staggered down onto one knee. Across the foyer, Devony had the death squad thug by the throat, draining away his power. But while that killer began to slump in her grasp, his partner had found his legs.

"Devony, behind you!"

The thug lunged for her, knocking her into the wall. Plaster and millwork cracked with the terrible impact of her full-body crash against it.

Rafe felt it too, her pain. Her terror. Her fading hope that they would get out of this alive.

In that same moment, he called upon every ounce of speed at his command and pulled one of his guns free from its holster. He squeezed off a shot, hitting the big bastard between the eyes. He put a bullet in the second one's skull just to keep the son of a bitch down for good.

But that still left the problem of Devony's brother.

Winters clamped his huge hand on Rafe's shoulder

and squeezed. Rafe couldn't dodge the connection fast enough this time. He felt the other male's power begin to siphon away his own.

No.

Ah, fuck. He had to hold on.

Winters grinned, his eyes crazed and bright as lava. He reached for Rafe's weapon, using his mangled, bleeding hand to pull the weapon out of Rafe's slackening grasp.

Damn it. No.

Winters lifted the gun, his movements awkward after Rafe had nearly cleaved his hand in two.

Rafe watched the gun rise toward his face. He couldn't fight back now. He could hardly maintain consciousness as the barrel of his own patrol weapon was aimed point-blank at the side of his skull.

He heard the gunshot.

It exploded like cannon fire in front of him.

But as his vision wobbled in and out of focus, he realized it wasn't his head that had been cracked open by the discharged round.

Harrison Winters dropped to the floor, lifeless.

And standing behind him with one of the death squad thug's guns in her hand was Devony.

"Rafe," she gasped, setting the weapon down as she scrambled next to him on the floor. Her hands were cool and trembling as she ran them over him, emotion welling in her eyes. "You came after me. You saved me."

He gave a halting shake of his head. It took all his strength to lift his hand and rest it gently against her bruised cheek. "No, Devony. You're the one who's saved me."

CHAPTER 29

Somewhere over the Atlantic, Rafe woke up with Devony in his arms. They were aboard the Order's private jet, lying naked together in the bedroom cabin of the spacious aircraft.

Mathias Rowan and his team had reported to the Darkhaven to retrieve them and contain the situation following Rafe's call. The Order would take care of the bodies and the cleanup of the property. They would also clamp a lid on the stunning revelations about Devony's brother and his involvement with Opus Nostrum.

Rafe still couldn't believe how heinously Harrison Winters had betrayed his duty, his JUSTIS colleagues, and his family. That he had been willing to add Devony's life to that brutal tally made Rafe wish he had been the one to kill the bastard. Slowly. Excruciatingly.

The fact that he had arrived with only moments to spare before anything worse had happened to Devony made his heart clench.

He'd gone after her to try to save what they had together, but in the end it was she who saved him.

Not only with the power of her blood after her brother's attack had almost leveled him.

Her love was a gift he would cherish and protect for as long as he drew breath.

Now that Devony was safe in his arms again, he would spend the rest of his days, and all of his nights, striving to deserve her.

Nestled in his embrace, she stirred. Her quiet hum as she woke vibrated against his chest. "Are we almost there?"

"We still have a few hours to go." He dropped a kiss to her upturned forehead. "How do you feel?"

"I'll be okay," she said softly. "In time, I'll be okay."

Her injuries tonight had been healed with his blood too. But they weren't talking about physical wounds now. They were talking about the horror of what her brother had done. The horrors that had yet to occur, if Opus Nostrum was allowed to continue with their plans for war.

"I want to say I'm glad it's over," she murmured. "But it's not, is it? It won't be over until every member of that twisted organization is rooted out and unmasked."

Rafe nodded. "With any luck, that photo you have will help us do that."

They had already transferred a copy to the Order while they were in London. Devony's father had made the right call in ensuring the image ended up in his savvy, courageous daughter's hands. Rafe only wished Roland Winters knew how instrumental she had proven already in the quest to thwart this new evil.

"If men like that could get to Harry, they can get to anyone, Rafe. They're worse than monsters. I don't think I realized that until I heard my brother tonight."

He stroked Devony's bare arms, tracing the flourish of one of her pretty *glyphs*. "I'm sorry I didn't get there sooner. It kills me to think how close I came to losing you." He lifted her chin on the edge of his fingertips. "I don't mean just a few hours ago with your brother and those goons. I mean before . . . because of the way I hurt you."

Her warm bourbon gaze reached inside him like a caress. "You can't lose me, Rafe. I love you."

"Thank God." Although their bond told him as much, he didn't realize how much he needed to hear her say the words until just now. He'd needed to feel her forgiveness and know that he would have a lifetime to prove himself worthy of it.

Lowering his mouth to hers, he took his time kissing her, savoring the soft press of her lips against his. His blood ignited even though his intent had only been to comfort. Devony's pulse answered with a thrumming heat of its own.

"I'm sorry for everything I did," he murmured, stroking the side of her lovely face. "You were right. I should've trusted you. I love you. I should have chosen you, not my mission."

She frowned, slowly shaking her head. "It was unfair of me to say that, Rafe. It wasn't fair for me to ask—"

"I choose you." He slid his hand around to her nape and drew her closer, his mouth brushing over hers. "That's what I told my commander earlier tonight before I came to find you. I choose you, Devony."

"What are you saying? That you quit the Order?"

"I tried to. Chase wouldn't let me. But I will, if that's what it will take to have you." He kissed her again, more deeply this time, his heart belonging solely to this woman. "I love you, Devony. You're my partner, the only one for me now. And I'll do anything to prove that to you. Including giving up the Order."

"No." She shrank back from him. "That's not what I want. That's the last thing I want for you. The Order is your life, your family."

"So are you."

Her fingers caressed his jaw with tender care. "I want you to have both, Rafe. I want something more than that, actually." Her gaze searched his, steady with the strength and resolve he loved about her. "I want to share that life with you. All of it. I want to be part of this in whatever way I can be."

"What are you saying?" His brow furrowed. "You want to be part of the Order?"

At her nod, he blew out a sigh and rolled onto his back.

Devony moved up next to him, her head propped on her hand as she stared down at his bewildered face. A challenging gleam lit her gaze. "Before you try to argue, I'd like to remind you that you just said you'd do anything for me."

"I did say that, yes."

"But what?" She frowned. "You don't want to put in a recommendation for me?"

He turned toward her, gently cupping her face in his palm. "What makes you think I haven't already?"

"You did?" She blinked, clearly astonished. "When?"

"Before we left the London command center, I

spoke to Lucan Thorne and Commander Chase. I told them we were heading back, but we were a package deal now. If you wanted it, that is. Those were my terms. And they agreed."

"You did that for me?"

"I did it for us." He smiled, caressing her pretty mouth as the smile broke over her lips. "I did it because nothing would make me prouder, or happier, to have you at my side, Devony. As my partner, my lover. My mate."

"Rafe." On a quiet sob, she grabbed his face and kissed him, no gentle melding of their mouths, but a fiery claiming.

He loved that about her, how she could be both vulnerable and tender, yet the hottest, most exciting woman he'd ever known. She was headstrong and fearless. Innocent, yet wise.

But most important of all, she was his.

On a possessive growl, he rolled her beautiful body beneath him on the bed.

She was already wet and ready for him when he entered her, her tight sheath gripping his shaft as he sank to the hilt inside her heat. Devony cried out, her short nails raking his shoulders as they moved together in a rhythm they both knew well now, their shared need for each other both urgent and tender.

Earlier tonight, they drank from each other's veins for healing. Now, it was desire that ignited their mutual thirst. It was need that brought Rafe's mouth to the side of Devony's neck as he rocked against her. It was pleasure that made him shout in erotic torment the instant her fangs sank into the muscle of his shoulder.

God help him, he would never get accustomed to the

intensity of their bond.

He bit down on her delicate throat, moaning as the sweet taste of her blood roared over his tongue. Her climax swelled into a wave that broke against him as his own release reached its peak too.

And it was love—bright and hot and eternal—that powered through his veins and into every particle of his being as he wrapped Devony in his arms and prepared to take her over that steep edge with him again.

They had hours before they would touch down in Boston.

He was going to make the most of every second.

CHAPTER 30

"**R**elax. You'll do fine."

Rafe's reassurance as Devony stood in front of the mirror in their quarters at the Boston command center helped soothe her, but she was nervous. She couldn't help it.

They had arrived from London yesterday, and tonight everyone was gathering to meet her and welcome her into the fold as one of their team.

She smoothed her palms down the front of her new black pants and V-neck top, the outfit a gift from Carys and Tavia. As soon as they'd heard Rafe was bringing her back with him, the two women had stocked half of the large closet with brand-new clothes, boots, and every other item she could possibly need in order to be comfortable when she arrived.

She'd never had a sister, but Carys seemed excited to step right into the role. Even Jordana had been gracious and forgiving, so much so, she'd actually hugged Devony upon meeting her despite the terrible way they'd first been introduced at the museum.

But in just a few minutes, Devony would be meeting her teammates and some of the Order elders in the command center's war room.

Rafe came up behind her and pressed a kiss to the curve of her neck and shoulder. His aquamarine eyes met her gaze in the mirror's reflection. "You look beautiful. And you've already got a room full of support down there. Gideon's been raving about your fieldwork to anyone who'll listen."

She smiled. "I just want to make you proud."

"You already do, so cross that worry off your list."

She turned around to face him, unable to resist putting her arms around him. "Do you have any idea how much I love you?"

He smirked, pulling her against the hardness of his body. "I think I have some idea, but why don't you give me a hint right now?"

He didn't have to ask her twice. She caught his mouth in a passionate kiss, her veins lighting up with the pleasure of his mouth on hers. When she drew back from him, he groaned, his eyes glittering with amber.

"I think I'm getting the idea now," he said, his lips curving. "I'm getting several interesting ideas, in fact."

She kissed his squared chin. "Is that right?"

"Mm. The best ones involve a lot fewer clothes than either one of us is wearing at the moment."

"Sounds intriguing so far."

From behind them at the open doorway, someone cleared his throat. The deep voice belonged to a big Breed male with golden-blond hair and eyes of the same leaf-green shade as Tavia's. A dimpled grin broke over his handsome face. "Bad timing?"

Rafe grunted. "The only kind you have."

"You must be Devony."

She nodded. "And you must be Aric."

"Ah. My reputation precedes me," he said, crossing Rafe's quarters to greet her. She expected a handshake, but got a brief embrace instead. "It's great to meet you, Devony."

"You too, Aric. Rafe's told me so many nice things about you."

Rafe chuckled. "All lies, obviously."

Aric glanced at Devony. "You really like this dickhead, huh?"

"I love him."

"I guess someone has to." He shook his head and reached for Rafe's hand. As soon as he had a hold on it, he pulled him in for a tight hug too. "I heard what happened in London. You gotta stop almost getting your ass killed, or I'm going to need to find a new best friend."

Devony's nerves calmed as she watched the two men catch up. After a moment, Aric's attention returned to her.

"Everyone's already gathered in the war room, but I wanted to catch both of you before you head down there. Especially you, Devony."

She nodded. "All right."

"I don't know if Rafe told you, but I've been recruiting for a special unit these past few months."

"The daywalker team," she said. "Yes, I've heard."

"Good. Because I'd like you to be part of it. If you're interested, that is."

She could hardly hold back her excitement. Except .

. . "I'd love to, Aric. But I don't want to be part of a team that doesn't include Rafe."

"Yeah, I had a feeling you were going to say that." He swung a look at Rafe. "I've got a spot for you too, if you want it. The team will be based here in Boston, but our assignments can take us anywhere our specialized skills are needed."

"Sounds interesting," Rafe said, wrapping his arm around Devony.

Aric nodded. "We can talk about it some more after the introductions downstairs. Lucan just arrived with Gabrielle and Gideon and Savannah. Your parents are here too."

Devony stared at Rafe. "I'm meeting your parents tonight?"

"Of course. They've been dying to meet you since I told them about you."

Oh, God. Now, her nerves came back with a vengeance.

"Wait a minute," Aric said, a strange look coming over his face. "You mean, Tess hasn't seen Devony yet?"

Rafe shook his head and his friend arched a brow.

"Why?" Devony asked, worry washing over her even though Rafe's blood was utterly calm. "What's going on?"

"Some time ago, my mother saw a vision in a seer's eyes. Mira's eyes."

"One of the Order members from Montreal," Devony said, recalling Rafe mention some of the other warriors' names since they'd arrived in Boston. "What did your mother see?"

"I don't know. A vision of me with my mate, apparently. And our children."

Devony gaped. "You never told me this before."

He gave her a nonchalant look. "Didn't I?"

"No." God help her, she wanted to throttle him. "Rafe, what if I'm not her? What if you're supposed to be with someone else? What if we—"

Rafe silenced her with a slow, toe-curling kiss. When he drew back, the love shining in his gaze was undeniable. "There is no one else for me, vision or not. Whatever my mother saw makes no difference to me. You're my mate, Devony. You're my heart." He pressed a loving kiss to her temple. "Now, are you ready to go say hello to them?"

She blew out her breath and looked into his confident, affectionate gaze. "Okay. I guess I'm as ready as I'll ever be."

"That's my girl," he said, lacing his fingers through hers.

With Aric accompanying them, she walked into the war room holding Rafe's hand. His grasp was her lifeline, her steady anchor as she met the expectant, friendly gazes of Rafe's teammates, friends, and family.

They were hers now too.

She felt it as the introductions were made and she was welcomed into the fold by everyone from Lucan Thorne and his beautiful, auburn-haired mate, Gabrielle, to each member of the Boston command center. Aric brought his gorgeous mate, Kaya, over to meet her, then motioned for two hulking Breed males and a pretty female to come forward.

"Devony and Rafe, meet the rest of the team: Grayson, Jade, and Lachlan."

They spoke for a few moments, but Devony couldn't keep her eyes off the stunning blond who watched her from across the room and the dark-haired warrior with her, whose confident male swagger was so similar to the Breed male who'd stormed into Devony's life and turned it upside down.

There was no question who that couple was.

Rafe must have sensed her curiosity. "Shall we go say hello?"

"Yes," she said, meaning it completely. "I'd love to meet them."

Making their excuses to the rest of the room, they walked over to greet his parents. Rafe didn't let go of her hand, not even when they were standing in front of the couple.

"Mom, Dad. I'd like you meet Devony. My mate."

"Hi," she said, feeling somewhat awkward in the prolonged, unreadable silence.

"I'm Dante," his father said, his deep voice rolling over her senses like velvet and whisky.

He held out his big hand, but Devony felt a burst of affection for the people who gave her the man she loved. She hugged Dante, then turned to look at Rafe's mother, Tess.

"Hello," she said, then waited in breathless dread for her reply.

A tender smile curved Tess's kind mouth.

"Hello, Devony. I've been waiting a long time to welcome you to our family." Tess drew her into a tight embrace and held her there. "It is so wonderful to finally meet you."

~ * ~

Never miss a new book from Lara Adrian!

Sign up for Lara's VIP Reader List at
www.LaraAdrian.com

Be the first to get notified of new releases,
plus be eligible for special VIPs-only exclusive content
and giveaways that you won't find
anywhere else.

Sign up today!

ABOUT THE AUTHOR

LARA ADRIAN is a *New York Times* and #1 international best-selling author, with nearly 4 million books in print and digital worldwide and translations licensed to more than 20 countries. Her books have regularly appeared in the top spots of all the major bestseller lists including the *New York Times*, USA Today, Publishers Weekly, Wall Street Journal, Amazon.com, Barnes & Noble, etc. Reviewers have called Lara's books "addictively readable" (Chicago Tribune), "strikingly original" (Booklist), "extraordinary" (Fresh Fiction), and "one of the consistently best" (Romance Novel News).

Visit the author's website at
www.LaraAdrian.com.

Watch for a sexy new contemporary romance standalone set in Lara Adrian's 100 Series!

Coming Soon

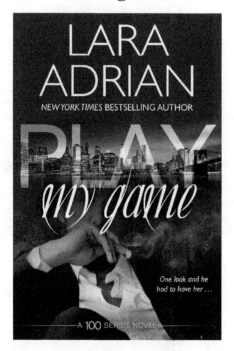

Play My Game
Available Fall 2019

"Lara Adrian not only dips her toe into this genre with flare, she will take it over... I have found my new addiction, this series."
--The Sub Club Books

The Hunters are here!

Thrilling standalone vampire romances from Lara Adrian set in the Midnight Breed story universe.

AVAILABLE NOW

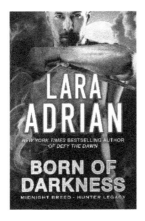 

COMING EARLY 2020

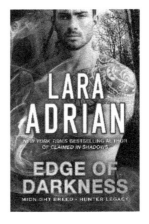

Turn the page for an excerpt from this recent release in the Hunter Legacy vampire romance series

Hour of Darkness

Available now in ebook, trade paperback and unabridged audiobook

For more information on the series and upcoming releases, visit:

www.LaraAdrian.com

Hunters. They are the most lethal Breed vampires in existence—and Cain is as cold as they come. Until a fiery Russian beauty stirs a dark, dangerous hunger in the icy assassin's blood.

Born and raised as an assassin in the notorious Hunter program, Breed vampire Cain has since put his specialized skills to use as a mercenary willing to clean up any problem for a price. Or so he thought. After a job in Las Vegas strains even his dubious code of honor, Cain pulls up stakes and lands in Miami for a much-needed break. All he wants is time away to clear his head and regroup, but then a beautiful young woman is nearly killed in front of his eyes and the ruthless former Hunter becomes the only thing standing between her and a sniper's bullet.

As the niece of a Russian organized crime boss, Marina Moretskova's grown up around killers and criminals. But her uncle wants out now, and he's enlisted her help in buying his freedom by delivering valuable intel to a secret contact. Not even Marina's bodyguards are aware of her mission, so when an attempt on her life is averted by a handsome, steely-eyed vampire, the last thing she needs is the shrewd Breed male nosing around for answers. Cain's cold, haunted gaze and merciless abilities attest to his brutal nature, yet the rough, solitary Hunter stirs a powerful longing in Marina--a darkly seductive hunger she can neither afford nor resist. With a target on her back and covert enemies closing in from all sides, trust is a risk that can prove deadly . . . and the safest shelter she may find is in the arms of the most lethal man she'll ever know.

Chapter 1

Cain sank his fangs deeper into the brunette's neck, closing his eyes on a low snarl as bitter, coppery red cells filled his mouth. Seated beside him on the sofa of his palatial Miami hotel penthouse suite, the female he'd met only minutes ago clung to him and whimpered as he drank from her opened vein.

He was rough about it, eager to take his fill and be done. Cain made no secret of what he was. In the twenty years since humans had learned of the existence of the Breed, it wasn't unusual for his kind to mingle among their mortal neighbors. Some, like the blood Host he'd hired to service him tonight, seemed to find the open coexistence of the past two decades not only an acceptable arrangement but a profitable one too.

Cain gave the small punctures a brisk, businesslike swipe of his tongue to seal the wounds and conclude the transaction. Unfortunately, his Host didn't seem to grasp the limitations of his interest in her. As he drew away, her moan held a whining edge of complaint.

"Mmm, don't stop now, lover. Let's move to the bedroom and keep this party going." She reached for him, licking her cherry-red lips in invitation. "Look, I know you're only paying me for blood, but if you want something more—"

"Your cash is on the table in the vestibule."

Cain was already on his feet, wearing nothing but a pair of dark jeans. He reached for the black dress shirt he'd removed before sitting down to feed a few minutes ago. He slipped it on, not bothering to button it as he turned to meet the disgruntled face staring up at him.

Although the female was pretty and he wasn't the type to deny himself pleasure or sustenance, he rarely mixed the two. Repeat performances weren't his thing. He kept to a strict one-and-done policy, even when it came to the human women who offered him their veins. Life was simpler that way, cleaner.

No strings.

No complications.

No exceptions.

He lifted a black brow, impatient to be done now. "There's a bathroom down the hall if you need to clean up before showing yourself out."

The female frowned, muttering something under her breath as she stood and grabbed her purse off a nearby chair. Her spiked heels clacked sharply over the beachfront suite's polished tile floors in her swift march into the foyer. The hotel door closed behind her with a bang.

Cain blew out a breath, glad for the return to his solitude.

He had been in Miami for more than a week now, having eventually drifted to the very edge of the East Coast after leaving Las Vegas and a job that had been slowly devouring his soul. He'd assumed all he needed to clear his head—and his conscience—was enough time and miles put behind him. Now, a couple of months on the road, with nothing to keep him busy outside of feeding and fucking whenever the urge arose, about the only thing he was feeling was bored.

And restless.

Turns out, he wasn't built for idling. None of his kind were, but especially the Breed boys and men born into the infamous Hunter program. Twenty years of freedom from that hellish enslavement was hardly enough to erase the brutal discipline and training that had made Cain and the rest of his assassin half-brothers bred inside that laboratory anything close to civilized.

As much as Cain enjoyed life's endless luxuries—all the things his mercenary existence provided him—inside he was still shackled to the program. There had been a time, once, when he'd longed for a different life. A simpler, normal life. But those dreams belonged to better men than him.

Deep down, he was still the cold, detached killer his master had made him. Still the solitary predator existing on the shadowed fringe of the real world.

And lately, every one of his Hunter instincts was beginning to tell him it was time to move on.

He hadn't survived this long by ignoring them.

Strolling barefoot across the expansive living area of his suite, he pulled a bottle of whiskey from the fully stocked bar and poured a glass. As Breed, he couldn't drink the liquor but he swished it around in his mouth to erase the metallic tang left over from the human's blood then spit it into the wet bar's polished steel sink.

On the other side of the ultraviolet-blocking shades that covered the floor-to-ceiling glass doors overlooking the beach and ocean beyond, the sun had finally dipped below the horizon. Blue hour. The fleeting moments between day and night when he could stand outside with no threat of searing his Breed skin and eyes.

Cain walked to the sliding doors and opened them wide. He stepped out to the terrace ten stories above the hotel pool and courtyard below. Warm salty air stuck to him, carrying the drifting aromas of blooming flowers and grilled foods. Just off the blanket of white sand still littered with beachgoers, an old reggae song being sung live in one of the tiki bars competed with the pulse and racket of a dance club down the street.

Christ. He'd left the nonstop glitter and noise of Las Vegas for some peace and solitude, but had only traded one circus for another.

He shook his head. Hell, maybe he'd roll out tonight yet. He'd already gone about as far south as he intended. Nothing but swamplands and a lot of bad memories in that direction, anyway. Instead, he thought he might venture north for a while, eventually end up in the Dakotas or Montana. As one of the Breed, he needed living human blood every few days for sustenance, but the idea of getting far away from people—even his own kind—was beginning to sound like a damn good plan.

He turned to go back inside, but paused when he glanced down at the hotel pool. A woman swam alone in the glowing turquoise water, slender arms and legs propelling her with effortless grace and speed across the Olympic-sized length. She wore a skimpy black bikini, with her thick blond hair bound in a long ponytail and floating like gossamer waves over her back as she swam.

Her gorgeous body alone would have been enough to make Cain pause to admire, but it was the delicate body art that decorated her limbs and torso that drew him to the railing for another look. That and the fact that it was next to impossible for anyone to have the entire pool to themselves no matter what hour of the day.

And now that he was looking closer, he realized she wasn't exactly alone after all.

Four big men in dark suits were positioned around the vacated pool and courtyard garden. Their grim faces alternated between watching her swim and scanning their surroundings. Cain didn't have to see the faint outline of firearms holstered beneath their jackets to know they were professionals.

So, who was this woman?

Whoever she was, the female was a knockout. Curves and lean muscle in all the right places. Smooth, alabaster skin that only made the contrast of the ink even sexier. Twisting vines and blood-red roses wrapped her upper arms and long legs, the unbroken chain continuing all the way around her ankles. Each movement of her body made the roses appear alive, begging to be touched.

Cain angled for a better view of her face as it dipped in and out of the water with her sleek strokes, but all he could discern was the hint of high-cut cheekbones and a lush mouth.

It was plenty for his libido to take an interest. Arousal coiled inside him as he fixated on her gliding trek back and forth across the pool. He watched her face lift out of the water in rhythmic motion, her parted lips taking in air between each fluid stroke of her arms.

The illuminated water licked every inch of her body the way he suddenly wanted to do. Each fluttering kick of her strong legs made him hunger to have them wrapped around his hips as he drove inside her. He'd just fed, and yet hunger coiled in him. The urge to feel her throat giving way beneath his sharp fangs was nearly overwhelming.

He closed his eyes on a growl, entertaining a swift and powerful image of the two of them tangled together in his bed. His cock went heavy and hard at the thought, his fangs erupting from his gums.

Fuck.

When he lifted his lids a second later, his eyes burned with unearthly heat. He watched her pivot at the end of the pool and begin another lap. Her loose blond hair undulated around her shoulders and down her spine, and Cain's fingers clenched with the desire to feel those silken strands clutched in his fist as she writhed naked beneath him, begging for everything he gave her and more.

He let the fantasy play out as he watched her swim, trying to ignore the bulge growing more unbearable behind the zipper of his jeans.

He was so transfixed, he hardly registered the quiet pop that sounded from somewhere nearby. But in that next instant, a bloom of red erupted from the back of the woman's head.

Blood. It streaked into the pale blond tendrils of her hair, a growing stain that grew and grew, swirling around her like scarlet tentacles.

Her strokes stalled. Her body went instantly limp, collapsing lifelessly under the water.

Holy shit.

She'd just been shot in front of his eyes. Executed. The massive wound in her skull erased any doubt about that..

Ten stories below him, her corpse began to sink to the bottom of the pool as her security detail scrambled in to retrieve her.

"Son of a bitch." Cain closed his lids in disbelief.

When he opened them again, the blood was gone.

The blonde was still swimming her lap, alive and well. Totally unharmed.

At least she was for now.

Because the killing he'd just witnessed hadn't happened yet. What he'd seen was a sixty-second glimpse of the future. Her future, coming to a violent, watery end.

It wasn't the first time he had experienced a sudden flash of precognition foretelling someone's death, but it had been years since the last one. His unique Breed ability had been with him since he was a boy. He hadn't learned to hate it until he was a man and his cursed gift had failed him when he'd needed it the most.

Failed not only him, but someone else too.

Cain bit off a dark curse, refusing to let the memory—or the shame—take hold of him. He had buried that part of his life and moved on. He'd been damn glad his unwelcome gift had seemed to abandon him altogether in recent years.

The visions had been gone so long, he assumed they'd never return. And good riddance, so he had thought. Yet as much as he wanted to ignore what he'd just witnessed in his mind's eye, he couldn't.

If he didn't do something, his vision would become reality and she would be dead.

The last thing he wanted was to get involved. He shouldn't care what happened to a random woman he had no business craving, let alone thwarting destiny to protect.

But none of that stopped him from palming the railing of his tenth-floor balcony and leaping over the edge.

He sailed down in a flash of motion, faster than any human eye—or sniper's sight—could track him. Feet first, he plunged into the water and grabbed the woman into his arms.

She screamed. One of her bodyguards jumped in from the side of the pool, but Cain was already well out of reach, moving her out of the bullet's path just as the assassin's round tore into the water where she'd been only seconds before.

Cain swiveled his head and glanced up toward the roof of the hotel, scanning for signs of the sniper. The would-be killer was already gone from his post, not a trace of a weapon or a hunkered shooter anywhere above. Meanwhile, the woman struggled to get loose.

Her body was lean and strong in his arms, and warm. She twisted around in his grasp, crushing her curves against the front of his body in her efforts to break free. Everywhere her bare skin touched him, he burned with awareness of her.

She fought the firm bands of his arms, finally shoving him away on a shocked curse. Long-lashed eyes in an arresting shade of warm burgundy stared at him in confusion and fury. "What the hell are you do—?"

Her voice, tinged with a Slavic accent, cut off as she looked at him. She glanced from the sharp points of his elongated canines to the Breed skin markings that covered his wet torso. The tangle of multi-hued *dermaglyphs* prickled everywhere her gaze touched him.

.

He couldn't hide what he was, even if he tried. His fangs were bared in battle-readiness, and in response to the feel of her curves having been pressed against him.

"Are you okay?" he asked her.

She didn't answer, merely looked around his shoulder to where her guard now sagged lifeless in the pool, his blood staining the water instead of hers. Cool and collected in spite of what just happened, she returned to Cain's gaze.

"You saved my life." She swallowed, her intelligent wine-dark eyes searching his face. "But how did you— where did you come from?"

He shrugged, unsure how he would explain what just happened. Not that he was going to have the chance. Two of her men were at the edge of the pool, lifting her out of the water while the remaining one held his pistol on Cain.

"Yury, *nyet*." Her voice was crisp with command. She held up her hand, giving the gunman a tight shake of her head. She said something more in their language, orders that had all of the guards snapping to attention.

God, she was beyond attractive. Those sharp cheekbones and pouty lips were even more striking up close, but combined with her burgundy gaze and delicate bone structure, her beauty was both angelic and exotic. Her attitude was pure confidence, though, and Cain had hardly seen anything hotter.

The weapon trained on him lowered immediately and the third man moved to her side, adding his bulk to the human shield surrounding her.

Without another word, she and her guards were moving hastily away from the pool. Cain watched her go, standing in the waist-high water along with the corpse that might have been her if he'd allowed fate to have its way.

And the question that had intrigued him from high atop his penthouse terrace only deepened now.

Who the hell was she?

The woman glanced back at him only for a moment, a silent connection of their gazes that shot through Cain like a physical caress. He saw the curiosity in her eyes too. And the flicker of awareness that made the memory of her bare, wet skin against his burn even more intensely.

She blinked once, then turned around and hurried into the shelter of the hotel surrounded by her bodyguards.

HOUR OF DARKNESS
is available now at all major retailers in eBook, trade paperback, and unabridged audiobook.

Each novel in the Hunter Legacy vampire romance series can be enjoyed as a standalone.

Thirsty for more Midnight Breed?

Read the complete series!

. . . and more to come

Discover the Midnight Breed
with a FREE eBook

Get the series prequel novella
A Touch of Midnight
FREE in eBook at most major retailers

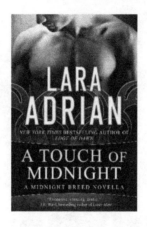

After you enjoy your free read, look for Book 1 at a
special price: $2.99 USD eBook or $7.99 USD print!

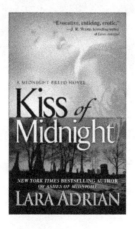

Go behind the scenes of the
Midnight Breed series with the ultimate
insider's guide!

The Midnight Breed Series Companion

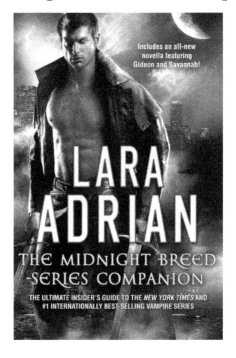

Available Now

Look for it in eBook and Paperback at
major retailers.

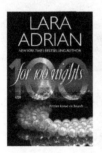 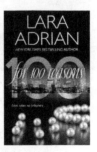

Gabriel Noble barely survived the war that took his leg, but now the stoic Baine International security specialist's honor is put to the test bodyguarding beautiful Evelyn Beckham.

A 100 Series Standalone Romance

Available Now

eBook * Paperback * Audiobook

"Lara Adrian has managed once again to give us a story with heat, high emotion, and angst that touches our heart. I absolutely loved it."
—*Reading Diva*

Award-winning medieval romances from Lara Adrian!

Dragon Chalice Series
(Paranormal Medieval Romance)

"Brilliant . . . bewitching medieval paranormal series." –Booklist

Warrior Trilogy
(Medieval Romance)

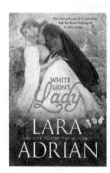 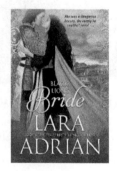 

"The romance is pure gold." –All About Romance

A dark knight abducts the daughter of his enemy as the price of her father's sins. Can the bold but innocent beauty tame the beast?

Lord of Vengeance

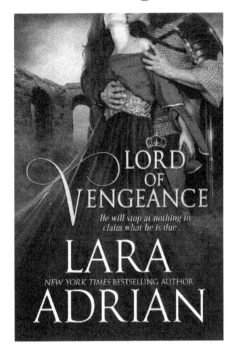

Available Now

eBook * Paperback * Audiobook

"A truly wonderful read."
—*All About Romance* (Grade A / Desert Isle Keeper)

Connect with Lara online at:

www.LaraAdrian.com

www.facebook.com/LaraAdrianBooks

www.instagram.com/laraadrianbooks

www.pinterest.com/LaraAdrian

www.goodreads.com/lara_adrian

CPSIA information can be obtained
at www.ICGtesting.com
Printed in the USA
LVHW041534080819
626994LV00005B/695/P